The Cretan Prophecy

The Cretan Prophecy

P. R. Farmer

On January 31 2018 Crete witnessed a spectacular blood supermoon eclipse. For some it marked the end of days. For others it was a sign to act ...

Chapter 1

Mid-June 2018

Houmam sat huddled with his wife and twelve-year-old daughter in an overcrowded boat off the Turkish coast, clutching bags containing their entire worldly possessions. He had sold almost everything to pay for their passage from Aleppo in Syria, and even then he had been forced to beg and borrow from his family in America to pay the extortionate price demanded by the Turkish people smugglers.

Houmam and his family were exhausted, having hardly slept for days. From Aleppo they had been taken in an old bus to a remote place near the Turkish border, where they had been ordered to get out and continue on foot. They had carried their bags for more than an hour over rough terrain in order to evade the border guards. Packed with thirty or more other refugees in the back of an airless truck, they had then made the long and arduous journey to a makeshift transit camp near Izmir on the Turkish coast, where they had spent two days in filthy tents without sanitation and with limited food and water.

Now, at least, they had left Turkey behind. The sea was calm and the weather good, a warm early summer's day without the blistering heat that would follow in this part of the world in a few weeks. Ahead of them were Greece and the EU. A new life. The smugglers were unfriendly and unsympathetic, but they had assured Houmam that he and his family would be welcome in the EU. They would be safe there and he would be able to find work. He should not believe the TV news reports saying that people were being turned back or kept in camps. This was just sensationalist reporting by unscrupulous western journalists trying to make a name for themselves.

He was still hoping eventually to go to America to join his family there. They were well connected and had tried to help. But getting visas for Syrian refugees under the current administration was hard and would take time. So for the moment he had been obliged to settle for Europe.

Houmam was excited by the prospect of a new chapter in their lives, but also sad at leaving his beloved homeland Syria behind. One day he would return. But for the moment the country was torn apart by a seemingly endless conflict and it was too dangerous for his family to stay. He was sure he had made the right decision despite the hardships.

The smugglers had announced that they were going to rendezvous with a larger vessel that would take them direct to the Greek mainland. From there they would be taken overland to Germany. After about twenty minutes a large freighter came into view. The boat carrying the refugees moored alongside. They were told to climb up the steps that led up the side of the vessel. For Houmam and his family this was manageable. But for the older refugees it was too much after the long tiring journey. Houmam tried to help them but he was pushed on by the smugglers.

His relief at arriving on deck turned to anxiety when he saw they were surrounded by men dressed in black combat gear, armed with rifles and machine guns. They were ordered to sit down and put their hands on their heads. It took a few minutes for the remaining refugees who were able to climb the steps to come on board. The smugglers then came up on deck. They too had guns but were less heavily armed than the freighter's crew. Their leader went over to the ship's commander. Houmam was close enough to overhear their conversation.

"So forty in all. The others are too frail to come up the steps. I'm surprised they've even survived the trip. Where's our money?"

"Don't worry. You'll get your reward," replied the commander. He gave an almost imperceptible signal to his men who opened fire, gunning down the people smugglers. They died before they had time to react.

"Throw their bodies over the side," the commander ordered, "and kill anyone left in the boat. Then cut it loose and sink it."

The smugglers' bodies were unceremoniously dumped over the side. Two of the crew trained their machine guns on the boat, shooting the refugees who had been unable to climb up the freighter's steps. They then went down to the boat and cast it adrift. Waiting until it was a safe distance from the freighter, the crew had fun lobbing grenades into it, blowing it apart.

At first the refugees on deck had watched in startled silence but now many of them began to scream. Houmam was scared but found the courage to remain calm and console his wife and daughter. The commander fired his gun into the air.

"Silence," he shouted.

The screaming continued. He fired again and shouted even louder.

"Silence, I said. Do as you're told and you'll not be harmed. Keep screaming and you'll be shot."

The screams died down to be replaced by whimpering and sobbing.

"Good. The men will now take you to your quarters and then we can get under way. Leave your bags on deck and hand your mobile phones to the guards."

With that the refugees were ordered down a stairwell at gunpoint and, after being searched, led into a hold below deck. A metal hatch door shut behind them, leaving them in darkness apart from the scant light coming through two small portholes.

Chapter 2

Southeastern Crete 2493 BC

Princess Hemite sat on a sedan chair carried by four servants as she entered the courtyard of the Cretan palace. Four of Pharaoh's guards walked before her holding ornate ceremonial sceptres.

Dressed in a white, tight-fitting kalasiris, carefully designed to show off her shapely figure, she wore a magnificent golden necklace with matching tiara and bracelets, presented to her as a wedding gift by her father, King Userkaf of Egypt. Unusually for such a high status Egyptian woman, she was not wearing a wig. She had no need. Her thick, raven-black hair, braided with colourful beads, framed her face, showing off her high cheekbones and delicate features. Even the chair she sat on was beautiful. Specially made for the occasion, it was decorated with ebony panels and golden hieroglyphs.

Princess Hemite was accustomed to the finery and grandeur of a royal court, but she could still scarcely believe her eyes as she entered the Cretan palace. She had not expected to find such splendour and opulence outside Egypt. Like her father's court, the palace was awash with gold and other precious metals and the vivid frescoes covering the palace walls equalled anything she had seen in Egypt.

She had been excited when her father had first told her of her forthcoming marriage to the Cretan king. But as the day drew nearer she had become increasingly anxious about leaving Egypt and her father's palace. She feared that his courtiers, keen on arranging an alliance with an important trading partner and naval power, had exaggerated the youth and charms of her husband to be.

In truth she had little choice in the matter. The daughter of a minor wife of the Pharaoh, her exquisite beauty made her one of her father's favourites, but it also meant that she was a valuable pawn in the affairs of state. Her father's courtiers cared little for her well-being. They would be more than happy to marry her off to an ugly, ageing foreign king if it served their purposes.

But her fears evaporated when she caught sight of the Cretan king. Before her stood one of the most handsome men she had ever seen. He was magnificent. In keeping with Cretan male fashion of the time, he was dressed in a brightly embroidered loincloth with a wide belt, his toned muscular body on full view, obscured only by the multi-coloured necklace hanging from his neck. He wore tall leather boots and elaborate head gear, flamboyantly decorated with lilies and peacock feathers. His beauty was matched only by his charm. As her servants lowered her chair, he stepped forward, going down on one knee before her and offering her his hand.

Her heart leapt with delight. For once her father's courtiers had been truthful.

Chapter 3

Early July 2018

Giovanni Rossi sat at his computer in the National Archaeological Museum in Naples, Italy. The museum was housed in an imposing stuccoed building in central Naples that had previously served as cavalry barracks and later as the seat of Naples University. Established in the late eighteenth century, the museum possessed one of the world's finest collections of Graeco-Roman artefacts.

Giovanni had been busy all day. He was preparing a forthcoming exhibition of finds from the Villa dei Papiri, a residence in ancient Herculaneum named after the papyrus scrolls contained in its extensive library. Owned at one time by Julius Caesar's father-in-law, Lucius Calpurnius Piso, the building had been buried by the eruption of Vesuvius that destroyed Herculaneum and Pompeii in 79 AD. The finds included not only papyrus scrolls from the library but also bronzes, sculptures, coins and pottery. The scrolls had been packed in crates ready to be evacuated away from the eruption, but time ran out as the building was overwhelmed by the pyroclastic flows hurtling down the mountainside. The scrolls were transformed instantly into carbonised sticks which until recently had been unreadable.

Giovanni was studying images produced using a new scientific technique, known as multispectral imaging or MSI, which allowed the scrolls to be read. He found the images fascinating, marvelling at how the fragile remains had been made to reveal their secrets. The library's collection had included numerous Greek and Latin philosophical texts. But the scroll Giovanni was reading was unusual. It was an autobiography recounting the life story of a Herculaneum merchant who had plied his trade for many years across the Mediterranean Sea, or Mare Nostrum as it was known to the Romans.

Giovanni had been staring at his computer all day. Noticing that the light was fading outside, he looked at his watch and, to his horror, realised he was going to be late for his dinner date with Korina. Hardly a way to impress a new girlfriend.

He was about to shut down his computer when he came to a passage of the scroll which brought him up short. "Dio mio!" he exclaimed.

He quickly printed off the images and tucked them in his jacket. Closing down his computer he sped towards the exit, willing his watch to slow down. He crossed the Piazza Museo and headed down the Via Santa Maria di Costantinopoli towards the restaurant where he was meeting Korina. As he walked, he used his phone to email the museum Director to tell him about his discovery.

**

Alessandro Ferrari lounged on his sleek black motor yacht moored in the Porticciolo di Santa Lucia, a small marina in Naples. He tended to spend much of his time on the yacht over the summer months, occasionally making trips out into the Bay of Naples and over to Capri. He was in his usual attire of white chinos with turn-ups, a crisp collared shirt and a double-breasted navy jacket with gold-coloured buttons and braiding on the cuffs.

He'd had a productive day and was enjoying a glass of *Franciacorta*, in his view Italy's finest sparkling wine, more than a match for the best France had to offer. His was a busy and challenging life, but he always took a few moments towards the end of each day to remind himself how fortunate he was. It was good for the soul and enabled him to keep a sense of proportion in dealing with the irritations of everyday life.

He had a beautiful young Ukrainian wife, a tall former model, and two handsome boys from his first marriage, with whom he was on good terms. His relations with his ex-wife were also good. Mind you, so they should be. He looked after her well enough. She continued to live a life of luxury at his expense despite their divorce. But he didn't mind because he could easily afford it. Money really wasn't a problem. In fact, life would be perfect if he could just find better staff, men he could trust to act on their own initiative without messing things up. He really couldn't carry on micro-managing things forever. He would soon be too old for it. But for the moment he had no choice if he wanted to avoid mishaps.

His mobile rang, interrupting his thoughts. It was his old friend Mario Lombardi, Director of the Naples Archaeological Museum.

"Ciao, Mario," he said with genuine delight. "Come stai?"

"Bene, molto bene! I have something which may interest you. You may need to act quickly though."

"You have my undivided attention as always, Mario."

"There may be an opportunity to acquire a very interesting artefact." The Director told Ferrari about Giovanni Rossi's email.

"Hmm, very interesting," said Ferrari. "I think we should keep this as quiet as possible until we've been able to explore the lead ourselves."

"I agree," said the Director.

"What's your employee's name again?"

"Rossi. Giovanni Rossi."

"Do you think Rossi can be trusted to be discreet?"

"I'm not sure," replied the Director. "To be candid he isn't the most discreet person in the world. I thought you might ask me that and so I had his computer checked. It seems he printed off some images shortly before closing it down this evening. It may be a coincidence of course, but I'm told Rossi had been talking all day about how excited he was to be taking his new girlfriend out to dinner this evening. Apparently she's an archaeology professor at the university."

"What's her name?"

"Kouklakis, Korina Kouklakis. She's Greek. Cretan. She's on secondment from the University of Crete."

"And do you happen to know which restaurant they're meeting at?"

"Yes, it's the *Gran Gusto* near the ferry port, not far from the university area."

"I know it. OK. Leave it with me," said Ferrari. "I'll look into it."

"You will deal with this discreetly?"

"Of course, old friend. When have I ever let you down? And as usual I'll make sure you're handsomely rewarded."

***

Rob Martin was at his desk at the National Security Agency in Maryland when his phone rang.

"Good morning, Admiral, I was expecting your call. So the cell phone was last located off the coast of Turkey. The odd thing is that the phone was functioning but stationary for a good ten minutes before it went dead."

"Yes, that is odd," said the Admiral. "So they may have had problems?

Perhaps they had engine trouble?"

"That's possible. Or maybe they rendezvoused with another vessel?"

"That's a thought. Do we know whether there was any other shipping nearby at the time?"

"Yes. I checked. There was, but nothing really close. The location was slightly outside the normal shipping lanes."

"OK. Well thanks for your work."

"There is something else though," said Martin. "It's a bit speculative but I may as well tell you anyway."

"Please do. I'm fine with informed guesswork."

"I widened the search area and checked the satellite AIS messages for shipping in the eastern Mediterranean."

"Good thought. All large vessels have Automatic Identification System equipment."

"Yes. Again there was nothing, except that there was a vessel which was heading direct for the last location of the phone but stopped transmitting shortly before. The timing fits perfectly."

"So either its AIS system broke down or it was switched off?"

"Yes," said Martin. "When it started transmitting again it was stationary, just off the southern coast of Crete."

"Interesting. What do we know about the vessel?"

"It's called the *Princess Ariadne*. It's registered to a large Greek shipping group headquartered in Crete. As I said, it may be nothing, just a coincidence."

"Thank you anyway," said the Admiral.

***

Federico Mancini was sitting in a white van parked in the Passaggio Castel dell'Ovo, a small street which led to the seafront castle of the same name and ran alongside the Santa Lucia marina. From there he was able to keep watch on the sleek black motor yacht moored in the marina. He had chosen the van because it blended in well with other vehicles which were parked there to make deliveries to nearby restaurants and businesses. The narrow road was busy with tourists and locals walking over to the castle and to the restaurants and cafés by the marina.

A member of the art squad of the Carabinieri, the Italian Military Police, Federico had been tracking a suspected art and antiquities gang for a couple of months and gradually collecting evidence. He had taken numerous photos of the gang going about their business, secretly meeting dealers and collectors. The photos included several close-up shots of them handling artworks and antiquities which Federico presumed to be stolen. On one occasion he had followed them out of Naples to a remote farmhouse which he suspected they were using as a storage depot.

Federico had taken what he had so far to show his boss, Brigadier General Romano.

"Excellent work, Federico," the Brigadier had said. "Truly excellent!"

"Do you think it's enough to bring them in for questioning, sir?"

"Oh yes. Most certainly," said the Brigadier. "The thing is though that these are the foot soldiers. I'd really like to get my hands on Il Capo, the boss."

"How do you know one of them isn't the boss, sir?"

"Because I know who the boss is," said the Brigadier with a knowing smile. "It is Alessandro Ferrari."

"What THE Alessandro Ferrari?"

"Yes," said the Brigadier, "the well-known businessman and playboy."

"How do you know that, sir?"

The Brigadier gave Federico a piercing look over the top of his reading glasses.

A question too far, thought Federico.

"Well, if we brought them in for questioning, sir, they might be persuaded to talk," he suggested.

"They might. But there's a serious risk that they wouldn't. Don't forget that Ferrari can afford to hire expensive lawyers, and his men will most likely have been drilled on what to do if arrested by the police. We may just end up looking foolish."

"I see that," said Federico. "The problem though is that, if Ferrari is the boss, he's more elusive than his men. I've never seen him with the gang and there's been no sign of his meeting any of the dealers and collectors the gang does business with. If he is the boss, he's like a phantom."

"Yes, Federico," said the Brigadier, "and I think I know why. What I'm going to tell you must remain strictly between us. For some time now I've suspected we have a leak in the department, someone who feeds Ferrari information. What you've just told me reinforces my suspicion."

Federico was shocked. He hadn't considered that possibility. "Do you have any idea who it might be?"

"Yes. I do."

Federico didn't pursue it. If the Brigadier General had wanted to tell him whom he suspected, he would have done so.

"So, what you're saying, sir, is that Ferrari has been one step ahead of me the whole time? He's been avoiding any contact with the gang while I've been watching them?"

"Yes. That's precisely what I'm saying. I suspect he's been conducting his business by phone."

"Couldn't we get a phone tap?" asked Federico.

"We don't really have enough yet to get authorisation to tap his phones. I don't want to risk doing it unofficially because it would give his lawyers a field day. Ferrari is high profile. We need to play everything by the book. Here's what we'll do. We'll announce within the department that I've decided to drop the investigation and that you've been assigned to another matter, one of our cold cases. Complain to your colleagues about it if you like. Say you think I'm getting too old for the job."

"I won't say that, sir. No one would believe me!"

"Too kind, Federico. I do appreciate your work on this and I want you to continue, but discreetly. You speak only to me about it. Make up a story about the new matter I've asked you to work on. In the meantime I suggest you start quietly keeping an eye on Ferrari's yacht. He more or less lives on it at this time of year. But please be careful. Stay alert at all times. I've reason to believe Ferrari is extremely ruthless. I suspect he and his men are behind several recent murders and disappearances."

The conversation with the Brigadier had been a couple of weeks ago. Federico left it a few days, making sure that everyone in the department knew he had been assigned to another case. He then started keeping watch on Ferrari's yacht as the Brigadier had suggested. Hopefully, once word got to Ferrari that his gang was no longer under investigation, Federico might be able to photograph some of the gang members coming to the yacht. If he could get evidence to link Ferrari with the gang, he would then have enough for a phone tap. To make real progress with the investigation he really needed to be able to listen in and record Ferrari's conversations.

Federico had been sitting there in his van for several hours. It was now early evening and he decided to take a break. He opened the van door, planning to go to one of the nearby cafés. As he was getting out, a black *Mercedes SUV* came speeding past him, heading down towards the castle. Federico immediately recognised it as the SUV often used by the gang. He jumped back in and reached for his camera with its telescopic lens. The SUV pulled in farther down the street and two men got out.

"Gotcha," exclaimed Federico, recognising the two men as members of the gang.

"The Big Man was right," he murmured, using the nickname affectionately given to the Brigadier General by his men.

Federico snapped away as the two men walked round the road to the marina and over to Ferrari's yacht. He was so excited at getting photos linking the gang with Ferrari that he forgot to take his normal precautions. When keeping watch in a vehicle he always made a point of locking the doors and leaving the key in the ignition ready for a quick getaway. But on this occasion, elated at seeing the SUV as he was getting out, he did neither when he jumped back in. Even worse he was no longer alert to what was happening around him and failed to notice two men sneaking up behind his van. The first he knew about them was when one of them opened the passenger-side door and jumped in. The man poked a gun into the side of Federico's neck and told him to put his hands on the steering wheel. The other man stood by the van and made a call on his mobile.

***

Ferrari had been waiting impatiently for Luigi and Giuseppe to arrive. He had ordered them to come to the boat urgently after the museum Director's call. He had not met them there recently because he had been tipped off by his old friend Emilio Ricciardelli at the Carabinieri that his gang was being watched. It had been hard conducting business over the last few months without being able to brief his men in person. He could do so much on the phone, but his men tended to be accident-prone unless he could brief them face-to-face and drill them on every detail of an operation.

He had, however, been informed by his contact at the Carabinieri that the investigation had now been dropped. His gang was no longer being watched. The museum Director's call required immediate attention and so he decided to risk it. His mobile rang.

"Boss, there's someone out here parked in a van who has been taking photos of Luigi and Giuseppe boarding the yacht. Shall I terminate him?"

Dammit, thought Ferrari. *They're still watching us.*

"No, you idiot, not here. It's too public."

Sighing, he asked himself what he had done to deserve being surrounded by such brainless imbeciles.

"Take his van and drive him to the farmhouse. Discreetly please! Find out who he is and what he knows. Then get rid of him. Make sure it looks like an accident. Just to be clear, that means no bullets in the head! A road accident will do fine."

Why was it that he had to spell out every detail for them? Couldn't they sometimes work things out for themselves? Trying to relax and calm himself, he turned to greet Luigi and Giuseppe. He had asked them to come because they were among the brighter of his men.

"Now there's something I need you to do…"

Chapter 4

"I'm so sorry," began Giovanni, kissing Korina on both cheeks and taking his seat at the table in the restaurant. The *Gran Gusto* was located on the Via Nuova Marina just opposite the ferry port. An unpretentious, modern-looking restaurant attached to a café and delicatessen, it had a casual atmosphere and a reputation for good food. Giovanni had suggested it because it was handy for the museum and for Naples University's Department of Humanities, where Korina worked.

"Don't worry," replied Korina, "I came prepared." She pointed to the pile of exam papers she had to mark. Korina was getting towards the end of her year's secondment from the University of Crete, where she was an assistant professor of archaeology.

"I do, however, have a peace offering," said Giovanni, producing the images he had printed off and placing them on the restaurant table.

Korina looked amused. "And to think some stupid girls like flowers!"

Giovanni smiled. He knew this would interest Korina far more than any flowers. Giovanni let Korina order the food as she knew the restaurant and, after a couple of dates, was familiar with Giovanni's tastes. He concentrated on the wine list, choosing a small bottle of white as an aperitif and a Tuscan red to accompany the food. Both were expensive but this evening he felt like celebrating.

While eating the seafood starter, Giovanni recounted the story told by the Roman merchant in the scroll. Like all good raconteurs, he took time to build up to the climax of the story and was about to get there when the main course arrived, polpette or meatballs in tomato sauce, a Naples speciality and one of Giovanni's favourites. He paused to compliment Korina on her choice but she wasn't interested. Slapping the palms of her hands on the table, she said impatiently, "Come on, Giovanni! You can't keep me in suspense. What happened next?"

Delighted, Giovanni completed his story. Korina, leaving her main course untouched, listened intently as he told her what the merchant had said.

"I thought you might be interested," said Giovanni with a satisfied smile. "I think though we need someone to help us decipher the MSI results. There's a lot of detail in the scroll I can barely read. Do you know anyone at the university who might be able to help? Discreetly though. When I emailed my Director he came straight back with strict instructions to keep it quiet."

Korina thought for several seconds. "Yes. I think I know someone. There's a professor from Harvard doing a series of guest lectures at the university."

"Who's that?"

"Dan Baker."

"Ah yes. I know the name," said Giovanni. "He's an expert in ancient Mediterranean and Middle Eastern texts."

"As it happens, the Rector just rang me and asked me to step in to chair one of his lectures tomorrow. I'll see whether I can have a word with him."

They finished supper and headed towards the door.

"Well, to use a well-worn phrase," said Giovanni, "my place or yours?"

"Hardly original, but very tempting," said Korina, smiling. "Sadly I still have a pile of papers to mark by the morning. Can you do tomorrow, or perhaps the day after? With a bit of luck I'll have had a chance to talk to the American professor by then."

"OK," said Giovanni, a little disappointed. He'd been looking forward to a pleasurable finale to what had been an exciting day. "But please be careful or I'll be in trouble with the Director."

"Don't worry," replied Korina, tucking the envelope containing the images in her bag. "I'll emphasise the need for discretion."

They left the restaurant, embraced and went their separate ways.

***

After leaving Giovanni, Korina walked swiftly towards her apartment in the Via Santa Caterina da Siena, a short walk from the university area. She loved strolling through the streets of Naples. For many, Naples was a noisy, dirty, crime-ridden city, but Korina found it intoxicating. She loved the colours, the shops and markets, the smells and the bustle. For her the edginess and faint sense of menace were part of its charm. She could easily have afforded a larger apartment in a more expensive area of the city, but she had chosen to rent one in the Spagnoli area close to the centre because it was more atmospheric.

Tonight she took the most direct route. It didn't bother her that it led her through a number of dimly lit back streets. She always remained alert as she had been trained to do by her tutor, but so far she hadn't had any problems during her stay despite the city's reputation. Tonight though she noticed that there had been a guy not far behind her ever since she left the restaurant. He had kept at a discreet distance, speeding up or slowing down as she increased or reduced her pace. He was no immediate threat, she decided, but he did seem to be following her. She wondered vaguely whether he might be a stalker of some kind. A student from the university perhaps? She had been warned when she arrived in Naples that it wasn't unknown for female professors to attract unwanted attention from students.

She reached her apartment and bolted the door. Leaving the room in darkness she peered through the window into the street. The guy walked past, casting the most cursory of glances towards her apartment block. No one she had seen before. She continued looking but he didn't reappear. It may be nothing, she thought, but she would keep an eye out for him over the next day or two just in case. She pulled her phone out of her back pocket and called her father in Crete, as she did every day. She told him about Giovanni and the scroll. Her father was hugely excited by the scroll and wanted to know every detail. When it came to Giovanni she sensed a slightly disapproving tone. It was always the same. No man was ever right.

She had to admit though that, unwittingly, her father was right about Giovanni. He was a handsome guy and a lovely one. He had been as giddy as a schoolboy telling her about his find, and he genuinely didn't understand why the museum Director would want him to keep quiet about it. But she knew that she would never have any romantic interest in him. The chemistry just wasn't right. There was something missing. Maybe he was just too nice. Anyway, whatever the reason, great guy though he was, Giovanni would have to go.

***

Giovanni was more wary than Korina about walking around Naples at night. There were constant reports of street muggings in the papers, and indeed a number of his friends had been robbed at knife point. The Università Metro station was not far away from the restaurant though, and this wasn't a bad area. So he decided to walk and take the Metro.

The side streets in this part of Naples were lined with tall apartment blocks, some old and dilapidated, others recently renovated. The streets were dimly lit by lamps mounted on cables which sporadically crossed overhead between the blocks. At this hour it was quiet with hardly any traffic or people around. The shops and other businesses occupying the ground floors would have bustled with activity during the day, but they were now closed with their shutters down.

Giovanni's thoughts went back to the scroll and the MSI results. He was pondering why the Director had been so insistent that he tell no one about the scroll. It could provide the clue to a wonderful archaeological find and would be fantastic publicity for the museum. He had walked a short distance from the restaurant up the Via Porta di Massa and was turning left into another street, the Via Lanzieri, when he noticed two youths about fifty metres behind him. He wasn't too concerned. They were busy chatting and weren't particularly looking his way. But after turning the corner he glanced back and saw that they had followed him. Giovanni had planned to walk the whole length of the street before turning right towards the Metro. But having spotted the two men he decided, as a precaution, to turn right sooner. This would take him more quickly on to a main thoroughfare, the Corso Umberto I, which should be much busier.

Giovanni looked back again to see whether the men were still following him. They were. What's more, they'd stopped chatting and were now staring straight ahead towards him. He began to worry and increased his pace, walking as fast as he could. When he reached the end of the street he checked on them again. They had broken into a jog and were now no more than thirty metres behind.

Giovanni started to panic. He turned left on to the Corso Umberto I and ran. The road wasn't as busy as he had hoped. After about fifty metres he looked round again and saw the youths were still making ground on him. He quickened his pace even further, sprinting as fast as he could. His heart was pounding and he was struggling for breath. He now regretted drinking the lion's share of the wine at the restaurant.

After what seemed like an age, the Metro came into view about one hundred metres ahead. Looking behind again, Giovanni nearly tripped but was relieved to see his pursuers were no longer gaining on him. The street was also becoming reassuringly busy as he approached the Metro.

He'd made it, he thought. The Metro would still be crowded at this hour and they surely wouldn't dare assault him once he was inside. There would be cameras and too many witnesses. Reaching the entrance Giovanni was pleased to see a throng of people going in. He rushed down the escalator, squeezing past anyone who was standing still or walking down slowly. At the bottom he paused to catch his breath and looked back up. To his relief he saw that the two men were nowhere in sight. They hadn't come into the Metro; they had given up.

Giovanni began to relax, his breathing and pulse returning to normal. Following the crowd on to the platform, he made a mental note to keep to his rule of taking taxis at night in future. Feeling calmer now, his thoughts went back to Korina. He was really taken with her. Her dark hair, olive skin and striking features oozed sex appeal, and her eyes were so hypnotic he hardly dared look into them.

Those pleasant thoughts were sadly Giovanni's last. Lost in thought he had failed to notice the two youths coming on to the platform behind him. Standing at the edge he was pushed from behind just as the train came in. He fell into its path, his head colliding with the front of the train. His death was mercifully instantaneous.

Chapter 5

Dan Baker, Harvard Professor of Classics and Historical Linguistics, was in full flow giving a public guest lecture at the Department of Humanities at Naples University.

"So Theseus is of noble birth. He's either the son of Aegeus, King of Athens, or the son of Poseidon, God of the Sea, depending on whom you believe. What we know for sure is that he's a bit of an adventurer. He volunteers to join the seven maidens and seven youths sent by Athens every nine years to the palace of King Minos in Crete to be sacrificed to the Minotaur. Half man half bull, the Minotaur is the offspring of King Minos' Queen, Pasiphae, and a bull – I'll spare you the lurid details."

Chuckles from the audience.

"So off he goes from Athens and I guess everyone thought that would be the last they'd see of him. Fairly safe bet you'd think. The Minotaur was kept in an underground labyrinth in which everyone got hopelessly lost. So once you were cast into it, sooner or later the Minotaur would get you. Not great news! But they hadn't bargained for Theseus. He was smart. He was also, to be frank, a bit of a chancer. He woos the beautiful Ariadne, King Minos' daughter, who is mistress of the labyrinth. She falls madly in love with him and so when it's his turn to be sent in she gives him a ball of red thread so he can find his way out. So he kills the Minotaur, escapes from the labyrinth and gets the girl. A regular Greek superhero, Hollywood style."

Laughter from the audience.

"There was one slight blemish on his character though which would doubtless have been edited or airbrushed out of any Hollywood movie. He'd impetuously told Ariadne he'd take her away from Crete and marry her. But our intrepid hero conveniently forgets this – well he does take her away but he quickly dumps her on the island of Naxos. Not such a bad place to be dumped, but hardly the bright lights of Athens."

More chuckles from the lecture hall.

"But it gets better for Ariadne. She's picked up by a god, Dionysus, the God of Wine and Ecstasy in fact. Definite upgrade on Theseus, despite his heroics."

Dan had been invited over from the States, and before that from Oxford in England, to give summer guest lectures in Naples several years in a row. He always made an effort to make them lively and fun. For many people linguistics lectures could be really dull and so he found ways of spicing them up. Today he had decided to use the Greek story of Theseus and the Minotaur to introduce the main subject of his lecture, the languages of ancient Crete.

"The story varies a bit depending on whom you read," he continued. "But just as archaeology has shown the story of Troy to be an echo of historical events, so too it has shown that the myth of King Minos and the Minotaur was fuelled by a real-life civilisation which flourished on Crete long before the heyday of Athens and even before the heroic age of Achilles and Odysseus. We know that civilisation as the Minoans, named after King Minos. What we don't know is their real name, what they called themselves. What I want to explore today is why it is that the Minoans are so mysterious and elusive. Why is it that we still don't know what language the early Minoans spoke and we are unable to decipher their writing?"

After speaking for about an hour he sat down and handed back to the chair, an attractive female academic, Korina Kouklakis, who was on secondment from the University of Crete. She thanked Dan for a marvellous speech and opened the floor for questions.

The lecture was well attended, the audience comprising the usual mix of academics, students and members of the public. The customary representation from the Carabinieri art and antiquities squad was hard to miss. They sat in imposing silence in full uniform near, but not at, the front.

As always the most interesting and genuine questions came from the general public. The students' questions were mainly intended to impress their professors, whose own interventions served as a platform for mini lectures on their latest pet theories. Dan treated the students kindly but teased the professors. He knew they would take it in good part; they had become friends over the last few years.

Dan admired how Korina handled the audience, politely but firmly refusing to allow the professors to dominate the session and ensuring that everyone had a fair chance to speak. After about half an hour she announced that it was time to draw the session to a close. Before she did, she gave an impressive three-minute summary of the conference. She then invited everyone for drinks in an adjoining room.

"That was fascinating," said Korina as she stood up from the speakers' table. "I must confess I was very honoured when the Rector asked me to chair your session, star-struck almost!"

Dan didn't quite know what to say, unsure whether she was being serious.

"There are a number of questions I'd like to have asked myself," she continued. "I don't suppose you'd be free for lunch tomorrow?"

Dan, who had been wondering how to arrange a further meeting, couldn't believe his luck. "Sure. Or I could do dinner this evening if it works?"

"That would be great. Where would be convenient? Where're you staying while you're here?"

"I'm living on a motor yacht I chartered. It's moored in a small marina here in Naples, the Porticciolo di Santa Lucia. I do a bit of sailing at weekends and thought after my final lecture in a couple of months' time I'd take the opportunity to do a longer trip round the Med."

"How wonderful," said Korina. "Perhaps you should drop in on me in Crete."

"I'd love to," said Dan, again not sure how serious her remark was.

"My apartment's not far from the marina," she added. "There's a restaurant I sometimes go to near there. It's called the *Zi Teresa*. It's quite relaxed and has good food and a nice terrace. Shall I book a table?"

"Sounds great. I've seen it but never been."

"Shall we say 7.30?"

"Perfect," replied Dan.

Dan didn't see Korina leave as he was engulfed by a swarm of conference groupies hoping to speak to him. He had spent about twenty minutes talking to them when they suddenly parted, rather like the Red Sea is said to have parted to allow the Israelites across. A very large Carabinieri officer approached. Not fat, just massive in a way that even his well-cut uniform could not disguise. He held out his large hand.

"Professor Baker, I'm so pleased to meet you. I'm Brigadier General Romano. I've attended a number of your lectures and always found them fascinating."

"I'm flattered," said Dan genuinely.

"I was wondering whether I might invite you to lunch. Let me be quite straightforward. Part of my command deals with antiquities theft, sometimes ancient manuscripts. It would be useful for me to know an expert such as yourself should the need arise. I don't know if you've ever worked with the police before?"

"Not as such," said Dan, "but of course I'd be delighted to assist if I can."

"Excellent. Here's my card. Please give my secretary a call and we can fix something up."

"Just one thing, if I may," said Dan. "I've been very honoured to have your fellow officers attend my lectures so often. But I've noticed they never ask questions?"

The big man moved closer to Dan and winked. "Well, we wouldn't want people thinking we weren't omniscient, would we?"

***

Alexandria 48 BC

Ptahhotep sat, as he had for most of his adult life, in a large room surrounded by the collections of the Great Library of Alexandria. One of the Library's longest serving and most esteemed keepers, he was responsible for the Library's oldest and most prized collection, the ancient artefacts from the Old Kingdom. Even after so many years Ptahhotep remained devoted to his work, putting his encyclopaedic knowledge of the collection to good use. He was a favourite with visiting scholars and students and was generous in sharing his knowledge with fellow keepers.

There was, however, one item which intrigued Ptahhotep more than any of the others in the collection. In fact in recent years it had become an obsession. It was a large golden disc commemorating a wedding between a daughter of Userkaf, a Pharaoh of the Old Kingdom, and a king of one of the city states of Crete, or Keftiu as it was known to the Egyptians. Ptahhotep had no difficulty reading the ancient Egyptian hieroglyphics on one side of the disc, although he'd never heard of the city state of Keftiu to which it referred. The other side of the disc bore strange symbols he couldn't read. He concluded that this must have been the writing of Keftiu at the time when the wedding took place. Yet this was not the Greek script now used in Keftiu. It must, he concluded, be the writing of a civilisation that had long since disappeared.

Ptahhotep spent many hours at the Library studying the disc. But his popularity with visitors and other keepers meant that he had precious little time to give the disc the attention it deserved. And he feared his time was running out. His cough was getting worse by the day and he'd started spitting up blood. He was also suffering from constant fatigue. He longed to remove the disc from the Library so that he could study it at his leisure. But this was impossible. Security at the Library was tight, even for trusted keepers like himself. It was strictly forbidden to remove items from the Library, and transgressions were severely punished. If he were caught the consequences for himself and his family would be unthinkable.

But then one day his opportunity came. The fire started in the port after the Egyptian Navy was set ablaze by Roman fire ships sent in on the orders of Julius Caesar. The fire quickly engulfed the buildings in the dockyard, consuming warehouses, arsenals and other buildings. It then began to sweep into the city, heading in the direction of the Great Library. As soldiers and sailors struggled to contain the blaze, the fire and smoke sowed terror in the overcrowded city. The panicked mob fled through the narrow streets towards safety. When word reached the Library, fear began to spread among its occupants. The Library's guards could only stand by as the scores of people inside forced their way past them and out into the street.

Ptahhotep was horrified at the threat to the Library and its precious contents. There was little he could do though. He had to go. But he was not going to leave without his beloved disc. He furtively tucked it under his robe and joined the throng of people pressing out into the street.

***

Dan arrived at the restaurant early and listened to RAI news while having a beer in the bar.

We have some breaking news. Reports have just come in that an undercover agent of the Carabinieri art squad was killed early this morning. He has been named as Federico Mancini. He was married with two children. The circumstances surrounding his death remain unclear. His van is thought to have crashed off the Amalfi coast road into the sea around 2 am. I'm told we can now go over to a live press conference with a senior Carabinieri officer.

The camera cut to the massive figure of Brigadier General Romano, whom Dan had met at the conference.

Brigadier General, what can you tell us…

Dan was distracted from the report by Korina arriving. They took their table in the restaurant.

"So you're on secondment from the University of Crete?"

"Yes. I've spent the whole academic year here," said Korina. "Back to Crete in a couple of months. I wish I were staying longer. Crete's going to seem a bit dull after Naples. And you? Can I just check by the way? You are actually American? Your accent sounds British. I probably sound more American than you!"

"Yeah, I spent a lot of time in the UK when I was young and then I taught at Oxford until a few years ago. Boston's hardly like the Deep South though. Some of the pronunciation's quite British. For example, Gloucester, near Boston, is pronounced Glawstah, not much different from the way the Brits say it."

"Well ya lecture's wicked awesome," said Korina in her best Boston accent.

"My grandpa would have said 'wicked pissah'," said Dan laughing. "But you're too young to know that! Where did you pick up your Bostonian?"

"I spent a year at Hahvad," she replied, again mimicking the Boston accent.

"Anyway, it was very good of you to chair my lecture even if you think my accent's weird."

Korina looked stunning in her sleeveless light blue dress. From her neck hung a golden pendant which Dan recognised to be a replica of the famous 'Bee Pendant' exhibited at the Heraklion Archaeological Museum in Crete. It depicted two bees with their wings outstretched, clasping a honeycomb into which they were placing a small drop of honey. But what struck Dan most of all as he sat opposite Korina were her eyes, the translucent blue depths of her irises drawing him relentlessly into the intense blackness of her pupils. They reminded him of eyes he had seen before somewhere, but he couldn't think whose and where. They were utterly captivating.

"It was a pleasure," said Korina. "Obviously I couldn't refuse the Rector's request but actually your lecture was great. I almost came away thinking linguistics was interesting!"

Dan smiled. She had been the epitome of professionalism at the conference, but he was beginning to realise that hidden beneath that veneer was a cheeky playfulness.

"Coincidentally I've come across something that I'd appreciate your help with if you wouldn't mind, something my boyfriend Giovanni at the Naples Museum came across?"

"Sure," said Dan, trying not to show any reaction to the news she had a boyfriend. He wasn't sure he managed it though. Her eyes seemed to peer directly into his mind.

"I've brought what he found with me." She showed Dan the MSI images that Giovanni had printed off for her. "They're images of a carbonised scroll found in excavations of the Villa dei Papiri near Herculaneum."

"Ah yes, I'd heard there had been further MSI analysis."

"I did study Latin," said Korina, "but never really took to it. Giovanni tells me the scroll records the life story of a Roman merchant who plied his trade around the Mediterranean in the first century AD. He talks of a treasure he acquired in Alexandria from the grandchildren of a keeper of the Great Library. The keeper had fallen ill and died but the piece was kept by the family. The grandchildren, now desperate for money, sold it to the merchant. He says he paid them a very handsome price because he took pity on them."

"Or maybe he just wanted to look honourable in his memoirs," commented Dan.

Korina smiled. "You old cynic! Don't spoil my romantic story."

Less of the old please, thought Dan. He wondered how old Korina was: late twenties, thirty maybe?

"The piece, if it still exists, sounds interesting in itself," she continued. "It's a large disc made of solid gold recording the marriage of an Egyptian Princess to a Cretan king. The Princess is the daughter of Userkaf, the Old Kingdom Pharaoh who founded the Fifth Dynasty."

"So we're talking middle of the third millennium BC?"

"Yes," said Korina. "But what's really fascinating is that the disc was inscribed with text in both Egyptian hieroglyphs and some other symbols which were unknown to the keeper at the Library. My guess is that they must be Cretan hieroglyphs or Linear A."

Dan was stunned. "Gosh, a Minoan equivalent of the Rosetta Stone! I hardly need explain to you the significance of this if it could be found."

The world-famous Rosetta Stone was found in 1799. Carved in black granodiorite, it recorded an Egyptian decree written in ancient Egyptian and Greek. The stone proved to be the key for deciphering Egyptian hieroglyphs, which until then had remained a mystery.

"It would be a fabulous find," said Korina. "The Egyptian hieroglyphs on the disc would allow us to decipher the writing of the first great European civilisation, Minoan Crete, my ancestors."

By the middle of the second millennium BC Cretans were speaking Mycenaean Greek, the language of the Greek 'heroic age'. But the Minoan civilisation on Crete went back further, at least a thousand years and possibly longer. The language they spoke, recorded in hieroglyphs and later in a script known as Linear A, was as yet un-deciphered. Nothing equivalent to the Rosetta Stone, written in both ancient Cretan and another, known language, had yet been found.

"But," asked Dan, "does this golden disc still exist? Does the scroll give any clue where it is?"

"Yes and no. The merchant sailed across to Hispania, modern-day Spain, to exchange some of his cargo for other goods. As he sailed along the Spanish coast he was taken by surprise by a storm that came from nowhere."

"Yeah," said Dan ruefully, thinking of his planned sailing trip, "I've been warned the Med can be very unpredictable."

"This must have been a very bad storm because his vessel sank just off the coast. It seems he lost most of his cargo but managed to save the disc. He got a berth back to Rome on another vessel but decided that it would be safer not to take the disc on a strange boat. After all, I suppose, it was made of solid gold and would have been a target for thieves. So he hid it until he could go back."

"Do we know where he hid it? And did he ever go back?"

"This is where Giovanni says the manuscript becomes fragmentary and hard to read. I'm hoping you might be able to help."

Dan looked at the images. "May I borrow them?"

"Yes of course. But please don't show them to anyone. Giovanni was warned by his Director to keep quiet about them and he's worried about getting into trouble."

"I understand. This would be a major find if it still exists. One art thieves would kill to get their hands on, literally."

"But surely," said Korina, "this would be too hot to handle, too unique?"

"You'd be surprised. There are many unscrupulous collectors who would pay a fortune to have this in their collection. They take pleasure in collecting pieces even though they can't show them off."

"You sound like you've had some experience of this?"

"Some," said Dan. "From time to time I've been offered handsome fees by collectors to help them decipher manuscripts they've acquired. I tend to refuse on principle, but have to confess that on a couple of occasions my curiosity got the better of me. I've always declined to take payment though."

Korina smiled. "Very noble."

Once again Dan wasn't sure how to read Korina's comment, but his thoughts were interrupted by the arrival of two appetizing plates of seafood. The conversation switched to the delights of Italian food and wine. Dan quickly demolished his own portion and was happy to oblige when Korina asked him to help her finish hers. She insisted on paying the bill, saying that as chairperson she had a budget from the university.

"Well that was wonderful," said Dan, as they headed towards the door. "I hope you'll allow me to reciprocate soon?"

Korina didn't respond. She was no longer with him. Dan turned round to find she had stopped several paces behind and was staring at the television screen in the corner of the bar. The screen showed a photo of a man.

Long delays on the Metro last night. A man fell under a train at the Università Metro station. He died at the scene. He's been named as Giovanni Rossi, an employee of the Naples Museum...

"I'm so sorry," said Dan, gently placing his hand on Korina's arm. "Shall we sit for a moment or can I walk you home?"

Korina turned her gaze from the screen and fixed Dan with her mesmerizing eyes. "Thanks. No need."

"Are you sure? I feel unhappy about leaving you on your own."

"I'd rather be on my own right now, if you don't mind?"

"Of course. You have my number. Please call me if you want to. Any time."

"Thank you. I do appreciate that. I'm sorry. I'll be in touch."

***

It was already dark by the time Korina approached her apartment. She was deep in thought. How could Giovanni have fallen off a Metro station platform? She hadn't known him long but he seemed such a cautious guy. She couldn't help thinking it might not have happened if she had gone back with him and hadn't made the excuse about having to mark exam papers. But she had decided there was no future in their relationship. The only reason she hadn't ended it that evening was that Giovanni was in such good spirits after his find that she hadn't wanted to spoil his evening, so she had decided to postpone telling him. But there was no way she could go to bed with him.

As she reached her apartment she was distracted from her thoughts. She was sure she saw a dim light moving around in the apartment. The light abruptly disappeared. Odd, she thought, perhaps a trick of the light. But then there had been the guy who had followed her the previous night. Perhaps he had somehow broken into her apartment. She climbed the stairs and opened the door.

***

Ferrari's men, Luigi and Giuseppe, had spent over an hour in Korina's apartment, fruitlessly searching for the images which Giovanni had printed off.

They had turned the apartment upside down, emptying wardrobes and cupboards. Clothes and papers were strewn all over the floor.

"Perhaps the Boss got it wrong," said Luigi. "Maybe she doesn't have them. Rossi may have printed them off for someone else."

"Or it's possible they're still in his apartment and we just didn't find them. I think we'd better wait for her and find out what she knows."

Luigi gave a mischievous smile. "Why don't we have a bit of fun with her at the same time?" He used his phone to look her up on the university website and showed Giuseppe her photo. "She's pretty. Completely wasted on that loser I did for last night."

Luigi's thought level was poor, although to be fair probably above average for a Naples thug. What he hadn't bargained for was that Korina was in no mood for fun, at least not the sort of fun he had in mind.

They heard a key in the lock. The door swung open. No one came in.

Luigi walked over to the open door. He didn't see the need for caution. This was just a woman, and so he wasn't worried. He should have been.

As he reached the door frame a leg shot out and swept him off his feet. The last thing he saw was the tip of a flattened hand smashing down into his throat. Choking, he blacked out. Giuseppe hardly had time to recover from the shock when Korina climbed him like a ladder and somersaulted over him. Wrapping her legs and arms tightly around his abdomen and throat from behind, she held him in a choke hold until he too blacked out.

***

Korina checked the intruders' pulses. They were both unconscious but alive. She was pretty sure that one of them was the guy who had followed her back to her apartment the night before. Looking round, she realised they hadn't touched her laptop or her jewellery, the high value items burglars usually went for; they had obviously been looking for something else. She stood for a few moments in thought and then, coming quickly to a decision, gathered some things and put them in a suitcase. Grabbing her laptop she left the apartment and, as she walked along the street, rang Dan on the number he had given her.

"Dan, I was just burgled. They were obviously looking for something. I fear it may have been the MSI images. I'm not sure Giovanni's death was an accident. I think he may have been pushed off the platform. I just wanted to warn you in case they were watching us at the restaurant and followed you back to your boat."

"Thanks," said Dan. "Are you OK?"

"Yes. I'm fine. Thank you for asking."

"That must have been quite a shock. What are you going to do? You can't stay at your apartment. They might come back."

Korina decided not to mention the two unconscious bodies she had left on the floor of her apartment. "I'm going to book into a hotel for the night. There's one close by. I can then work out what to do."

"No need. Come down to the marina. You can stay on my boat. I have two spare cabins."

After a few moments' thought Korina accepted Dan's offer. She was impressed by his decisiveness. The offer had come in an instant, and he hadn't seemed at all concerned that he might be making himself a target.

Chapter 6

Spain, first century AD

The Roman merchant ship neared the Hispanic coast, heading for the port of Carthago Nova in the southeastern part of the peninsula. The merchant had sailed from Alexandria with a cargo of grain, a commodity which Egypt exported on a large scale to Rome and other parts of the empire. He planned to exchange some of it for Hispanic goods which he would sell in Rome.

On this trip though the merchant carried another item he had acquired in Alexandria, a magnificent ancient disc made out of solid gold. He planned to keep the disc for himself as an addition to the private collection at his lavish villa near Herculaneum.

He had bought it from the descendants of a keeper of the Great Library. They had approached one of his trading partners in Alexandria in the hope of selling the piece. A trusted friend after many years of dealing, the trader had assured him that the family were genuine. They had insisted on meeting him in person as they wished to impress upon him the importance of the piece and what it had meant to their grandfather. He could see that they were emotionally attached to it and that it was hard for them to let it go. They felt they were letting their grandfather down. The merchant was a little angry with himself for paying too much for it. They were desperate for money and he was sure he could have beaten them down. But at the end of the day he was wealthy and could afford the odd indulgence and, although as a hard-nosed businessman he didn't like to admit it to himself, he felt sorry for them.

The long sea journey across the Mare Nostrum to Hispania had been uneventful. No pirates, and Neptune, the God of the Sea, had looked down upon him favourably. Perhaps his generosity to the family had won him favour. Having put into port at Carthago Nova he did some profitable business exchanging his Egyptian grain for Hispanic goods. Hispania was a major producer of olive oil and garum, a strongly flavoured fish sauce to which the Romans were addicted.

The merchant then set sail up the Hispanic coast, planning to head east towards Rome once he had favourable winds. But a day after leaving Carthago Nova his good fortune changed. The winds became stronger and more unpredictable, and storm clouds began gathering over the tall mountains which swept down to the sea. The sky suddenly went completely black, and his vessel was engulfed by one of the fiercest storms he had ever experienced. It came from nowhere. The merchant was used to the notoriously unpredictable Mare Nostrum and in deep water he would have known precisely what to do. But this time he was trapped in shallow waters just off the coast. The ship was driven on to the rocks and then sucked back out to sea. Holed below the waterline it began to sink. He was now alone as his crew had been swept overboard. Then, just as suddenly as the storm had arrived, it started to abate. His ship and its cargo were doomed but, grabbing a bag of gold coins and the precious piece he had acquired in Alexandria, he took to the small boat that he kept on deck.

He made for a coastal town he had just passed, where he was offered hospitality by a family. They asked for nothing in return, but they were poor and he insisted on paying them handsomely for their kindness. His problem now was how to get back to Herculaneum. The choice was between a long land journey and a sea crossing. The land route, following the coast to the north of Hispania and then across Gallia Narbonensis before turning south down the length of Italia, was fraught with danger. There were many stories of travellers being attacked by bandits. So he chose to pay for a passage back on another merchant vessel. He felt uneasy though about taking the disc on board with him. There would be no way of keeping such an attractive object safe.

So what to do? He didn't really know the family he was staying with and, despite their wonderful hospitality, he couldn't risk leaving the disc with them. In the end he decided to hide it so that he could collect it when he was able to return with his own boat. But where? He hired a small sailing boat and headed north along the coast looking for a suitable hiding place. After a couple of hours he found a promising site, a small cove surrounded by steep cliffs. He placed the disc in a bronze chest and covered it in sack cloth for protection. Dragging the chest up the cliffs was hard work, but once he got up there he realised it was the perfect spot. There was no way anyone would find the disc there. In fact the place was so remote and inaccessible he doubted anyone had ever set foot up there. He buried the disc in one of the caves in the cliffs to provide protection from the wind and rain. The chest was shallow but also quite wide, and he struggled to dig a hole large enough to conceal it in the bone-dry red earth. But eventually he managed it, concluding that the dry conditions would be perfect for preserving the chest and its precious contents.

***

Dan met Korina by the *Zi Teresa* restaurant where they had dined earlier, near the Santa Lucia marina. He took her to his yacht and showed her to her cabin. Dan had quickly prepared it, placing fresh towels on the bed. Korina dropped her bag in the cabin, had a shower and came back on deck. Dan was studying the images of the merchant's scroll.

"You must be exhausted," he said, looking up. "You should try to get some sleep."

"I doubt I'd sleep at the moment. I see you're looking at the MSI images."

"Yeah, they're fascinating. Giovanni was right. A lot of the text is completely unreadable, but there are some clues as to where the merchant hid the disc. The shipwreck took place north of Carthago Nova, modern day Cartagena in southeastern Spain. It happened on the second day after leaving Cartagena as he sailed past a small town. Unfortunately he doesn't say what the name of the town was. After being shipwrecked he sailed another, smaller boat along the coast for about an hour, passing a large bay and several headlands. He eventually spotted a small, remote cove surrounded by steep cliffs. He scrambled up the cliffs until he found a cave. He buried the disc in a shallow bronze chest in the earth, which he describes as unusually red."

"I guess he didn't want to give too much detail in case he managed to get back there," said Korina.

"Yes. On the other hand the fact that he was telling the story at all may suggest he was old or seriously ill and was worried he wouldn't get back. The question is what to do about it. I was just thinking about that before you came. My next public lecture is not for a while. It's tempting to go and have a look. I don't know how you're fixed. Would you consider joining me? We could take the boat across. It's all ready to go because I'd been planning a trip over the weekend. On this boat it would just be a couple of days' cruise over to Spain."

"But where would we start looking? Somewhere north of Cartagena is a big area to search."

"It is. But we know he'd sailed for less than two days and was shipwrecked near a small Roman town. He also says the coastline was very mountainous at that point. I have a friend in Palma de Mallorca who is a marine archaeologist. He's a leading expert on Roman wrecks. Maybe he'll be able to help narrow it down for us. If he's there we could drop in on him on the way. We would be stopping over in Mallorca anyway."

Korina thought for a few moments. "Well, it would be a shame if the disc ended up in a private collection and was lost to the world. Besides, I could do with getting away from Naples for a while. Let's do it. I'll call the university. I'm sure they'll understand in the circumstances."

***

"Admiral, good to see you. It's been a while," said Diana Klaas, holding out her hand as she walked up to the Admiral's table. A striking brunette in her early thirties, she wore a light blue dress cut just below the knee with a smart white jacket.

"Too long," said the Admiral, jumping to his feet and grasping her hand between his, "far too long." A tall, broad-shouldered man in his early sixties, he had an attractive, if rugged, face with a strong jaw bone and a full head of sandy coloured hair. He had chosen to meet Diana at the *1789* restaurant in Georgetown, a favourite of his whenever he was in DC. They exchanged pleasantries while they studied the menu.

"If I may make a suggestion," said the Admiral, "the scallop and rockfish crudo and Icelandic cod are both excellent if you don't mind two fish courses."

"Perfect," said Diana.

"A little wine?"

"Oh, since it's a special occasion I'm sure I could manage a glass of white."

Diana didn't normally drink at lunchtime, but knew the Admiral liked to have wine when dining out and felt it would be churlish to force him to drink on his own.

"Excellent. I know just the thing to go with the crudo. So still travelling the world?"

Diana was a senior international correspondent with CNN. The Admiral had met her about ten years earlier when she had just started with CNN as a junior correspondent. She had been assigned to cover a naval operation in the Mediterranean that he was commanding. They had hit it off well and had stayed in regular touch ever since, Diana even dating his son for a short period at one point. The Admiral was Diana's go-to person whenever she had to cover naval affairs, and in turn she had become a valuable media contact for him, especially in recent years after his promotion to Vice Chief of Naval Operations. They had a relationship of qualified trust. There were limits and both knew the game.

"Yes," said Diana, "still travelling. I just got back from covering the refugee crisis in Syria and Turkey. Terrible situation. The human suffering is immense. The war itself has killed hundreds of thousands of people, and there are over eleven million displaced, incredibly that's half the population! Over five million have fled the country, three million to Turkey."

"What route do they take?" asked the Admiral.

"Many of them go through Gaziantep and on to Izmir, which has become the main hub for smuggling people over to Europe. The refugees pay around fifteen hundred to two thousand dollars each to cross to Greece, a huge amount for most of them."

The Admiral topped up Diana's wine glass. "I guess the journey must be pretty dangerous?"

"Yeah, the risks are massive. The smugglers, as you might expect, are unreliable. Some of them are outright con men and are into human trafficking. There are real safety issues for women and children. It's a nightmare for the agencies trying to protect them. And if the refugees get to the coast, the sea crossing is hazardous. The waters round there are notoriously treacherous."

"Yes. I've seen your reports. Many never make it across."

"The boats are generally small and overcrowded. And then that only gets them to the Greek islands. From there they still have a long way to go. They usually travel overnight by ferry to Athens and then overland through Macedonia. Many hope to get to Croatia, Austria and Germany. The worst is that there's no obvious end to the crisis in sight. This has been going on since 2011. The population are just victims of one huge geopolitical game between Russia and the West."

"Where're you heading to next?" asked the Admiral.

"Well that's the problem. I don't know from one day to the next which country I'm going to be in. I'm thinking of a change. It's beginning to get to me covering these sorts of stories. I'm in talks with CNN about moving to an anchor role. The constant travel is also getting too much, and it plays havoc with my private life!"

"I bet, but won't you miss it?"

"I might, but I guess if I do I can always go back to it after a break. Talking of life changes, I hear you retired at the end of last year. What are you doing? Have you thought of being a part-time naval correspondent for CNN?"

"It's a thought," said the Admiral laughing.

"I'm serious. I bet CNN would love to get you on board, if you'll pardon the pun," she said, smiling. "Shall I have a word with them? You could be my go-to naval person when I move into my anchor role."

"I'll certainly think about it. Right at the moment though there's some business I still need to take care of. In fact I was hoping you might be able to help me with it."

"Sure. Fire away."

"I need to find a reliable contact in Crete, someone who's familiar with local affairs and politics, someone with an ear to the ground. Do you have anyone in Crete you would recommend and could put me in touch with?"

"I do in fact. I have a close friend there. She's an Aussie, from Sydney, but her family come from Crete and she's living there now."

"Ah yes. I believe there're a lot of Aussies whose families come from Greece," said the Admiral.

"Yes. She's bi-lingual, an investigative journalist. Works independently, although she does a lot for the *Cretan Daily News*. She mainly does stories on local crime and political scandals, that sort of thing."

"Sounds perfect. Would you be able to put me in touch with her? There may well be a good story in it for her eventually."

"Sure. On one condition. If there's a good story you cut me in on it too," said Diana with a smile.

"Deal," said the Admiral. "My son's over in Europe and will be doing the leg work for me. I'll get him to call her and arrange a meeting."

"I meant to ask how he was."

"He's good, thank you."

"What happened to his girlfriend was just dreadful. I was in Afghanistan at the time and covered the story about the air raid on the Trauma Centre. Some people think CNN didn't exactly cover themselves in glory that day. They say we sat on the fence for too long about the US involvement."

"Well that's always easy to say with hindsight. If you'd blamed the US and got it wrong you'd have been criticised for that too."

"Yeah, I guess so," said Diana, "although it still keeps me awake at night. Has he got over it? It's been a couple of years now."

"No I don't think he has fully. It'll take time I think. He was talking to her right at the moment when it happened. I think there's some guilt mixed in there too."

"I must make time to catch up with him," said Diana.

"I think he'd like that. He often speaks of you."

"Yeah. It's why I need to change jobs. With all the travel I never seem to be able to hang on to relationships."

***

Dan and Korina left Naples as dawn broke. After moving slowly through the boats moored in the marina, Dan gunned up the powerful twin marine diesel engines, heading out into the Bay of Naples and past the island of Ischia and onwards towards southern Sardinia. Neither of them spotted the sleek black motor yacht which slipped out shortly after them.

Korina was tired and heavy-headed after barely sleeping, but she felt her spirits lift almost as soon as they left Naples. The strain and tension started to dissipate, and her head began to clear. The weather was fine and settled, and the crisp morning coolness soon gave way to the shimmering heat of the day. Lounging on deck Korina revelled in the sea breeze as Dan took the yacht up to cruising speed. She was no stranger to boats. Her father owned an entire fleet of them, but sailing on this sleek powerful craft with Dan was an exhilarating experience. He wasn't as classically handsome as Giovanni, who with his slick, dark hair and smouldering Latin looks had an almost feminine beauty. Dan was very different. His hair was sandy coloured and his face more rugged, more masculine. She wondered about his age. Mid to late thirties? His tall athletic frame probably made him look younger than he was, she concluded.

Dan seemed to sense she was looking at him and turned his head towards her. "Are you OK?"

"I'm OK, thanks," she replied.

"I'm so sorry about what happened last night. It must be hard."

Korina paused for a few moments before replying. "I hadn't known Giovanni all that long. I wasn't in love with him. But he was such a wonderful generous guy. Life is so cruel."

"Yes. I'm afraid it can be."

Korina looked into Dan's eyes, thinking he might elaborate. But he didn't.

"I keep blaming myself," she said. "He wanted me to go back with him but I said no. It wouldn't have happened if I had been with him."

"You can't blame yourself. You couldn't know what was going to happen."

The sea was relatively calm and they made good time on the first leg of their voyage. By early evening they reached the Marina di Bonaria near Cagliari in Sardinia. Having refuelled and completed the formalities, they moored in their allotted berth.

Dan announced that he was starving. *What a surprise*, thought Korina, who had already tumbled to the fact that he was almost permanently hungry. Handing Korina a glass of wine, he sprang into action in the galley. About twenty minutes later he reappeared with two bowls of delicious-looking pasta, and clutching a bottle of *Chianti*. They dined on deck against the romantic background of the beautiful Sardinian sunset.

***

"What's this pasta?" asked Korina. "It's fantastic."

"It's called Spaghetti alla puttanesca."

"Spaghetti in the style of a whore. Great name!"

"Yeah. I think it was once called 'Bad girl pasta'."

"Oh thanks," said Korina laughing.

"I'm reliably told in fact that, contrary to popular belief, the name has nothing to do with whores. It comes from the word 'puttanata' meaning garbage. The story goes that a restaurant owner had run out of ingredients and his customers told him to make up a dish from any old garbage."

"So what's in it?"

"That's the point, I think, very little. Tomatoes, anchovies, capers, olive oil and garlic. It's perfect boat food. Really quick and easy to do. I eat it all the time."

"Where did you learn how to cook it?"

"I'm often invited to dinner when I'm in Naples by one of the professors and his wife. They're great fun and his wife loves teaching me Neapolitan cooking. They do lots of fish and seafood pasta dishes. She took me down to the fish market one day to show me what she buys. I love it. I could eat pasta every day. But that's enough about my efforts at cooking. Tell me about yourself, Korina."

"Not much to tell really. Spoilt daughter of a wealthy Cretan businessman."

"You don't come across to me as spoilt. Brothers or sisters?"

"No. My father would've liked me to have a brother but it didn't work out. That's probably why he wanted me to go into the business. Still does. He got me to do a master's degree in management, an MBA, after my degree in archaeology, and he insists I spend a few weeks work-shadowing each year in different areas of the business. At some point I may have to go into it. After all, I guess I'll inherit it one day. I'm not in a rush though. I like what I do. And my father's not too unhappy either. He's obsessed with ancient Crete and all things Minoan. In fact he's even more obsessed than I am."

"He sounds quite a forceful character. Do you get on with him?"

"He's definitely someone you have to stand up to if you don't want to get walked over. We get on surprisingly well. I went through my childhood not seeing all that much of him. Still don't. He's away a lot. But I ring him every day. He likes to speak to me. I think he's reached an age when he's regretting the limited time we had together when I was growing up. I was mainly brought up by my full-time tutor and my mom."

"Full-time tutor?"

"Yes. He lived with us. Still does. He's now head of security for my father's villa and the business, but we still refer to him as 'the Tutor'. He was very stern when I was growing up. Quite fit though. I had a crush on him when I was a teenager."

"What about your mother? Do you get on with her?"

"Yes. She's stricter than my dad. He may be a strong character but I can wrap him round my little finger. I'm his little princess! My mom gets cross if she thinks I'm not being lady-like, which by the way is quite a lot of the time!"

"Is she involved in the business?"

"Not as much as my dad. She does a lot of entertaining of my dad's business and political friends. She and my father own the business jointly. It was my grandfather, her father, who founded it. He's dead now. He left it to both of them because my dad had helped him build it up."

"Are your mom and dad both Cretan?"

"Oh yes. My mom and I are of super pure Cretan stock. My dad's really proud of it. We were both DNA tested as part of a genetic survey of people in the Lassithi area of Crete. Mitochondrial DNA is passed down from mothers to their children and so it contains information about maternal ancestry. The survey suggested that Cretans living around five thousand years ago, when the Minoan civilisation arose, descended from a Neolithic population who had come over to Crete from the Middle East about four thousand years earlier. Our DNA is an almost perfect match. I keep telling my dad I should marry someone from outside Crete to add a bit of fresh blood. He isn't keen though. I wish I'd never done the DNA test. He's become obsessive about keeping the blood line pure."

Hmm, thought Dan, *where have I heard that before? Nazi Germany maybe?*

"Anyway, that's enough about me and my family," said Korina. "Tell me about yourself, Dan."

"Plenty of time for that over the next day or two. I think perhaps I should show you where we're heading."

Dan cleared the dishes out of the way and got the charts out. "Tomorrow is another longish day. We'll head for Mallorca and spend a couple of nights in Palma on the southern coast. I emailed my friend Antonio and gave him details of the merchant's story. He's around and will be happy to meet up."

"Great. I've never been to Mallorca."

"We'll then do a short hop over to Altea, a small town on the east coast of Spain. How we take it from there will depend on what Antonio says. Altea may be roughly in the right area as it's several hours' drive north of Cartagena, the port the merchant says he'd left a day or so before he was shipwrecked. My guess is that it could easily have taken a Roman merchant ship more than a day to get there. But let's wait and see what Antonio says."

Chapter 7

The Society's Inner Sanctum met in an elegant room decorated with vivid frescoes and alabaster statues. Mounted on the wall behind the Leader was a wooden sculpture of a bull's head with fearsome golden horns.

"The first item is the *Energia Corporation*," said the Leader. "This matter is rather urgent. As you are aware, keeping national ownership of key industries is an important aim of the Society. While we control many important companies a number remain in public ownership and are vulnerable to foreign takeover. On occasions we've been forced to take direct action to prevent companies from falling into foreign hands. This is another occasion when we need to act. It's been reported that a German company is about to mount a takeover bid for *Energia*, one of our key energy suppliers. We can't let control of our energy fall into German hands. I propose therefore that we take steps to prevent this from happening. Are we all agreed?"

Nods of agreement around the table.

"Excellent," said the Leader. "A plan has already been drawn up. I'll give the green light.

"Next item, the media. As you know, we've made a big effort to extend our control over the local media in the past few years. This is important to ensure that the people get the right messages. Perhaps, Georgios, you would like to tell us about the latest addition?"

"Yes, certainly," said Georgios. "I am pleased to tell you that my bid for the *Daily Echo* has been accepted. The lawyers are currently preparing the papers and, all being well, the deal will be completed next week."

"I'm sure you'll all join me in congratulating Georgios," said the Leader.

Loud applause from the members of the Sanctum.

"Now a quick word on another matter. This is more of an update really. January's extraordinary blood supermoon was seen by many in the Society as a sign. We agreed and decided it was finally time to embark on a project that has been a long-standing aim of the Society. We have since acquired the necessary human resources and are now in the process of procuring the materials we need. We will of course have to choose our precise timing carefully. The moment has to be right. I'll report back further at our next meeting."

Nods of approval around the table.

"Good," said the Leader. "So, as usual, the final agenda item is charitable donations. We're keen to use our charitable fund to do good works. Any proposals? I always value your input on this so please speak openly."

"We have an opportunity," said one member, "to help the local Chief of Police. His daughter has been taken seriously ill and needs to travel to Switzerland to receive treatment. It's going to be expensive for him. I'm sure he would be grateful for a contribution."

"Well I for one would certainly agree to this," said the Leader. "In fact, why don't we offer to finance it in full? He's a long-standing Society member and has been very helpful to us in the past. I'm sure he will continue to be so in the future; and of course it's a very good cause. Do we all agree?"

Everyone nodded their agreement and the donation was approved.

"There's also the possibility of helping the Commander of the 5th Airmobile Brigade," said another member. "His son is about to start university at Oxford. I'm sure he'd be grateful for a contribution to his fees."

"Oh yes absolutely," said the Leader. "Again, a long-standing Society member. Does everyone agree? This is precisely the sort of donation we should be making. A very worthy cause, and a good choice of university too."

"Indeed," said the member. "Not one of those Mickey Mouse American ones!"

Laughter around the table.

"Good," said the Leader. "Unless there's any other business let's retire to the courtyard for refreshments."

***

It was another clear bright morning and Korina rose early to exercise. Dan came on deck shortly afterwards and quietly watched her go through her exercise routine. He couldn't have taken his eyes off her if he had wanted. Dressed in tight black leggings and top, she performed a series of acrobatic movements punctuated by bouts of brutal aggression, during which she launched vicious and sustained punches and kicks at a tyre she had suspended from the radar arch.

Korina caught sight of Dan and paused her routine.

"Is that an oriental martial art?" asked Dan.

"No. It's an ancient Greek form of fighting called Pankration."

"I see," said Dan, "literally, 'all powers'. How long have you been doing it?"

"All my life. It's one of the things the Tutor taught me. We practised every day. I do it mainly now to keep fit and supple."

"Is it different from the Japanese or Chinese variety?"

"Yes. It's a mix of wrestling, boxing, kicking, strikes and, once you get down and dirty, strangulation! There were different variants. The Spartans did it differently from the Athenians for example. It didn't really have set rules, except that in athletic competitions certain things like eye-gouging were banned. Do you want me to give you a demonstration?"

"OK, but be gentle with me!"

"Have you ever done any martial arts?"

"No. Just a bit of boxing in the Navy."

"OK. Come at me as if you were boxing."

Dan moved forward with his fists half raised, doing his best impression of Muhammad Ali in his prime. He hardly saw her move before finding himself face down on the deck, his legs swept from under him. Before he could get up she had jumped on his back, encircling him tightly with her legs while applying a choke hold.

Dan had a definite preference for the tight leg scissors.

"The first move, bringing you to the ground, was called the 'hard leg sweep'," Korina explained. "It was a favourite of the Spartans. The hold I have you in now was called the 'Klimakismos' or 'ladder trick'. You can also do it while standing. I'm not applying any pressure though. Normally what I'd do now is strangle you." She placed her forearm across his windpipe and squeezed gently.

Dan understood why her mother didn't think her very lady-like.

Korina relaxed the hold. "Another stranglehold was called the 'Tracheal grip choke'. You grab your opponent's tracheal area, the windpipe and Adam's apple, between your thumb and forefingers and squeeze. Quite effective. Your opponent won't last long if you do it properly. You have to be careful though. You can do some serious damage if you don't get it right."

"I bet," said Dan, who was happy to pass on that one.

"So that's your first Pankration lesson," said Korina, tilting her head and peering into Dan's eyes. "I guess we should head now. I'll go and grab a quick shower."

Dan felt he could do with a cold one.

***

As they headed out to sea Dan asked Korina more about the martial art.

"It was introduced into the Olympic games in the mid seventh century BC, but some think it goes back much further, to Mycenaean and Minoan times. Theseus is said to have used it to defeat the Minotaur. I'd have thought you'd know that," she said with a cheeky smile.

"I didn't. Must remember it for my next lecture. Perhaps you could come and demonstrate?"

"I'd love to," said Korina laughing. "I think it might be a first for a chairperson. Not sure what the Rector would think!"

"Apart from you and the Tutor, does anyone else practise it today or did it die out with the Greeks?"

"Pankration was later adopted by the Romans but was then banned in the late fourth century AD when they did away with gladiatorial events. It was rediscovered in the late nineteen sixties, by a Greek-American."

"Why did the Tutor want you to learn a martial art?"

"He's a Pankration master and so I guess it was understandable he'd want to teach me. I think he'd probably see it as an essential life skill. It does give me confidence, knowing I can look after myself. But it's not the only thing he taught me. I learned other stuff as well, not just how to fight."

"What sort of stuff?"

"I went to school as well of course. He concentrated on life skills such as confidence, poise, making the right decisions under stress, suppressing and not showing emotion or fear, that sort of thing. I'm brilliant at Poker!"

"Very handy! Is there anything he couldn't teach you?"

"Only one thing," said Korina, laughing. "Sense of direction. I'm a brilliant map-reader but if you asked me now which direction Naples is in from here I would struggle to tell you. I have a navigation app on my phone though. It's set up so I can access it straightaway without having to put in my code. And it works even without a GPS signal. It's great. It's impossible for me to get lost."

"Clever."

"Yes, I guess it must track your movements somehow."

Once again they made good time in the calm sea and reached Mallorca shortly before sunset. The view of the island as they skirted round its southeastern coast was breathtaking.

"It's beautiful," said Korina. "So green and lots of pretty coves."

"Yes. It's no wonder that Mallorca and the other Balearic islands are so popular with tourists and sailors. If we hadn't been meeting Antonio in Palma, I might have suggested staying in one of the marinas along this stretch of coast. Cala Santanyi just over there for example is lovely. The little bays round here are perfect for swimming and there are some great restaurants."

They sailed on for another half hour along the southern coast heading towards the island's capital, Palma, which lay to the southwest of the island. The coastline flattened out as they turned into Palma Bay. They entered the Marina Moll Vell in Palma just as the sun set. The marina was centrally located not far from the magnificent La Seu Cathedral, which overlooked the sea and dominated the Palma skyline.

After they had moored the boat and completed the formalities Dan asked,

"Do you fancy a walk and a bite? I don't know Palma well but there's a little tapas bar in the pedestrianised old town called the Quina Creu which my friend Antonio recommends. He's a bit of a gourmet so I bet it's good."

"Sounds perfect after a long day's sailing."

They showered and strolled through Palma's medieval old town for a while before heading to the tapas bar. They ordered some drinks while looking at the menu.

"I'm tempted by the suckling pig," said Dan. "I'm a bit seafooded out."

Korina smiled. "I think it has to be the grilled tuna tataki for me."

As they ate, Korina asked about Antonio. Dan explained that he had met him many years ago when they were both doing postgrads at Oxford. They had remained close even though they only managed to see each other now and then. Whenever they met they picked up as if they had seen each other yesterday.

After leaving the tapas bar they walked back through the old town to the marina, enjoying the late evening coolness. When they got back to the boat Dan rang Antonio to make arrangements for the following day. Antonio suggested they come to his apartment around midday.

***

Gerhard Schaumberger sat looking at papers in the back of his chauffeur-driven *S-Class Mercedes* saloon on a German autobahn. He was on his way from his home in Königswinter, a small picturesque town on the river Rhine near Bonn, to a meeting of his group's board of directors in Frankfurt. This would be an important meeting. The board was being asked to approve a proposed takeover bid for the *Energia Corporation*, a large Cretan energy supplier. As majority shareholder and chairman, Schaumberger had ultimate power, but he was still keen to get the other directors, in particular the managing director and the directors appointed by the group's bankers, on board with the plan. All the directors took their responsibilities seriously, including their duties to the minority shareholders. He had prepared the meeting well, having talked to each of the directors individually and secured the backing of the main minority shareholders. He didn't anticipate any objection in principle. The acquisition was a bit of a no brainer. *Energia* was a good company that fitted in well with the group's overall strategic objectives. He expected the main debate to be about the bid price. The papers he was reading included a report on the subject prepared by the corporate finance team. He had of course read it before and approved it but he wanted to refresh his memory on the detail before the meeting. With the economic problems in Greece, *Energia's* shares, like many Greek assets, were currently undervalued. Schaumberger's group could easily afford to offer a premium to tempt the existing shareholders to sell.

Schaumberger's private mobile rang.

"Dr Schaumberger," said an unfamiliar voice.

"Who is this? How did you get this number?"

Schaumberger was puzzled as only his family and closest business associates had his private mobile number.

"Who I am need not concern you. What should concern you is that I have your daughter."

A spear of anxiety shot through Schaumberger's stomach and chest. "That's impossible. She's at school in Bad Godesberg."

"No. She never got to school. In fact she never made it to the ferry."

If Schaumberger had had any doubts about the caller being genuine he no longer had them now. The caller evidently knew that his daughter took the ferry each day across the Rhine from Königswinter to Bad Godesberg to go to school.

"What have you done to her?"

"Nothing, as yet," came the menacing reply. "She's sitting opposite me tied to a chair. Perhaps I should let you hear her voice."

"Daddy, please help me," his daughter screamed.

"Convinced?" said the unfamiliar voice.

"Let me speak to her."

"You'll be able to speak to her when and if I let you have her back."

"What do you want, you arschloch?" Schaumberger was trying to place the accent. Spanish? No, Greek maybe?

"I'm not sure it's a good idea to antagonise me, but I'll excuse you on this occasion as I suspect you may be a little stressed."

"What do you want?"

"You're attending a meeting of the board today to approve a takeover bid for the *Energia Corporation*. You shall tell the board that you've changed your mind and that the bid should not go ahead."

Schaumberger sat in stunned silence.

"Dr Schaumberger, are you still there?"

"It may be too late," said Schaumberger eventually. "The plans have all been drawn up and it has the backing of the directors and the other shareholders."

"I hope for your daughter's sake you're wrong. Unless I hear a public statement by this evening that the bid has been abandoned you will not see your daughter again. It's in your hands."

"And how do I know you won't harm her anyway?"

"You don't. But I've taken the precaution of not allowing her to see my face and she has no idea where she is. If you comply I'll have no reason not to release her. She'll be back with you tonight. If on the other hand you don't or I find out you have involved the police, you'll be fishing her out of the Rhine."

Chapter 8

The following morning Dan and Korina left the yacht and walked into Palma's old town. Korina was keen to visit the La Seu Cathedral.

"I think it'd be a good idea to go to the cathedral early," said Dan. "Antonio tells me Palma is a favourite destination for cruise ships and from late morning onwards the old town is often so packed it's barely possible to move."

"So what do you know about the cathedral?"

"Not a great deal. I know construction began in medieval times, early thirteenth century, but it wasn't finished until much later - turn of the seventeenth century I believe. I also remember reading that it has an unusual blend of styles: gothic but with American influences. Not sure what that means exactly."

Entering through a side door and passing the cathedral museum, they walked over to the nave and gazed up at the multi-coloured shafts of light flooding through the huge rose window, which was studded with countless small pieces of stained glass. They moved on to inspect the wrought-iron candelabra designed by Gaudí.

"It's OK," said Dan. "But I guess to be honest it's a bit of a disappointment after the outside, which is spectacular."

"Yes. I like the Gaudí stuff but it's limited. You really need to go to Barcelona to see his work."

After visiting the cathedral Dan announced he was hungry. They stopped at a café in one of the nearby pedestrianised streets and enjoyed a typical Spanish breakfast of coffee and tostadas. They then moved on to visit the Arab Baths, one of the few buildings left from the Moorish occupation of Mallorca, and sat for a while in the cool of its shady garden. They spent the rest of the morning wandering round the old town and browsing in the countless shops, before heading to Antonio's apartment.

A project manager at the Balearic Institute of Marine Archaeology, Antonio knew everything there was to know about Roman shipwrecks.

"Dan, que tal?" he said, embracing Dan as they came through the door.

"Muy bien gracias," replied Dan. "May I introduce you to my friend Korina?"

Antonio's eyes widened with pleasure as Korina entered. "Muy encantado," he said, kissing her on both cheeks. "Welcome to my humble abode."

Antonio's 'humble abode' was actually a magnificent duplex in the old town with spectacular views over the cathedral and the sea.

"Now, first things first," he said, opening a bottle of *Sa Vall Seleccio Privada*. "I know it's a little early but as this is a special occasion I chose a bottle of my favourite Mallorcan white wine."

"Excellent," said Dan.

"And to go with that I'm preparing one of my favourite local dishes, baby eels. I do hope you like eels. I bought them at the market this morning." He went to the kitchen and came back with a box of small eels.

Dan was horrified. "Are they supposed to be still wriggling?"

"But of course," said Antonio laughing. "They need to go into the pan alive."

"Dan, don't be such a wimp," said Korina, winking at Antonio. "They look wonderful. We eat a lot of eels in Crete. I'll be interested to see how long you cook them for. Not too long I hope."

"Just enough to stop them wriggling," he replied, winking back at Korina.

Dan felt sick.

Korina joined Antonio in the kitchen and watched attentively as he prepared and cooked the eels.

"Now," said Antonio, after they had settled at the table, "I've read your translation of the merchant's account of the shipwreck. There are several possibilities, but given the timing and the description of the coastline, there is one that stands out."

"Great," said Dan.

Antonio produced a large-scale map of southeastern Spain. "The merchant said he'd sailed north for a day or so from Carthago Nova, modern day Cartagena."

"Yes. I wasn't sure how far a Roman merchant ship would get in that time," said Dan.

"Well it would obviously depend a lot on conditions, but on average it would be in the region of four or five knots per hour. So by the second day we could be looking at this sort of area."

Antonio moved his finger up the coast from Cartagena to the region north of Alicante. "Now an important clue is the merchant's reference to the coastline being mountainous with large cliffs. Once you get round the headland from Cartagena the coastline is pretty flat until you get north of Alicante. Then you start to get cliffs."

"Yes. I know the area because I have a friend at Alicante University. She's driven me along that coastline."

"That would be María Sanchez I guess?"

Dan nodded. "Yes. Of course, I'd forgotten you'd met her."

"The other clue," continued Antonio, "is that the merchant talks of being shipwrecked near a small Roman town, where he was offered hospitality by a family. Now there are a few candidates. One of them is Villajoyosa, a town a few miles north of Alicante. Modern-day Villajoyosa is built on the site of the Roman town of Allon."

"I know it," said Dan. "María and I passed by it on the way up to a dig she was doing just north of there in the little village of El Albir in the Bay of Altea."

"Interestingly," said Antonio, "there's a wreck of a Roman merchant vessel just off the coast of Villajoyosa. It's called the *Bou Ferrer* after two local divers who discovered it. It was carrying the sort of Hispanic produce that the merchant is likely to have taken on board in Carthago Nova if he planned to head back to Italy. It could just be coincidence of course. But it does fit timing-wise as the wreck dates from the first century AD, and the terrain fits perfectly. Until you get to the Villajoyosa area the coastline is still flat, but once you go north from there it gets quite mountainous, with cliffs sweeping down to the sea."

"So all things considered," said Dan, "you think it's the best place to start?"

"Yes. I did look at other possibilities, but in every case there was something that didn't fit: the date of the wreck, the distance from Cartagena or the terrain. The *Bou Ferrer* is the one that stands out for me."

Dan was hoping that no one had noticed that he'd hardly touched the eels. Fortunately, in Spain it was customary to serve food in a single dish for sharing rather than as individual portions. Korina had evidently noticed though because she pushed the bowl Dan's way.

"Dan, with all the excitement you've hardly eaten any eels," she said innocently, serving him a sizeable portion.

Dan glared at her. *Oh, thank you so much*, he thought, gritting his teeth and forcing some down.

When they got back to the boat Dan got out a map of the Valencian region. He pointed to the town of Villajoyosa that Antonio had mentioned, just north of Alicante. "That's the Roman town of Allon, modern day Villajoyosa where Antonio's *Bou Ferrer* wreck is located. It's not far south of Altea where I was proposing we stay."

"Your guesswork maybe wasn't far off the mark then," said Korina.

"Let's hope so. The merchant said he hid the disc in a cave. The only significant caves in the immediate area are just inland from there, the Cuevas de Canelobre. They're now a tourist attraction."

"Should we go and check them out?"

"I don't think so. Chances are that if there was anything hidden there it would have been found by now. And the manuscript talks of the merchant sailing in a small boat along the coast before spotting the cave, so the site is too far inland. I don't think the coast will have silted up round there. If anything it's more likely to have eroded. The cliffs are mainly soft sandstone and limestone."

"Let's hope the merchant's cave hasn't disappeared into the sea then."

They studied the map for a few moments. "As Antonio says, to the south around Alicante the coastline looks pretty flat," said Korina. "I can't see there being caves and steep cliffs down there."

Dan agreed. "To the north on the other hand, around Altea where we'll be staying, there are a number of bays with cliffs going down to the sea. I think that's where we should start looking. We could head down the coast from Altea to Villajoyosa, and the site of the *Bou Ferrer* wreck, and then work our way back up along the coast. The merchant talks of sailing for about an hour in a small boat, so that could fit."

***

Korina had insisted on taking Antonio and Dan out in the evening to *Adrian Quetglas*, Antonio's favourite restaurant in Palma, to thank Antonio for his research. The restaurant was not far from the marina and the old town in the direction of Santa Catalina. It was 1 am by the time they left the restaurant. They walked a little way together and then went their separate ways, Antonio heading towards his apartment near the cathedral. At this time of night it was much quieter in the pedestrianised alleyways and squares of the old town. The cruise-ship loads of tourists who had thronged the narrow streets during the day had long since left and the shutters were now down on the numerous gift and souvenir shops which lined the streets. The dimly lit alleyways and squares took on a different, eerier character, shrouded in shadowy darkness punctuated by patches of light from the occasional lamps attached to the walls of buildings.

Antonio wasn't bothered. He often walked through this area late at night on the way back to his apartment and had never had any trouble. He was miles away, reflecting on the fun day he'd just had. Dan was a good friend and it had been great to see him, but his thoughts were mainly about Korina. He had picked up that she was single but hadn't had the chance to ask Dan whether they were an item. If they were then he would be delighted for Dan after the tragic loss of his long-term girlfriend. But if not, Antonio would try to engineer another meeting. He loved her playfulness, the way she had winked at him before serving Dan a helping of eels and forcing him to eat them. As archaeologists she and Antonio would surely have a lot in common and they obviously shared an interest in food. He would use those common interests as an excuse to contact her. Next time he cooked something special he would send her a photo.

Lost in those happy thoughts, he sauntered through the Plaça de la Seu by the cathedral and turned into the Carrer del Deganat, a narrow alleyway lined with elegant four-storey buildings. He was about to turn left at the end when something startled him. Antonio normally paid no attention to the distorted shadows cast by his body which grew taller and thinner as he walked past the intermittent street lamps. He had walked this way so often at night he scarcely even noticed them. But tonight, as he reached the end of the alleyway, he spotted not just one shadow but three. He turned back towards the lamp to look, half expecting it to be a trick of the light. But it wasn't.

Two men wearing identical Slam polo shirts and Bermuda shorts had come up behind him. One of them raced past him, stopped and turned round to face him. Antonio was trapped between the two of them. The man in front took out a knife and pointed it at Antonio's neck, forcing him back against the wall of the alleyway. "Try to run and I'll slit your throat," he said in Italian.

Antonio didn't speak Italian but the language was close enough to Spanish and Catalan for him to understand what the man was saying.

"What did the professor and the girl want?"

"The professor?" asked Antonio, trying to keep calm. This was no ordinary street mugging, he realised. These guys had obviously been following him since he left the restaurant.

"Yes. The professor and the girl you had dinner with, what did they want?"

"They just happened to be visiting Mallorca and invited me out to dinner."

The man took the knife away from Antonio's throat and stuck it in his leg. Antonio fell to the ground clutching his thigh, his face contorted in pain. The two muggers stood over him and grinned. The one with the knife then knelt on his chest. "Tell us what they wanted or I'll stick this in your eye," he said, moving the blade to within a centimetre of Antonio's face.

Antonio was terrified. He was wondering what to say when the other mugger suddenly collapsed on to the pavement, clutching his throat. The man kneeling on Antonio was in the process of looking round to see what had happened when he received a vicious kick in the side of the head, sending him sprawling against the side of the alleyway.

A third man stood over Antonio and peered down at him. His dark hair tied back in a short ponytail, he wore a silk scarf which concealed the lower part of his face.

"Go," he said to Antonio in English. "Go quickly. Do not look back."

Antonio didn't need further encouragement. He pulled himself up, clutching his wounded leg, and limped off as quickly as he could. He did as instructed and didn't look back, but hurrying away he saw the silhouette of his guardian angel projected on the wall in front of him. The silhouette raised a boot and brought it down sharply towards the ground.

Antonio got back to his apartment and bolted the door. He was trained in first aid and kept a fully stocked medical cabinet in case of accidents when rummaging around underwater archaeological sites. His hands were still shaking but he managed to clean the leg wound, which fortunately was not too deep, bathe it in antiseptic and dress it. He then tried Dan's phone but there was no answer. *Probably asleep already*, he thought, looking at his watch. He poured himself a large glass of brandy to steady his nerves.

***

Alessandro Ferrari was sitting at breakfast with his Ukrainian wife on his elegant yacht in the Port de Mallorca marina in Palma. He had spent the last two nights there with seven of his men. He had chosen the marina so that he could keep an eye on the professor and the Cretan girl, who had moored just across the harbour in the Marina Moll Vell. He had been following them at a discreet distance ever since they left Naples.

The museum Director had sent him a copy of the passages of the scroll telling the Herculaneum merchant's story. With a little help from an old friend in Rome he'd been able to understand enough to guess they were heading to Spain to search for the golden disc. His plan was simple: he would follow them and, if they found it, he would snatch it.

He had been a little surprised when they spent the day in Palma. He had expected them just to overnight there and continue over to the Spanish mainland. His men were despatched to keep a discreet eye on them, which they had done all day, reporting in regularly as instructed. But then in the early hours two of his men failed to ring in and stopped answering their mobiles. He sent his other men out to look for them but in vain. They reported that there was a lot of police activity in the old town, with whole areas cordoned off. Ferrari decided to abandon the search and ordered his remaining men back to the boat.

While at breakfast he was listening to Onda Italia, a local Mallorcan radio station that broadcast in Italian. He nearly choked on his coffee when he heard the news headlines.

Two men thought to be Italian were found dead in the old town early this morning. Their identity is as yet unknown, as is the precise cause of death. According to sources at the Guardia Civil, both men suffered multiple fractures to their limbs. Police are keen to interview a man who was observed leaving the scene. He is reported to be in his late thirties to early forties and have dark hair with a ponytail.

Dammit, thought Ferrari. Thankfully he had taken the precaution to make sure the men had nothing on them which would connect them with him, but it probably wouldn't be long before the police started checking the marinas for Italian boats, particularly since the two of them were wearing identical Italian-made Slam sailing outfits. He ordered his men to get the yacht under way as quickly as they could. They sailed out of the marina and stood off shore. Ferrari then asked his men to watch for other boats coming out. A little while later the professor's boat appeared and they began to follow it at a discreet distance.

Ferrari was trying to work out who might have murdered his men. It was too much to believe that they were simply mugged. This had to be connected with the disc. Perhaps someone else knew about it. Had Rossi spoken to someone other than the girl about it before Ferrari's men silenced him? Or had the professor or the girl told someone? Was it conceivable they had back-up?

The report of the multiple broken bones worried him. It sounded as though his men might have been interrogated. He didn't have much sympathy for them. It was their problem if they were stupid enough to get themselves caught. What worried him was what they might have said. Whoever did it would now have the drop on him. They would know who he was while he had no idea who they were.

He decided there was little he could do and so there was no point in worrying about it, but he would be more vigilant from now on. He ordered his men to break out the guns and rifles that were hidden in the secret compartment below deck.

***

The Society's Inner Sanctum met at the usual place.

"So, the main item to report on," said the Leader, "is the attempted foreign takeover of the *Energia* group by a German company. You'll remember that at our last meeting we agreed to take steps to halt the takeover. I'm pleased to tell you that following our timely intervention the bid has been dropped."

Applause around the table.

"There's one further matter I should mention," said the Leader. "It's just by way of information at this stage. The possibility has arisen of acquiring what might be a significant artefact of great interest to us all." The Leader went on to explain in more detail.

"Won't there be competition?" asked one man.

"You're right to ask. There is already in fact. But I've taken steps to eliminate it."

"And will there not be some bureaucracy involved?"

"Another good point. I've taken action to bypass it. I hope to report on the successful conclusion of this matter at our next meeting. So if all business has been concluded let's retire to the courtyard and join the rest of the Society for more pleasurable activities. We have another theatre piece to watch this evening."

***

Dan and Korina left the marina in Palma to complete the short hop over to the town of Altea on the Spanish mainland. Once again the weather was kind to them. It was a clear day and the sea was calm. After leaving the marina they headed west along Mallorca's southern coast before turning southwest out to sea. Korina noted that Dan seemed relaxed after their day in Palma and was taking it steadily, enjoying the final leg of their journey. After an hour or so they reached Ibiza, the holiday island famous for its clubbing scene. They sailed along the stunning northwestern coast of the island before turning towards the Spanish mainland.

As they crossed to the mainland the weather began to turn. Dark clouds gathered over the distant mountains and the sea became choppier as the wind picked up. Korina had just come back on deck with two mugs of coffee when Dan's mobile rang.

"Hi, Antonio," he said. "What a great day and thanks again for your help." He then fell silent as he listened to Antonio.

"Thank God you're OK," he said finally. "Do take it easy over the next few days. Call me anytime."

"Is Antonio OK?" asked Korina after Dan had rung off.

"Yeah he's fine," said Dan, who stared ahead towards the horizon seemingly deep in thought. "Would you mind taking the helm for a while please? I just need to make a quick call."

"Sure," said Korina, puzzled and annoyed that Dan hadn't shared with her what Antonio had said.

Dan picked up his phone and punched in a number.

"Hi, Antje," she heard him say before he disappeared out of earshot.

About five minutes later he returned.

"All OK?" asked Korina.

"All fine. Thanks. I'll take back control now." He rammed the throttles forward and took the boat up to full speed. He kept it there until they were in the approach to Altea marina.

***

By the time they got to Altea the threatened storm had passed over and it was a beautiful summer's evening. Dan had booked a hotel for a couple of nights to give them a break from the boat, choosing the *Hotel Altaya* just across from the port. After they had checked in, Korina took the opportunity to ring her father and have a relaxing soak in the Jacuzzi. Meanwhile Dan dropped his bag on the bed, jumped in the shower and headed back across to the marina. After Antonio's call he had kept a close eye on the radar and had noticed a boat some way behind that seemed to be on the same course. When he had taken the yacht up to full speed the boat had speeded up and kept pace with them. He had calculated it was about ten minutes behind them as they entered Altea marina.

Dan walked into the marina to see a sleek black motor yacht arriving. The stylish craft was unmistakably Italian. Dan counted six men and one woman on board. Five of the men, presumably the crew, wore identical dark polos and

Bermuda shorts, the uniform Antonio had told him the muggers were wearing. The sixth, the captain and possibly the owner, wore white chinos and a navy jacket, with a peaked cap embroidered with gold lace. The tall slim woman lounged in a bikini and sunglasses on the rear deck. Incongruously three off-road motorbikes were strapped on to the front deck of the elegant vessel.

Dan headed back to the hotel, meeting Korina in the bar. They decided to stay locally for a bite and ate at *Casa Jaume*, a small bar on the seafront near the hotel. The bar served delicious seafood tapas, which were a perfect match for the excellent house wine. Before turning in they had a quick stroll along Altea's seafront promenade. Dan was grateful that Korina didn't press him about Antonio's call. He'd kept it to himself because he didn't want to worry her. For the same reason he didn't mention the arrival of the Italian yacht.

Chapter 9

Alexia Psaltis woke with the alarm and noticed the inert male body in bed next to her. *I really shouldn't do this*, she thought. She had met the body the night before at a party. She didn't normally go in for one-night stands, but after a while without a boyfriend she had needed the sex.

She got up and made herself a coffee. Walking over to her desk, which was littered with papers, photos and newspaper clippings, she gathered what she needed for her 10 am meeting with the editor of the *Cretan Daily News* and placed them in a leather bag before heading for the shower. Pulling on a smart white jeans skirt and black top, she left a note for the body telling it where to find breakfast, quietly closed the door of her apartment and slipped out into Louka Petraki Street in central Heraklion in Crete.

"Over the last ten years," said Alexia, sitting down opposite the editor, "Crete has seen its media, including this newspaper, and key sectors such as telecommunications, armaments and shipping all come under the control of just four people, and one man in particular, Stelios Kouklakis."

"That's hardly surprising really. Crete's a small place," said the editor.

"And all four happen to be members of the Minoan Cultural Society, a society whose stated mission is to resurrect the values of ancient Minoan Crete."

"So what? So are a lot of people," said the editor. "It's a great society. Supports historical research and puts on wonderful theatre pieces and lectures. I'm a member myself."

"What it means though is that the four of them know each other well and meet regularly."

"What's your point, Alexia?"

"I'm not sure. I just think it isn't healthy having the media and key industries controlled by a small group of people."

"You're going to need more than that if you want to do a piece," said the editor. "We'll have their lawyers on us like a ton of bricks if we make the slightest suggestion of collusion or anti-competitive behaviour."

"I suspect there's even more to it than that. I think these guys may have plans we don't know about."

"What plans?"

"Well the Society is all about harking back to some Cretan golden age. I think…"

"Alexia. Come on! I see where you're heading and it's pure speculation. I know you have good instincts but I think you're letting your imagination run away with you on this one. It's becoming an obsession."

"There's other odd stuff going on too. In the last five years we've had a seventy percent reduction in organised crime. The foreign gangs we had a few years ago have mainly vanished."

"That's a good thing. It means the police have been doing their job."

"But there have hardly been any convictions. I checked the figures. The conviction rate has stayed the same. Where have the criminals gone? Have they all decided suddenly to go home? It doesn't stack up."

"Well that is a little odd, I must admit. Have you asked the police about it?"

"I've tried. And I've got nowhere. In fact word has obviously got round about my inquiries and they've started refusing me interviews. To get to talk to them I have to tell them it's about something else. There's definitely something going on, and I think the police are complicit in it."

"Alexia, you always do great pieces. But on this one you've no real evidence. And to run a story like this would be massive. I'd need a smoking gun, clear proof that there was a conspiracy of some sort. And there's no way I could run it without management approval."

"You mean Stelios Kouklakis?"

"There you go again with your conspiracy theories. Stelios doesn't get involved with editorial control. That's left to the editorial board."

"And then there's something else," continued Alexia, "the failed takeovers. In the past five years, since the financial crisis in Greece, there have been multiple attempts by foreign private equity companies, mainly German, to acquire Cretan assets. All but one has failed. When I looked into them the prospective purchaser backed out right at the last minute."

"Well again that could just be coincidence. It probably often happens for one reason or another. Have you tried to interview them about it?"

"I tried to talk to the chairman of a German company, Gerhard Schaumberger, about the latest one. It was weird. The takeover was all set up but his company pulled out at the last minute without explanation. I tried to disguise what I was inquiring into. I said I was doing a general piece about inward investment in Greece. When his secretary found out I was from Crete, she told me she had instructions to refuse all requests by Cretan journalists."

"Again you could be reading too much into it. It's not all that surprising that he didn't want to tell the press about the company's reasons for dropping the bid."

"There's something going on. I know it. And I think it has to do with the Minoan Cultural Society."

"Look, Alexia, I know I'm not going to dissuade you. You're unstoppable once you get started on something. It's why you're so good at what you do, I guess. But you'll need a whole lot more than you have right now if we're going to run this story."

"I'll keep digging. Don't you worry."

"I'm sure you will. Now, Alexia, what about the piece on the local councillor who we think is taking bribes? What's his name?"

"Christakos. Yes, it's nearly done. I'll send it over to you later this morning. I had a long alcoholic lunch with him. I pretended I was an agent acting for a local developer seeking planning permission. We agreed a 'fee' for his efforts with a bonus contingent on planning permission being granted. He tried to get me into bed as well, the randy old goat. I told him I wasn't part of the deal! I recorded the whole thing."

"Excellent, Alexia. That's more like it. If you can get it to me by lunchtime today we can publish it tomorrow. I'll put our legal department on notice that I have a story for them to vet quickly. Can you give me the recordings to pass on to them? Oh yes, and a short headline piece for the front page. And we need some photos."

"Already done. A photographer friend of mine secretly snapped our lunch."

"Brilliant. Send those over as well."

***

Dan and Korina, refreshed after a good night's sleep in the hotel, left the marina in Altea around 10 am and slipped out into the bay. The forecast was for a scorching hot day and they were both dressed to stay cool, Dan wearing a T-shirt and swimming shorts and Korina cut-off jeans and a top.

Dan had been keeping one eye on the radar screen and saw that they were again being followed by another boat. Once they were out of the bay and a good distance from the shoreline, Dan turned the boat south and took it up to full cruising speed. After a minute or so he looked at the radar screen to see whether their tail had stayed with them. It had.

After about half an hour Dan pointed to a town on the coast off the starboard side. "So that's Villajoyosa, Roman Allon."

Slowing the boat down a little he turned in towards the shore. A few minutes later he throttled right back and slowed the boat down to a virtual halt. He checked the GPS. "The *Bou Ferrer* wreck is somewhere around here. This is where we begin to retrace our steps."

Turning the boat round he headed back north along the coast towards Altea. He handed Korina a pair of binoculars. "We'll go back more slowly and stay closer inshore so that we can inspect the shoreline."

Their 180 degree turn meant they were now heading towards the boat that had been tailing them. Dan wasn't surprised when the sleek Italian craft that had moored in the Altea marina the night before appeared off the starboard bow. He steered towards it and passed close by, waving.

"Beautiful boat. Bellissima," he shouted.

Two of the men on the boat waved back, rather awkwardly he thought.

***

They continued back towards Altea and passed the headland north of Villajoyosa. Korina, who had been scouring the coastline with her binoculars, pointed to a small cave above a cove. "Is that a possibility?"

"Let's take a closer look," said Dan, turning the boat towards the cove.

Having dropped anchor, he took the binoculars from Korina and inspected the cliffs. "The one thing that's missing is the unusually red earth which the merchant mentions. This is just limestone rock."

"I guess," said Korina, "the colour of the earth is unlikely to have changed so radically?"

"Probably not. Two thousand years isn't all that long in geological terms. Let's continue along the coast to see whether there's a better fit. We can always come back."

It was now late morning and already very hot. Dan decided to have a swim to cool off. Korina quietly admired Dan's lithe muscular physique as he stripped off his T-shirt and dived into the turquoise waters. *Not bad*, she thought, *for a professor. He must work out to keep in that sort of shape.* She noticed though that he had a number of scars here and there on his body and wondered how a professor would have got those.

A few minutes later Dan emerged from the water and announced that he was starving. Korina, anticipating this, had gone out early to visit Altea's indoor food market. She rustled up a lunch of bread, cheese, tomatoes and Iberico ham, which Dan tucked into appreciatively.

He studied the map while they ate. "Interesting. I don't know how I missed it. In the Bay of Altea, where we're staying, the Sierra Gelada mountains sweep down to the sea and are the site of a disused nineteenth-century red ochre mine."

"So red earth?"

"Yes. All we need is a cave. But I hope it's not too near the mine as our disc will have been discovered."

"OK. Let's go and have a look," said Korina, packing away their lunch.

"Yes. But before that I'll introduce you to the delights of Benidorm."

***

Dan started the engines and they headed north around a headland to be greeted by a scene that looked like Gotham City on sea, a sweeping sandy bay circled by huge skyscrapers.

"Welcome to Benidorm. It's incredible to think that just over fifty years ago this was a picturesque fishing village. Like many villages along the Spanish coast it was transformed, some would say ruined, when developers took advantage of the tourist boom in the 1960s."

"In a funny sort of way I rather like it," said Korina. "And the beaches look terrific. I guess that's the big draw."

"And the climate. It has one of the best all-year round climates in Europe. It's a shame really. Lax urban planning gave the developers free rein to build monstrous tower blocks like the one over there." Dan pointed to a huge skyscraper with twin towers supporting a strange funnel-like structure.

Korina smiled. "I bet you have a great view from the top. I must admit though Benidorm is very different from Altea where we're staying. Altea's much quainter."

"The Benidorm old town on the hill over there is pretty but it's surrounded by tall modern buildings. Happily the town councils in some of the smaller resorts north of Benidorm learned the lesson and introduced stricter controls. The Brits love it though. It's one of their favourite holiday resorts. I once read an article by a British female journalist who complained she was the only person who was not getting laid that night in Benidorm, and it was all her fault."

"Only bad girls go to Benidorm," replied Korina sternly.

Dan thought better of pursuing her remark and changed the subject. He pointed to Benidorm Island in the middle of the bay. "There's an interesting myth attached to that rock, the legend of Roldán's slice. He was one of the commanding officers of Charlemagne, King of the Franks. He is said to have fallen in love with a local maiden. But then a curse predicted she would die the moment the last ray of sunshine touched her skin. Roldán, hero that he was, climbed to the summit of the mountain over there, the Puig Campana."

"I see it. It's an odd shape. There's a bit missing from the ridge at the top."

"The story goes that Roldán drew his sword and cut out a slice of the mountain in order to delay the sunset and prolong her life. But when the sun finally set she died and a grieving Roldán hurled the piece of rock he had hewn out down into the sea. It became Benidorm Island."

"Roldán sounds like a young girl's dream. A sad ending after his heroics."

Dan steered the boat round the headland to the north of Benidorm. "This is the Sierra Gelada National Park. The cove with the red ochre mine is on the north side of the park, just as we enter Altea Bay."

It took them ten minutes or so to cruise round the national park and past the Albir lighthouse, which marked the entrance to the bay. Before them stood the old hill town of Altea and its church with its blue-tiled dome. The town stood against the backdrop of the Mascarat Mountain, its whitewashed buildings reflecting the early evening sunlight. Further round the bay was the modern resort of Calpe with its famous Ifach, a large rock jutting out into the sea.

"The bay is very dramatic when you see it from the boat," said Korina.

"Yeah, it doesn't have the all-important sandy beach though, which is what saved it of course." Dan pointed to a tiny cove just after the lighthouse. "So that's where the red ochre mine used to be."

Korina looked at the map. "Yes. I see it. In fact it's called Cala de la Mina, Mine Bay."

Dan sailed into the cove and tied the boat to a mooring buoy. "Well there's your red earth."

The mine was just above the cove in a ravine. Korina pointed to the remains of a series of stone pillars that led down from the mine. "I imagine the pillars supported rails for wagons that carried the ochre down to the cove to be loaded on to boats."

"I guess sea was the only route out. The cliffs behind are really steep. This whole area would have been very remote in the nineteenth century."

"And even more remote in the first century," replied Korina. "I bet there was hardly anything in this bay then."

"There was a Roman villa in Albir, the one my friend María from Alicante University helped excavate, but I think it dates from a couple of centuries later."

Picking up the binoculars, Korina inspected the cliffs which rose steeply behind the cove to a height of several hundred metres. She pointed to what looked like a large cavern near the top of one of the cliffs. "I suppose we're going to have to put our climbing boots on and scramble up."

"Hmm, it's been a pretty hot day. I don't want to seem unenthusiastic but right now I'm more interested in a beer. I see there's a track about halfway up to the cave that winds round the cliffs towards the lighthouse. Why don't we call it a day and explore the track tomorrow? It should make the climb a bit shorter. I guess it must come from Albir on this side of the bay, about a twenty minute walk from Altea. Tomorrow's Monday. It should be fairly quiet, particularly if we go at the crack of dawn."

Korina agreed. Dan started the engines and they headed out of the cove and across the bay back to the marina in Altea.

"So, drinks," asked Dan as they arrived at the hotel, "and then a stroll up to Altea old town for dinner? I know a little restaurant up there with a great view of the bay."

"That would be lovely. Can you give me an hour? I need to freshen up and call my father. He'll be worried if I don't ring."

"Let's make it a bit later as the restaurant I'm thinking of doesn't get going much before 8.30 anyway. Drinks in the bar at 8?"

***

After her meeting with the editor Alexia went back to her apartment. The body had gone. He'd had the decency to leave a thank-you note, but no telephone number or message saying he would ring. She hadn't really expected it and wasn't particularly bothered.

Making herself another coffee she sat down at her desk. She finalised her piece on the local councillor and sent it to the editor before his lunchtime deadline. She had no qualms at all about the sting. She wouldn't do this sort of thing to just anybody but the guy was a corrupt sleaze ball. He had it coming.

She thought back to her conversation with the editor about the Minoan Cultural Society. He was right. She needed more. But how to get it? She had tried to interview Stelios Kouklakis but hadn't even got past his secretary, who had politely informed her that he didn't give interviews to the press.

"But this isn't a business matter. I want to speak to him about his favourite topic," she had said, "the Minoan Cultural Society."

"I'm sorry," the secretary had replied. "He doesn't like speaking to the press. The Society has a press officer though. I can give you her contact details if you like?"

"I already have them. I wanted to do a more in-depth piece on the founder of the Society."

"I'm sorry. I can't help you."

Alexia went on the Society's website and continued her reading of its annual reports. She began to wonder whether the editor was right. Perhaps she was just becoming obsessed and letting her imagination run riot. The Society's members were plainly fanatical about Minoan history and culture, but there was no hint of anything sinister.

She then came across a section of the report on the activities of the Society's finance committee. *That's interesting*, she thought, reading the list of members of the committee. So Stelios and the other three tycoons are all on the finance committee. They must meet privately all the time. She knew it still wasn't enough though to get her editor's attention. He would dismiss it as a coincidence or say it was logical to have the wealthiest entrepreneurs in charge of the Society's finances.

She was about to close the website when a news item popped up. The Society was putting on a theatre piece, *Theseus and the Minotaur*, which would be open to the public. The performance would be at the *Kazantzakis Theatre* in Heraklion on Saturday evening the following week. *Perfect*, thought Alexia, booking herself a ticket online.

***

Dan had noticed that the Italian yacht had remained with them all day and had been stationary as they inspected the cove with the red ochre mine. It had then followed them over the bay and slipped back into the Altea marina shortly after them. He dashed upstairs and showered. Within five minutes he was in a taxi heading towards Alfaz del Pi, a town just behind the coast in the Altea Bay.

The Alicante region had a tram network which ran up the coast from Alicante past Benidorm to the town of Denia. The Alfaz del Pi tram stop used to be on a main road to Benidorm but was now on a disused side road. Next to the platform was a bar, converted from the old station house. Dan knew it from previous visits. It was a strange affair, having the feel of somewhere that had seen better times. But for rock enthusiasts it was THE venue on Sunday evenings. Every Sunday local and visiting musicians of various nationalities met for a jamming session. Some weeks it was better than others. When it worked it was fabulous.

This was July and so the venue was outside. Dan got out of the taxi and immediately saw Antje, whom he had rung from the yacht the previous day. Not that she was someone you easily missed. A tall, athletic-looking woman with shortish blonde hair slicked back over her ears and a ring in one ear, she sat watching the band in leopard-skin leggings and a black strappy top, revealing her toned muscular physique. Dan sat down on the seat next to her to the sound of *A Girl Like You* by Edwyn Collins.

Without taking her eyes off the band she said,

"I wondered when my cunning linguist would turn up. What can Antje do for him?"

Antje had Caesar's habit of using the third person. While in Caesar's case it may have been a mark of arrogance, in Antje's it just betrayed her supreme self-confidence.

"I'm a linguistics professor way out of his depth."

Antje turned her head very slightly, her eyebrows raised. "And so what's in it for Antje?"

"Well, obviously I'll pay…"

"Don't be insulting! You know what I want."

Dan sighed. "OK. I guess so. But you'll have to be gentle with me. I'm not as young as I used to be."

"No way. No conditions, no limits," said Antje uncompromisingly.

Dan groaned. He needed her and she knew it. "OK. No limits."

Antje gave a satisfied smile. She pointed to the drummer and lead singer. "He's my latest by the way. I really like this one. I may keep him."

God help him if he has different ideas, thought Dan. "Then why do you need me to…"

"He doesn't have your endurance yet," replied Antje.

"Well, I don't want to deny him practice," said Dan feebly.

"Oh come on! Where would you get your kicks otherwise as a boring old professor?"

I wish people would stop calling me old, thought Dan. He gave up and changed the subject.

"Does he know about…?"

"Yes. He's the first one I've told for a while. I had stopped telling them. They normally can't handle it."

Antje often cut people off mid-sentence, which some found irritating. It wasn't that she didn't listen when she needed to; it was just that she didn't see the point in wasting time waiting when she knew what was coming. She rarely guessed wrong.

Dan had first met Antje ten years earlier when he was in the US Navy. She was a member of a Norwegian Special Forces unit that took part in a joint operation. She was now nearly thirty but she hadn't really changed much. Born of Dutch and Norwegian parents, Antje was a force of nature. Eccentric bordering on crazy, super bright and extremely calm under pressure, she was one of the world's most accomplished professional killers. Dan trusted her completely.

She had recently left the Norwegian armed forces and was now freelance, working mainly for Norwegian and other governmental agencies.

"I should warn you though," she said, continuing on the subject of her new boyfriend, "he has scruples. He's made me promise to be selective. I only kill people who are really bad."

"Do I have to certify that?"

Antje smiled. "Hmm. I guess in your case I'll take it as read."

Their conversation was interrupted by another of Antje's favourites, AC/DC's *Highway to Hell*, sung by a middle-aged vocalist whom Dan remembered from previous visits. His powerful throaty voice was a perfect match for the song and compelled everyone to join in.

The band then stopped for a break and Antje's boyfriend came over to say 'Hi'. They chatted for a few minutes. His name was Bert, which was short for Bernardus. Dan made a mental note to check why it was that the Dutch often went in for Latin-sounding names. Catholic influence maybe? He learned that Bert was in his forties. He'd spent a long time in the Netherlands Navy. When he left he came down to Spain and was making a living as a musician in the clubs in Benidorm, which was where he met Antje. Dan found he took an instant liking to him. He somehow seemed a good fit for Antje.

The music resumed and Dan took the opportunity to brief Antje, telling her everything he knew. He told her about Giovanni Rossi and Korina, the story in the scroll, the events in Mallorca and the Italian yacht with the three off-road bikes strapped to its deck. He also told her about their plans for the following day.

Antje listened in silence. "If you're going to get back into these sorts of adventures," she said once he had finished, "you should re-assemble some of your team. Joe and Ed are as bored as hell since they left the Navy."

"It's a thought," said Dan. "I hate to admit it but I may be a bit old for this sort of thing. I think I should stick to the classroom. Anyway let's see what happens. Most important thing is I have you. I may be worrying unnecessarily but I have a bad feeling about this."

"I've never known your instincts to be wrong."

Despite the warning Dan left the tram stop feeling much happier, knowing that Antje would be keeping an eye on the Italian gang who, in all probability, had attacked Antonio and murdered Giovanni Rossi.

***

By the time Korina came down from her room Dan was sitting in the bar of the hotel. It was a warm evening. Korina had chosen a cool white linen dress with thin shoulder straps and was wearing her favourite bee pendant and matching gold earrings.

Dan waited for Korina to be served a glass of white wine before opening a large-scale map of Altea Bay. "So the lighthouse track now frequented by tourists was only opened in the 1960s. Before that there was just a mountainous trail up to the lighthouse. The whole area was very remote. I fear even from the path it's going to be quite a scramble up the cliff to the cave."

"In a way that's encouraging. If it is the site it may not have been discovered."

"Let's hope so. Anyway, there's only one way to find out, but it should be much cooler, at least, first thing in the morning."

They finished their drinks and walked up from their hotel on the seafront to Altea's old town perched on a hill behind. They climbed the steep alleyways leading up to the Plaça de l'Església, the small square next to the Nuestra Señora del Consuelo, the pretty church with its blue-tiled dome they had admired from the yacht. The church was a landmark that could be seen from all over the bay.

Korina pointed to the plaque showing the name of the square. "Tell me, what language is that? Is it Catalan? I didn't think Catalonia came this far south."

"It's called Valenciano, which is related to Catalan. It's widely spoken in the Valencian region but they're not quite as obsessive about it as the Catalans. Here you get a mixture of Valenciano and Castellano, Castilian

Spanish, and most people are happy to talk to you in either. In Catalonia, Barcelona for example, my impression is they'd rather speak to you in English than in Castilian. You don't have the same separatist movement in this part of Spain."

"I don't think it's surprising you have a separatist movement in Catalonia. You have a local community with a different heritage who feel let down by the central government."

Dan was intrigued by Korina's remark. He didn't pursue it but made a mental note to ask her about Crete's relationship with Athens. He had been keeping an eye out for anyone following them as they had climbed up to the old town but had seen no one. They crossed to the southern edge of the Plaça de l'Església, from where there was a panoramic view across the bay and beyond to the silhouettes of the Benidorm skyscrapers in the distance.

"It's breathtaking," said Korina. "And with the Benidorm skyscrapers shrouded in sea mist this evening they look even more like something from a Batman movie."

Dan pointed to the resort of Albir, which lay at the foot of the mountainous Sierra Gelada National Park. "That's where we're heading in the morning. According to the map the lighthouse track begins at the top of the village, just below the pine trees."

They left the viewpoint and, crossing the square, strolled through the old town to the *Casa Vital*, a friendly, unpretentious restaurant with interesting tapas which were served on a large terrace overlooking the bay. They started chatting about the day ahead.

"What if we find the disc?" asked Korina. "What shall we do with it?"

Dan smiled. "Let's not get ahead of ourselves. As I'm sure you'll tell me, archaeology is rarely that easy. But I guess if we did find it we'd need to hand it over to the Spanish authorities. They'd have the first claim because the find would be in their territory."

"It doesn't seem fair," said Korina. "It belongs in a museum in Crete."

"I see your point. But I think Crete would have to negotiate with the Spanish authorities. There are serious penalties now in the EU and elsewhere for removing antiquities from a country without permission. I don't think we could risk it."

They fell silent for a few moments.

"It occurs to me," Korina said eventually, "that I haven't asked you whether you've ever been to Crete. You're very knowledgeable about Minoan history but have you had the opportunity to visit?"

"Yes, only once. It was quite a short trip. Too short. I was there for a conference. I did get to visit the Heraklion Museum and the Knossos palace though."

"Dan," said Korina, gazing into his eyes, "I've really enjoyed being with you the last few days. Do you promise you'll visit me in Crete?"

"I promise. I'd like that very much."

"Whatever happens?"

"Sure," said Dan, a little puzzled. He still couldn't work out where he had seen those eyes before, and it was bugging him. But he was relieved that he didn't seem to have upset her. She had gone very quiet after he had said they should hand the disc over to the Spanish authorities. Not that there was really much chance of finding it; the odds surely must be stacked against it.

They strolled back down from the old town to the seafront. Again Dan was keeping his eyes peeled for anyone following them but saw no one.

"So the night is young," said Korina suddenly. "Are you going to take me to Benidorm now?"

Dan was taken aback after her response on the boat. "I thought nice girls didn't go to Benidorm?"

"Who said I was a nice girl?" she asked in a deep husky voice, putting her arm through his.

Dan still struggled to read Korina. He had very little idea what was going on beneath the playful exterior. He gambled and put his arm around her. She responded by resting her head against his shoulder.

"Tell me about yourself," she said. "Do you have a partner?"

"No. I've had girlfriends in the past from time to time."

Korina laughed. "Yes, I bet. I saw the girls competing to talk to you at the conference."

"Hmm," said Dan, slightly embarrassed. "There was really only one that worked out."

"Tell me about her. What was her name?"

"Her name was Aliah. She was Afghan, a doctor like my stepmother. She was killed. She worked with Médecins Sans Frontières and was helping out at the Trauma Centre in Kunduz in northern Afghanistan. She got caught up in the civil war and was in the wrong place at the wrong time."

Korina raised her head from Dan's shoulder and look into his eyes. "That's terrible. What happened?"

"The Taliban had taken over the city and the US supported the Government forces with air strikes as they tried to get the city back. The Centre took a direct hit. It turned out that it had been deliberately targeted."

"Isn't that a war crime, to target a MSF facility?"

"MSF thought so. There were internal investigations in the US of course, but it was dismissed as an accident. I'm doubtful. It seems the pilots who launched the attack had questioned the legality themselves. Something went badly wrong in the US command chain."

"It must have been a terrible shock when you learned about it."

"I was talking to her on the phone when it happened."

Korina looked horrified. "My God, I'm so sorry. When was this? It must have taken you a long time to get over it."

"October 3 2015. Nearly three years ago. I still think about it every day. I keep reliving our last conversation. Virtually her last words to me were 'your guys are bombing the hell out of the place'. Then I heard a crash and people screaming. I kept calling her name but she didn't respond. Such a terrible fuck up."

"That's just awful."

"I keep having nightmares. They're always the same. Aliah is lying there trapped on the floor looking up at me. I reach out to her but she is beyond my grasp. She just keeps staring at me until I wake up."

"Dan, you have to stop blaming yourself. It wasn't your fault."

"I should have done more to stop her from being there. I should have talked her out of it."

"Do you really think you could have? It was obviously important to her to be there. She was doing what she wanted to do."

"I guess so. Thanks."

They walked on in silence for a while. Korina rested her head back on Dan's shoulder. "Tell me about your stepmother. So she's a doctor, too?"

"Yeah."

"Do you get on with her?"

"We get along great," said Dan. "I never really knew my mother. She died when I was quite young. My stepmother raised me and insisted on speaking Arabic to me. She's Syrian. So I grew up bilingual."

"Does she still have family in Syria?"

"Yes," said Dan.

"And your father?"

"My father was a US admiral until very recently. Now retired."

"How did he meet your stepmother?"

"He met her in the UK when he was posted there as a young officer. That was a few years after my mother's death. I stayed in the States and was looked after by my aunt down in Arizona. My father did another stint in the UK later when I was in my teens. My stepmother and I both joined him and I went to school there. She insisted that I go to a British school."

"How did he meet her?"

"In a hospital. She was caring for him," replied Dan.

"How romantic!"

"I'm not sure he thought so at the time. He had a badly broken leg! But he went back later and invited her out on a date."

They sat down on a bench on the promenade near the hotel and gazed out to sea, the darkening waters of the bay punctuated by the lights of occasional boats crossing towards the marina. Korina leaned against Dan and took his hand. "How long did you live in the UK?"

"About five years in all," said Dan. "Then we went back to the States."

"To Boston?"

"Yeah. My father had to travel but my stepmother was based in Boston and I finished my schooling there. My aunt in Arizona was keen to see me after looking after me when I was younger, and so I used to spend time on my uncle's ranch during the vacations. I learned to ride and herd cattle. I loved it. I look back on those days with fond memories."

"How did you come to be a languages academic?"

"I guess my interest in languages came from my stepmother. My father insisted though that after university I should go into the Navy for a while."

"What did you do in the Navy?"

"I was mainly with a special forces unit."

"Which one?"

"It was called SEAL Team Six."

"Did you see any action?"

"Some," said Dan, wondering whether she had noticed the scars when he stripped off for a swim.

"You seem reluctant to talk about it."

"It was a long time ago and I was much younger. It's not very relevant now. It was almost a different life."

"There must be some things that stay with you," said Korina. "It must give you confidence that you can cope with stuff that's thrown at you. I'm surprised you didn't receive some martial arts instruction though."

"It was just practical stuff. And I was a lot fitter then. I'd probably rupture something if I tried it now!"

"Why didn't you stay in the Navy and become an admiral like your father, or even better if that's possible?"

"The Navy was fun. But I was always hooked on ancient languages and wanted to be an academic."

"Must be a little dull though after the Navy?"

"Yeah. In a way I guess everything's a bit of an anti-climax after that, but it beats wearing a business suit on Wall Street, which is where a lot of my contemporaries ended up."

After several days together Dan sensed there was real chemistry between them. But, with Giovanni's death and the memories of Aliah evoked by their conversation, it wasn't the moment to take things further; and in any case getting involved with Stelios' daughter was really the last thing he should be doing right now. They returned to their hotel, agreeing to set their alarms for 5 am.

Chapter 10

Dan woke before his alarm and decided to go to the marina to check the boat. As he left the hotel he noticed a man standing on the promenade opposite. Dressed in the same dark sailing outfit worn by the crew on the Italian yacht, the man started stretching as if he had just completed a jog. By the time Dan returned to the hotel he had gone.

Dan and Korina met in the lobby of the hotel at 5.30 am. Dan had opted for jeans and a T-shirt ready for the scramble up the cliff. Korina was wearing the black leggings she had worn for her martial arts routine on the boat. Her bee pendant hung from her neck.

"Shouldn't you leave the pendant in the hotel safe? It looks valuable. You might damage it if we have to scramble inside caves."

"Thanks, I'd hate to lose it. It used to be my mother's. She gave it to me on my twenty-first birthday. But I think it's safer round my neck. And maybe it'll bring us good luck!"

It was still dark as they walked round the bay but the promenade was well lit. The only sounds were those of the sea lapping against the rocky shoreline and the occasional seagull. Dan discreetly cast a glance behind from time to time to check whether anyone was following. There was no one close but he noticed a figure keeping pace some three or four hundred metres behind.

Dawn was breaking as they reached the village of Albir. The only people around were cleaners sweeping up outside cafés and council workmen emptying bins and hosing down the pavements. Dan could have killed for a coffee but there was nowhere open yet. They left the promenade and walked up a steep road which led to a car park at the foot of the lighthouse track. The place was deserted. Climbing steadily upwards they followed the trail as it wound round the hillside through a forest of Mediterranean pine trees. It was now getting light enough to see the beautiful views down to the bay to their left.

After about a kilometre the track passed through a tunnel. It then began to twist sharply as it curved round the mountainside, the land falling away in a sheer drop down to the sea. Sandstone-coloured slabs had been placed along the edge to prevent unsuspecting tourists from tumbling down the cliff. Oddly there was a slab missing or broken here and there.

Dan could see no sign of Antje, but then he wouldn't have expected to. He checked his phone for texts. There was one which read,

She's pretty. Can I kill her? I'm sure she's bad.

Dan felt reassured. Antje was in position and watching the track.

After about another kilometre the track turned sharply to the left. Dan stopped and pointed to the ruined buildings down below.

"There's the red ochre mine, just above the cove where we were yesterday afternoon."

He turned and looked up at the cliff towering above them. At the top was the large cavern they had spotted from the cove, its wide entrance resembling the arch of a Roman bridge. "OK. So this is what you've been waiting for. This is where we leave the path and climb."

It was a steep scramble up to the cavern. In places the rock was very loose, the result of occasional torrential downpours which had broken chunks off the sandstone and limestone rocks and washed them down the mountainside. After about forty-five minutes' climbing they reached the cavern. Before entering they sat on a rock for a moment to catch their breath, inspecting the cavern from the outside.

"Well I can't imagine there are many people who come up here," said Korina.

"Yeah, I'm beginning to wonder whether our merchant would really have climbed all this way up with the chest. We've only come from the modern-day track. It's at least twice as far from the cove."

They began scouring the mountainside around them to see whether they could find a more promising site.

"Look," said Korina. "There's a small hole in the cliff over there. It's a fair bit lower down. Is that a better bet?"

"Yeah, it could well be. But as we've come all this way up, I guess we may as well have a look at this one first."

They went into the cavern and shone their torches around. It was wide but wasn't very deep.

"I really don't see the merchant hiding the disc in here. There's no obvious place to bury it," said Dan after a few minutes. "I think we should go and look at the little cave you spotted."

As they came out of the cavern Korina put her hand on Dan's arm. "Listen. I can hear motorbikes. It sounds like they're on the trail below."

From where they were they couldn't see the lighthouse trail. They waited and listened for a few moments. The noises got louder, echoing round the mountainside, and then stopped abruptly.

"Must be some local lads out early on their bikes," said Dan.

They scrambled down towards the smaller cave. From there they had a view of the track, but there was no sign of any motorbikes or people.

***

It had been barely dawn when Antje jogged up the trail to the Albir lighthouse, her telescopic sniper's rifle disassembled and neatly tucked away in a backpack. She had reluctantly abandoned the striking leopard-skin cat-suit she normally wore for her regular twenty-kilometre mountain runs in favour of a plainer outfit that blended in better with the limestone and sandstone cliffs. She knew the Albir lighthouse track well as she often used it as a warm up for the surrounding steeper climbs. Having reached the top of the track, she took up position on the ruined mediaeval watchtower situated just above the lighthouse. Concealed behind a wall, she had a clear view of the entire path but was virtually invisible.

Antje watched as the sun rose above the horizon and spread its rays across the sea, the dark waters of the bay gradually turning into a patchwork of blue and turquoise as they glinted in the sunlight. A pod of bottlenose dolphins gathered near the fish farm in the middle of the bay, leaping playfully out of the water as they chased each other while awaiting their morning feast. Antje loved observing the bay at sunrise, the morning light adding a particular sharpness to the outline of Altea old town and the ridge of the Mascarat Mountain behind it.

She was distracted from her thoughts as she saw Dan and Korina coming out of the tunnel halfway up the track. She texted Dan to reassure him she was in position. It took them another ten minutes to reach the bottom of the climb up to the cavern. They then left the path and started scrambling up the cliff, eventually disappearing from view.

Not long afterwards Antje heard the sound of motorbikes echoing through the tunnel. Three riders emerged on dirt track bikes one after the other. Peering through the scope of her rifle, she knew immediately they were the men from the Italian yacht. As Dan had predicted, they were wearing identical sailing outfits of dark polos and Bermuda shorts. Their only fashion accessories were their helmets and barely concealed rifles strapped round their necks.

"You've got to be kidding me," murmured Antje. "Don't you get proper baddies these days?"

She tracked them with her rifle as they rode along the trail. "Have these guys got dicks for brains? They're lining up like ducks in a shooting gallery."

She decided to take the opportunity to improve the odds and shot the last rider as he came to the first sharp bend. He went straight on, crashing into the low concrete wall skirting the track. He proceeded to somersault with his bike down the sheer two-hundred metre drop.

"Not bad," she murmured, "but only two somersaults. I'd say a five."

Antje had guessed correctly that the two riders in front would hear nothing through their helmets other than the noise of the bikes' engines. She took aim at the second one just before the next sharp bend. Once again the rider and his motorbike flew over the cliff, doing a number of somersaults as bike and rider fell even further now the path was climbing.

"Oh much better," exclaimed Antje. "Four and half somersaults. I think an eight. Would've been a nine if he hadn't landed on his head. Time to get down and dirty now though."

She ran quickly down the path from the watchtower.

***

The third and final rider was Luigi Carbone, the same Luigi who had helped Giovanni Rossi off the Naples metro platform and had hoped to have fun with Korina in her apartment. His luck with women was not about to improve.

Still unaware of what had happened to the other riders, he stopped above the red ochre mine. He took his helmet off and turned to look behind for the other riders. He was astonished to find they were no longer with him. Before he had time to think further a bullet struck the back of his leg, passing clean through the knee cap. He fell to the ground in agony.

He looked up to find an Amazonian blonde standing over him. She dragged him off the track behind some bushes and then placed her boot on his wounded knee, causing him to scream in pain.

"Ooh how satisfying," she said. "Sorry, but I just have to do that again!"

"No please," screamed Luigi.

"Oh come on! Have some backbone! Why is it so hard to find proper men these days? Oh well, I have a few questions for you. You can begin by telling me who you work for…"

Antje completed her interrogation of Luigi, which she recorded on her phone. When she heard what he had to say she was sorely tempted to throw him off the cliff, but decided against it. He might be more valuable alive. She couldn't resist one last stamp on his wounded knee though. "From Rossi with Love."

She took his bike and rode it down the track towards the tunnel. Concealing the bike behind a bush, she took another vantage point on the rocks above the tunnel. She then texted Dan.

Three down. Two to go. Owner on yacht screwing trophy wife. Have info. You'll have to earn it.

***

Dan and Korina had scrambled down to the cave they had spotted. It was much smaller and lower than the cavern they had explored. There was only room for one person to crawl in at a time. Leaving Korina outside, Dan went in on his hands and knees with a torch, searching for any sign of a hiding place.

"Well it's more promising than the other one, but I can't see anything obvious. Actually, wait a minute, maybe there is something."

Dan noticed there was an area at the back of the cave that was much smoother than the rest of the floor. He began scraping away the red earth with a small trowel Korina had thought to buy from a hardware shop near the hotel. Just under the surface he struck something solid. Clearing away more of the earth he realised that it was a large sheet of metal. He excitedly began removing the earth around it. It soon took shape as the lid of a bronze chest. He continued digging round the chest until it was free. Then he carefully lifted it out of the earth and dragged it slowly backwards out of the cave.

"Well I guess," said Dan, "this is where we find the note saying 'Fooled you. I did get back. Yours truly, The Merchant'."

Korina didn't respond. She stood in silence behind Dan waiting for him to open the chest.

OK, not in the mood for humour obviously. No pressure then, thought Dan.

Kneeling by the chest he opened it, revealing a large circular object covered in remnants of sack cloth. He carefully removed them to find himself gazing upon a large golden disc inscribed with symbols in a series of concentric circles.

Dan was stunned. They had found it. He had never really believed it possible. He began to inspect it.

"So on this side we have Egyptian hieroglyphs," he said, running his fingers round the outer circle.

He turned the disc over, placing it carefully back on the remnants of sack cloth. "And on the other…"

"Minoan hieroglyphs," added Korina from behind.

"Surely archaeology isn't meant to be this easy?" said Dan.

He had no sooner uttered the words than Korina jumped on his back, forcing him to the floor. Sliding her thighs under his arms she wrenched them upwards and yanked his head backwards with her left hand, holding him in a sort of camel clutch wrestling hold. She then brought her right hand forward and gripped his throat and Adam's apple between her thumb and forefingers.

Ah, thought Dan, *the dreaded Tracheal grip choke.*

Unable to move and hardly able to breathe, he gradually weakened.

"Make it easy on yourself, Dan. Don't struggle," he heard Korina say.

His last thoughts before he blacked out were:

I bet Benidorm girls aren't as bad as this.

***

Antje was still in position above the tunnel lower down the lighthouse track when she caught sight of Korina scrambling down the mountainside clutching a large bag. No sign of Dan.

"What has that bitch done to Dan?" she murmured.

She rang his mobile. No answer.

Korina came jogging down the path and went through the tunnel. Antje took a few seconds to decide what to do next. Dan hadn't anticipated this turn of events. "Trust your instincts, girl," she told herself, deciding to follow Korina. If Dan was dead there was nothing she could do for him. If he was alive it was what he would want her to do. She grabbed Luigi's bike and freewheeled down towards the car park at the foot of the track, not wanting to attract attention by starting the engine. She got there just in time to see Korina entering the car park. Antje pulled in behind the nearby tourist office.

As Korina walked by the parked cars two men dressed in the same sailing outfits as those worn by Luigi and his fellow thugs jumped out of a black *Alfa*, brandishing guns.

So there are the other two clowns, thought Antje. *I wonder whether this pair have more brains than the other three.*

"OK, bitch. Hand it over and we won't harm you," said one of the men. Korina stopped and stared at him.

"Don't I know you?" she asked.

"Yes. We met in your apartment, bitch."

"Oh yes. I'm so happy to see you're fit and well. I was really worried about you."

The man looked utterly confused.

Oh dear, thought Antje. *Nope. No brains at all.*

Antje had watched another man emerge from a nearby car and sneak up behind the two thugs while Korina distracted them. His dark hair gathered in a small ponytail, he was dressed in a black tunic not dissimilar to a Kung-Fu suit.

Hmm, nice outfit! Goes well with the ponytail, thought Antje.

He landed sharp blows to the kidneys of the two men, placing them on the ground in agony.

Wow! This guy is the real deal. Not like those other monkeys.

Having dealt with the Italian thugs the man walked up to Korina and kissed her on the cheeks. They got into his car and drove off.

"You treacherous little cow," murmured Antje. She started the engine on the bike and followed them at a discreet distance out of Albir and down the main road along the coast towards Alicante. Just before they reached the city they turned inland and headed to the Alicante aero-club, a private flying club nestled in the mountains just to the north of the city. Antje watched from outside the wire perimeter fence as they boarded a small private jet. She called a number stored on her phone.

"Tracking please for private jet about to leave Alicante aeroclub."

As Antje rode back to Albir she feared the worst. Nearing the lighthouse walk, she rang Dan for the fourth time. This time he answered.

"Where are you?" she asked.

"I'm back at the hotel."

"Shall I see you in the bar in five minutes?"

"Good idea. I need a beer. I have a very sore neck."

"No excuses," said Antje, "or no information."

Dan groaned.

Chapter 11

Dan rang the number on the business card given to him at the conference by the Brigadier General and asked to be put through to him.

"Professor Baker," said a familiar voice. "What a pleasant surprise to hear from you so soon. What can I do for you?"

"Brigadier General," began Dan.

"Oh let's not stand on ceremony. Just call me Brigadier."

"Brigadier. Some information has come my way which I think may be of interest to you. It concerns a murder."

"Murder?"

"Yes, murder," said Dan. "But I'm not sure how much I can disclose about how I came across this information."

The Brigadier took a few moments to reply. "Well I'm a pragmatic chap but, without knowing what it is you're about to tell me, I'm obviously not in a position to give guarantees."

"My information relates to a gentleman called Alessandro Ferrari and the murder of Giovanni Rossi."

"Ah," said the Brigadier. "That does change things a little. I've a score to settle with Signor Ferrari. I believe him to be responsible for the murder of one of my officers. I think you had better tell me what you know."

Dan told the Brigadier what Antje had learned from her interrogation of Ferrari's man Luigi, referring to her anonymously as an associate.

"Hmm, interesting," said the Brigadier. "There's more to you than meets the eye Professor Baker! I don't suppose there might be a recording of the... ahem... 'interview'?"

"There is. But I don't think it's something you could use in a court of law. The questioning was - how shall I put it? - a little robust."

"Let me have it anyway. Catching Ferrari and his gang is a top priority for me. In the circumstances I'll overlook your associate's, erm, excess of zeal. Can I reach you on this number if I need further help?"

"Yes. I'll be travelling. I have to go to Crete. But, yes, this number is fine."

"Thank you. Oh, and do be careful, Professor. You're not a Navy SEAL now."

"How did you know about that?"

"I told you. I'm omniscient," came the reply.

***

Alexia entered the *Kazantzakis Theatre* in Heraklion, where the Minoan Cultural Society was putting on its theatre piece, *Theseus and the Minotaur*. Founded during the Second World War, the theatre was later transformed into a large open-air venue for summer events such as theatre pieces, music, dance and opera. The play was to be performed by an amateur Cretan theatre group based in Myrtos in the south of the island.

It was a warm summer's evening and Alexia was wearing a red silk dress she had bought for the occasion. As soon as she had tried it on she had felt great in it. So nice to have a reason to dress up.

She took her seat near the front. Although she was there on business, she enjoyed the relaxing and atmospheric feel of the open air theatre as darkness fell. She really ought to come to this sort of thing more often.

The event was introduced by the President of the Society, Stelios Kouklakis, who gave a rather rambling speech about its history and activities. Its aim, he said, was to promote interest in Crete's ancient heritage and educate people about the importance of Minoan values in the modern world.

Alexia concluded he was a bit of an oddball. Her impression was reinforced when he introduced the cast, proudly presenting his daughter Korina as Princess Ariadne, daughter of King Minos and mistress of the labyrinth. Alexia wondered vaguely whether he saw himself as a modern-day King Minos.

She was surprised to find, however, that she enjoyed the theatre piece. It was well written and amusing. Korina was an excellent actress and could easily have been professional. And the Minotaur was really hot even with his bull mask on. There were squeals of delight from some female members of the audience when he removed the mask to take a bow at the end. Alexia found herself clapping enthusiastically.

Drinks and canapes were offered after the performance. Alexia went to work under the assumed name of Sheila Whitehead, an Australian teacher over on holiday from Sydney. She knew that her editor wouldn't be there as he was away on business. Just as well. He probably wouldn't have minded her attending the theatre piece, but he wouldn't have been impressed by the false identity, not at an event put on by his own Society.

She managed to squeeze her way through the crowd to the circle of people around Stelios, who seemed somewhat flustered by the number of people wanting his attention.

A bit odd for someone who is a leading businessman and President of the Society, she thought. He obviously doesn't like the limelight. Maybe he prefers to stay in the shadows and pull the strings?

Stelios was whisked off before Alexia managed to speak to him but she did succeed in having a quick chat with Korina, even though she too was in great demand. Alexia, speaking English with a broad Australian accent, congratulated her on her performance and asked whether she did it professionally. Korina, laughing, assured her it was purely a hobby and told her she was over briefly from Naples, where she was an archaeology academic. She showed a little too much interest for Alexia's liking in Sheila's background. Alexia felt as though she was being interrogated, a feeling compounded by Korina's piercing gaze.

"Which part of Sydney do you come from?" asked Korina, suddenly switching to Greek.

Alexia gave a puzzled look. "Sorry, I don't speak Greek."

"So how did you follow the theatre piece?" asked Korina.

Fortunately, before Alexia could answer, Korina was snatched away by her mother to speak to other, doubtless more important guests.

Alexia quietly cursed herself. When she was preparing a sting she always thought through and rehearsed her background thoroughly. But tonight her assumed name had been an afterthought. She hadn't really expected to be asked about her background and her cover story was pretty thin. She also remembered that she had booked her ticket online in her own name. She made a mental note to avoid lapses like this in future.

After Korina had moved on, Alexia remained in the same group of people and got talking to several members of the Society including, she was pleased to learn, Georgios Demetriou, one of the business tycoons on the finance committee. She quickly realised that Georgios had had one too many drinks and was in a talkative mood. After engaging in a few preliminaries she moved the conversation round to the Society and his role in it. She set out to provoke.

"It's all very well," she said, "and I heard what Stelios said about promoting the values of the great Minoan kingdom, but at the end of the day what relevance has any of this to the modern day? Crete is just a remote backwater of Greece. Hardly anyone where I come from in Sydney has even heard of it."

She feared that she may have overcooked it and angered him. Instead Georgios smiled and said,

"Ah, but you don't know what the Society is really about. Most of the members don't even know. Only a select few."

Bull's eye, thought Alexia. She asked,

"By the select few you mean the members of the finance committee?"

Georgios looked shocked. He was about to answer when Korina returned.

"Sorry to interrupt so rudely but my father needs to head off and would like a quick word with Georgios before he goes."

She put her arm round him and ushered him away. "Good to meet you, Sheila. I hope you have a good trip back."

Hmm, smart cookie, thought Alexia, noticing Korina's emphasis on the words 'trip back'.

She chatted to a few more people but the reception was now winding down. She decided to head home and get back to her computer.

***

The sleek black yacht slipped quietly into the Naples marina. It was late evening. Alessandro Ferrari looked immaculate as always in his white chinos, navy jacket and captain's hat, but his serene external appearance concealed an inner fury. He was livid at the sheer incompetence of his men. The trip to Spain had been an unmitigated disaster. They had failed to obtain the disc. Two of his men had been tortured and killed by some unknown assailant in Mallorca and two more had simply disappeared in Altea on the Spanish mainland. The remaining three were hobbling around injured and, despite the reports they had given him, he had no idea what had gone down.

Ferrari guessed it was the girl who was behind it. After Luigi's and Giuseppe's sheepish reports of how she had overpowered them in her apartment in Naples, he suspected there was more to her than met the eye. Giuseppe reported that the girl had come racing down the mountainside on her own carrying a large black bag, probably containing the disc. She had obviously done something to the professor. If she could incapacitate his men, she would have had little problem with the professor.

She appeared to have had at least two accomplices: the guy she made off with who took out two of his men in the car park and the tall blonde woman who shot Luigi. He wouldn't be surprised if it was one or both of them that were behind the disappearance of two of his men in Altea and the murder of his men in Mallorca. If this had been on home turf in Naples he would have done something about it. He would have had to in order to reassert his authority; he couldn't have let it pass. But he had no idea who these guys were or where they were from. It was too complicated to hunt them down. For the moment he would just have to cut his losses and move on, but if the opportunity came to put things right he would certainly take it.

**

Alexia sat at her computer. She was working on an article entitled *'Is there a darker side to the Minoan Cultural Society?'*

She had been at it all night after coming back from the theatre piece. She hadn't found it easy to write. After her conversation with Georgios Demetriou and his stunned reaction when she mentioned the Society's finance committee, she had no doubt she was on to something. But she still wasn't sure what it was. Her editor would doubtless say Georgios could simply have meant that the Society was more important than people thought; he wasn't suggesting anything sinister. If she was going to get any further with this piece she needed a break, a stroke of luck.

Her mobile rang.

"Diana, how are you? It's been a while."

"Four weeks and three days," said Diana.

"Precise as usual!"

"So have you got yourself another man yet?" asked Diana.

Alexia smiled. "What? No preliminaries? Like how have you been?"

"I reserve those for people who matter," said Diana, laughing.

Diana and Alexia were great friends who knew each other inside out. They talked about everything, from politics to their latest men or lack of.

"So what brings you to call me on this fine Cretan morning?"

"Oh don't rub it in! It's lousy here in Washington."

"Well you'd better get used to it if you're taking on an anchor role. So why the call? Are you going to put a knight in shining armour my way?"

"Well I do want you to meet someone."

"What kind of someone?"

"He's a professor. A Harvard professor."

Alexia groaned. "Oh great. A Harvard fucking professor. So fifty–five, balding with glasses and a paunch?"

"Not exactly. I dated him for a while actually."

Alexia sat up straight in her chair. "You have my full attention. But I must know him surely, or have you been secretly dating without telling me?"

"As if! No he was before your time."

"Why do you want me to meet him?"

"I had lunch with his father the other day."

"Oh wow! You ditched him for his dad?"

"Not quite," said Diana, laughing. "His father is a four star admiral, or was until he retired recently. I must say he isn't bad for a sixty something though!"

"Don't go there! Married? The son I mean, not the dad."

"No. Unattached but slightly damaged I think."

"Goes with the territory if he's been with you," said Alexia, laughing.

"Oh thanks. This was a bit more serious though. Listen, I'm getting cued in. I need to go. You should meet him. His father wouldn't tell me the whole story, but they're interested in finding out more about Stelios Kouklakis. The Admiral says there may be a story in it for you."

"Sounds great."

"Just one thing. If there is a story I want it too!"

"Of course, provided you get me live on CNN!"

"Deal," said Diana.

***

It was a beautiful early summer's evening in Crete as Georgios Demetriou drove back from Myrtos to his villa near Kalami in his brand new Ferrari sports car. It had been a splendid day. His lawyers had informed him that the paperwork for his purchase of the *Myrtos Daily Echo* was complete and the deal had been signed off. He had also had a meeting with his group finance director, who had told him group profits were up a full thirty per cent this year.

Georgios' sports car, with its sharp handling and low centre of gravity, was ideally suited to the winding Cretan mountain roads, and he enjoyed driving it at speed, preferably with the top down. But this evening he was taking particular care as he skirted the southern fringes of the Dikti Mountains. He had thrown a party in Myrtos to celebrate the newspaper deal. The drinks had flowed freely and, after such a great day, Georgios had got a little carried away.

He knew the road well though as he often drove this way, and it wasn't a particularly dark night with the moon and stars shining brightly in the cloudless sky.

His thoughts suddenly drifted back to the conversations he'd had at the reception after the theatre piece in Heraklion a couple of days ago. There was one in particular that kept worrying him. He had talked to an attractive young Australian tourist who goaded him a bit about the Society, questioning its value. He was trying to remember precisely what he had said. He was worried that after a few glasses of wine he had been a little indiscreet and said more than he should have. He tried to cast the thought from his mind. He was sure he couldn't have said very much and in all likelihood it would have got lost in the general conversation. In any case she was a tourist and was probably back in Australia surfing by now. He made a mental note to be more discreet in future and not let the wine do the talking.

He began to concentrate harder on the road as he had come to the start of a rather tortuous descent. He put his foot on the brake to slow the car down. Nothing happened. The brake just went straight to the floor. The car began to pick up speed as the descent became steeper and steeper. Panicking, he started pumping the brake but still nothing happened. He was now hurtling down the narrow pass at over one hundred kilometres an hour. To his horror he saw he was approaching a sharp bend to the left. He thought of using his gears to slow the car down and tried desperately to change down to second gear. But it was too late. As it hit the bend the car was still travelling far too fast to stay on the road. Georgios lost control as it smashed through the barrier and went over the side of the mountain. He screamed as it fell three hundred metres to the ground below, where it exploded on impact.

Georgios had not noticed the black SUV that had followed him at a discreet distance ever since he had left Myrtos. The SUV drew up at the bend where the Ferrari had left the road. A man with dark hair swept back in a ponytail got out and peered over the cliff. Seeing the car in flames in the valley below he got back into the SUV, turned round and headed back in the direction of Myrtos.

***

Alexia went in to meet to the editor, having finished her story about the Minoan Cultural Society and emailed it to him the previous day. She had decided in the end to retitle it '*Is there a darker side to modern-day Crete?*'

"Well to be honest it's still nowhere near your normal standard. It's largely speculation," said the editor. "Shame you couldn't get the police or Schaumberger to comment or Demetriou to be more forthcoming. All we have really are your theories and Demetriou saying there's more to the Society than meets the eye. That could mean anything."

"Yes I know. That's why in the end I didn't include the Society in the title. In essence I just set out the facts and ask whether there's something sinister behind them we should be worrying about. I don't point the finger."

"Yes. I realise that. I'll think about it. It's still explosive stuff and I'd feel much happier if we were on more solid ground. At least you recorded your conversation with Demetriou. Anyway, I forwarded it to the editorial board yesterday afternoon for their views. We'll see what they have to say. Now, how about the piece on Chania's procurement people getting all-expenses-paid trips to Florida in return for awarding contacts?"

"Coming on well. I've got stuff recorded again. One of the committee members invited me to go with him on his freebie. I was quite tempted to say yes. Just joking! I'll write it up. Will tomorrow be ok?"

"That'll be perfect. It should be another great story."

***

"We have a number of agenda items," said the Leader of the Inner Sanctum. "I fear Georgios can't be with us this morning, which brings me to the first item. It's slightly delicate and so I prefer to get it out of the way first. It came to our notice that, after drinking too much wine at the theatre piece which the Society put on in Heraklion, Georgios made some rather indiscreet remarks. What is worse, it turns out he made them to an undercover journalist. The Sanctum does not tolerate indiscretions. On this occasion, however, no disciplinary action is required. The matter is closed. Georgios had an unfortunate accident on the road to Kalami yesterday evening. He is sadly no longer with us."

The members of the Sanctum shuffled uneasily in their seats.

"What about the journalist?" asked one member finally.

"Don't worry," said the Leader. "I've taken steps to ensure that nothing embarrassing is published. But let this be a salutary lesson for all of us."

The Leader paused, peering at each member in turn, before breaking into a smile. "Let's move on to the second and rather happier agenda item, Georgios' replacement. I've considered a number of candidates. As you know, given our mission we are keen to bring into the Sanctum high-ranking members of the police and armed forces. We need to be careful of course and have discreetly been sounding out a number of Society members over the last year or so to check whether they share our convictions. My proposal is that we invite the Chief of Police of Heraklion to join us. He's been a faithful Society member for many years and has helped bring to justice a number of foreign criminals. My inquiries suggest he would be an enthusiastic supporter of our aims."

"Have you considered the Chania Chief of Police?" asked one member.

The Leader gave the member a withering stare. The other members looked down at their papers.

"Fair question," said the Leader eventually. "He's also a long-standing Society member and I certainly see him as a potential addition to the Sanctum. But I think we need to make further inquiries before we risk approaching him."

"I defer to your judgment as always," said the member hastily.

"Good. That's settled then," said the Leader. "While we're gathered together I should update you briefly on two other items. First, the American matter. I informed you at an earlier meeting that we had acquired the human resources and were in the process of procuring the necessary materials and equipment to carry out our plan. I'm pleased to tell you that everything is now in place. We just need to take a final decision on timing."

Nods of approval from the members.

"Secondly, I mentioned previously that an opportunity had presented itself for us to acquire an important artefact of great interest to the Society. I'm happy to tell you that we were successful. It's now in our possession. We can look at it together while we have refreshments."

Loud applause around the table.

"Good," said the Leader. "Unless there is any other business I suggest we move on to that now."

***

Shortly after his meeting with Alexia, the editor of the *Cretan Daily News* received a call from the chairman of the paper's editorial board.

"Excellent work on the councillor bribe story. It was picked up everywhere."

"Yes," said the editor. "Alexia's a great journalist. I don't know how she does it. She's doing another one about the procurement committee of Chania Council. Sounds like they have been on the take too."

"Great stuff. I wanted to have a word with you, though, about this piece on the dark side to Crete."

"Yes. It's obviously quite sensitive. I wanted to get your views."

"It's very good that you did. The editorial board have discussed it, and we want you to drop it."

"Well I agree it's premature but she has good instincts. She may well be on to something."

"Listen. You're a very good editor and a dear friend. We've known each other a long time. The board felt very strongly, and I mean VERY strongly, that it didn't want you or our newspaper associated with this. Please take my advice. It would be better if you tell her to drop it."

The editor had occasionally received instructions like this before. There were evidently reasons for dropping the piece that the chairman preferred not to share with him. He knew better than to pursue it.

"Very well," he said. "I'll tell her."

"Will she listen?"

"I don't know. She's very stubborn. She's like a dog with a bone once she gets her teeth into a story. It's why she's so good."

"You know her better than I do. I'll leave it to you to decide how to handle it. It's in her best interests."

***

After her meeting with the editor Alexia went to her favourite café, the *Hacienda Café* on Louka Petraki Street. She sat watching the local news on TV.

We're just receiving a report that local entrepreneur Georgios Demetriou died last night when his car came off the road in the Dikti Mountains. According to police reports the cause of the accident is unknown. Mr Demetriou's charred body was recovered from the wreckage of his car in a valley three hundred metres below the road. He appears to have been driving alone.

"My God," murmured Alexia.

She phoned her editor. "Have you seen the news?"

"About Demetriou, you mean?"

"Yes. So he speaks to me and mysteriously dies in a car crash."

"You're saying it wasn't an accident?"

"Well if it was it's an extraordinary coincidence, just after he spoke to me."

"You're jumping to conclusions again. The roads round there are notoriously treacherous and apparently he'd had a drink. In any case, how would anyone know he spoke to you?"

"Well I think Korina Kouklakis may have overheard our conversation at the theatre. She whisked Demetriou away as we were speaking. And of course you said you had sent my article to the editorial board."

"Yes. I did. But surely you are not saying…"

"I'm not sure what I'm saying," interrupted Alexia. "But as far as I know, other than Korina, they were the only ones who knew about my conversation with Demetriou, apart from you and me of course. Anyway, I must add Demetriou's death to my piece. At least we don't need to worry about libel now!"

The editor was starting to have a very bad feeling about this. "I want you to drop the piece."

"What?"

The editor repeated his instruction.

"Why? Surely you can see now that I'm on to something."

"I think it's too dangerous. I want you to drop it."

"You've been ordered to tell me to drop it, haven't you? You've been got at?"

"Alexia. For your own good. Drop it for God's sake!"

"Well if you're not interested maybe someone else will be."

"Alexia, no…"

She rang off.

***

The editor rang the chairman of the editorial board.

"I've spoken to her."

"How did she take it?"

"Badly. She accused me of being got at and threatened to offer it to another newspaper. I was wondering. If you're worried it's sensitive, wouldn't it be better that we keep it so we can control it? We can always water it down a bit in editing."

"Leave it with me," said the chairman.

Chapter 12

Southeastern Crete 2485 BC

The seventeen-year-old boy lay on the altar, his knees bent and wrists and ankles tightly bound. The Priestess stood beside him in a long skirt, sewn in patterned layers of purple and red, worn beneath an apron embroidered with gold lace, her bare breasts firmly supported by a tight-fitting red bodice. Her head, adorned with a golden crown, was raised towards the heavens as she uttered a long incantation. Beside her stood a temple servant, who was simply dressed in a blue and white loincloth. In the palms of his outstretched hands he held a long ceremonial dagger, engraved on both sides with images of a boar's head.

The boy had been one of seven youths selected for their flawless beauty as worthy sacrifices to the Mother Goddess. They had been taken to the palace, where they had been ordered to draw lots to determine which of them would have the privilege of laying down his life to appease the Goddess and protect the kingdom from her wrath.

After being chosen the boy had been led from the palace in a procession up to the temple, which stood on a nearby mountaintop overlooking the palace. His mother and sister had wept as he was led away. He had tried to console them, insisting that he was proud to have been chosen for this honour. But now, as he ascended the mountain, his feeling of pride had given way to one of fear and trepidation. He was fighting to banish the dark thoughts of resentment and self-pity that were overwhelming him.

For as long as the boy could remember the kingdom had been one of plenty, with a rich and varied diet of grain, vegetables, meat and fish harvested from the lush and fertile land and surrounding sea. But for several years now the climate had changed, becoming noticeably drier. The winter rains, so important for crops, had failed, leaving the countryside increasingly barren and arid.

Farmers were struggling to feed their livestock, and the normally abundant wildlife had become sparse.

King Titiku had dispatched the kingdom's merchant fleet to fetch produce from Egypt and other nearby kingdoms. But the drought was widespread and the neighbouring lands were also struggling. The Nile floods, so important for the production of grain, had failed several years in succession.

The King had been wise and had built up stores of grain during the years of plenty. But these were now running out. There was still produce to be had from the sea but without staples, such as grain and pulses, and with little meat the population began to go hungry. And with hunger came discontent. The people began to ask what they had done to bring down the wrath of the Mother Goddess in this way. They looked for a scapegoat. Some suggested that their hitherto popular young king had angered her by taking a foreign bride, Princess Hemite, daughter of an Egyptian pharaoh.

King Titiku had consulted the Priestess, the earthly personification of the Goddess, who had demanded more lavish sacrifices. Repeated offerings had been made of the kingdom's precious grain, vegetables and livestock. But it hadn't worked. In fact things had got worse. The kingdom had begun to suffer a series of earthquakes, small and irregular at first but then more frequent and violent.

The Priestess now demanded the sacrifice of a healthy young man. She had spoken of this before, but the King had resisted. The word was that he had been restrained by Queen Hemite, who as an Egyptian found the practice of child sacrifice abhorrent. But the Priestess proclaimed that only the sacrifice of a young male would appease the Goddess' anger. Only then would the earthquakes stop and the land return to fertility. And so the King had relented.

After the long walk up the mountainside the procession arrived at the entrance to the temple. The Priestess stood on the temple's steps with two servants awaiting his arrival. The boy walked forward to the steps, kneeling before the Priestess. She took his head between her hands and uttered some words which he did not understand. She then turned and entered the temple. The two servants took the boy by the arms and followed her in.

The temple, lit by blazing torches mounted along the walls, was rectangular in shape, comprising three rooms with an anteroom that ran alongside. The boy had been inside the anteroom many times before with his family. This was where offerings of grain and other produce that had been carried up the mountain were prepared with the help of the temple servants. Once the offerings were ready the servants would lead the family into the last of the inner rooms to present their offering to the Priestess. But today the boy was led into the first of the three inner rooms. Along two sides of the room ran stone benches and in the centre was a large stone basin. The Priestess looked on as the servants removed the boy's loincloth and washed him from head to toe with water from the basin. He was then dressed in a fresh white loincloth ready for his meeting with the Goddess. The Priestess expressed her satisfaction and left the room. One of the servants then handed the boy a golden cup containing a potion to give him courage. The potion had a strange taste and was like nothing he had ever drunk before.

The servants then led him back through the anteroom into the second inner room, where the Priestess awaited them. The boy had heard stories about this room. There was no mistaking the use to which it was put. In the middle of the room was a large stone altar, with deep grooves running from its centre and along its edges to channel the blood of sacrifices. But the potion the boy had drunk was now taking effect. He felt strangely detached from what was happening to him. The voices of the Priestess and the servants seemed distant and distorted. He was helped on to the altar by the servants, who tied his hands and ankles. He lay there in a state of relaxed contentment and euphoria. Blurred memories of his childhood flooded incoherently into his brain: his first wild-boar hunt on horseback; the bull-leaping and athletic competitions in which he had participated in the palace courtyard, with the King and Queen looking on; the long days spent fishing at sea; and his first clandestine encounter with a girl from the palace.

Ending her incantation, the Priestess took the dagger from the servant and leaned over the boy. The Priestess began to make cuts into his body, pausing between each cut to utter further words. In his blurry dream-like state the boy felt the wetness of the blood trickling from his body but he felt no horror or pain. He lost all sense of time as the Priestess continued her work. His only sensation was one of feeling increasingly cold.

But just as he was drifting into unconsciousness he sensed something was happening. The whole chamber seemed to be moving. The Priestess stopped her incantation and moved away from the altar, dropping the dagger. The last thing the boy saw was the roof of the temple coming down to meet him. This was the moment, he thought. He was about to meet the Goddess.

***

Korina received a call from one of her father's men. Dan had arrived at Heraklion airport on a flight from Athens.

"Well it took him long enough. Which hotel is he staying at?"

"I don't know."

"Follow him and let me know where he's staying."

***

"Thank you for meeting at such short notice," began the Leader of the Sanctum. "I have called this extraordinary meeting to deal with a matter of some urgency. But first, let me welcome our new member Leonidas, Chief of Police for Heraklion."

Applause around the table.

The Leader moved on to the urgent agenda item.

"As you're aware, following widespread concern among Society members we decided a few years ago to take action to stop the constant raids on members' businesses. Recent years have seen an influx of foreign criminal elements infiltrating our society and, as Leonidas has explained, the police simply don't have the resources to cope. When they manage to make arrests they struggle to secure convictions because clever lawyers often get the culprits off on technicalities. So the Sanctum embarked on a programme of building its own security force. It has been successful. We now have a force of two hundred men and have administered justice to a number of gangs. Our businesses have reported a significant reduction in the number of incidents."

Having outlined the background the Leader handed out copies of a photograph.

"Today we have a specific matter that requires urgent attention. This gentleman, if that's the right word, has been active here for about a year now. His name is Vladimir Romanov. He was previously involved in organised crime in Siberia, but evidently thought there would be richer pickings here. He has a gang of four men who've been targeting retail outlets. He's made the mistake of raiding some of our members' businesses. We ordered one of our teams to conduct a surveillance exercise. I'm told there's the possibility of bringing the gang to justice. I'd like your approval to give the team the go-ahead."

There was unanimous agreement.

"Very well. Thank you for your swift decision. I shall report back once we have apprehended them. Justice will be administered to the gang-leader, Romanov, in the usual way."

Dan took a cab from the airport to the *Atrion Hotel*, a modern business hotel in central Heraklion with balconies overlooking the sea. He knew it from his previous visit to Crete. Slinging his case on the bed, he took a quick shower and went down to the bar for a much needed beer. He made a point of never drinking on flights, but he was always thirsty as hell afterwards. He walked into the bar to find Korina sitting there. Her bee pendant hung from her neck as usual, but the casual clothes she had worn in Spain were gone, replaced by a smart business suit.

"So what does a girl have to do to give a guy the brush off?"

"Well strangling usually works!"

Korina smiled. "Oh I bet you quite enjoyed it really. You have to admit, I executed the Tracheal grip choke brilliantly!"

Dan wondered whether one day he might meet a normal woman.

"So where's the disc?"

"It's at my father's villa."

"Is it safe there?"

"Yes. The villa is heavily guarded."

"What are your plans for it?"

"The Heraklion Museum of course," said Korina indignantly. "What did you think? That I'm some sort of art thief?"

"The thought had crossed my mind."

"I've already informed the museum and given them some photos. They've given me permission to keep it for a couple of weeks while I study it. They know me. I've given them pieces I've found in the past. Look, I wouldn't have had to sneak off with it if you hadn't been so square-headed. If we'd handed the disc over to the Spanish authorities we might never have seen it again. At best we would have had to face years of bureaucracy before we got to study it."

Dan had to admit she did have a point there. "OK, but I suspect Egypt may think they have a claim too."

"True. But they're hardly going to miss it. They've so many artefacts in Egypt they've run out of space to display them."

That was true too. In fact Dan had read about plans to build a new archaeological museum in Cairo to house the thousands of finds that were stored away out of view.

"I'm sure an amicable agreement can be reached. This is hardly the Elgin marbles," added Korina. "Anyway, are you just going to sulk or are you going to help me find the palace?"

Dan looked up, his eyebrows raised. "The palace?"

Korina smiled. "Oh good. I finally have your attention. The Minoan King mentioned in the disc was called Titiku, by the way."

"Interesting. A Hurrian name from Anatolia."

"The disc says he ruled in the southeast of the island. If there was a king worthy of marriage to an Egyptian Princess, then there must be a good chance he had a palace. But the thing is that there is no known palace in that part of Crete. And we're talking middle of the third millennium BC, long before the palaces were built at Knossos and Phaistos. There were Minoan settlements in the area though which date back to the middle of the third millennium BC. Two have been uncovered near Myrtos at Fornou Korfi and Pirgos."

"So that may be the area to explore," said Dan.

"As it happens my parents have a villa in that part of Crete, near Myrtos. Why don't we go and stay there? It'll be the perfect base for exploring the area."

"I thought your father wasn't a great fan of foreign men."

"Only if he thinks they might sully my pure Cretan blood!"

Not much chance of that if you keep strangling them, thought Dan. "Why's your father so concerned? I thought it was your mother who had the pure Cretan DNA?"

"Yes it is. But she's less obsessive than Dad. In fact she's super keen to meet you. It was she who suggested I invite you to stay with us. Don't worry about my father. He's always very polite and in any case, he'll be busy with one of the Society's committees."

"The Society?"

"The Minoan Cultural Society. At least that's its short name. It has a fancy long one which I can't remember. My father founded it about twenty years ago."

"So what is it?"

"It's a club that brings together people who are interested in ancient Crete. It's quite big these days. It has about five hundred members."

"What does it do?"

"It promotes research and holds lectures, theatre pieces, enactments of Minoan rituals, that sort of thing."

"Enactments of Minoan rituals?"

"Yes. Why don't you ask my father when you meet him? He'll love telling you all about it."

"So what about the Minoan hieroglyphs? Do you have any clue as to the language?"

"Yes, I do. But I thought I'd wait until the great Professor Baker had been able to inspect the disc himself."

"How did you know I'd come?"

Korina gave a puzzled look. "I invited you over dinner in Altea and you promised, remember?"

You're a dark horse, Korina, thought Dan. *I wonder what other little surprises you have in store for me.*

Korina got up to leave. "I'll pick you up at 8.30 sharp tomorrow morning."

***

After Korina had left, Dan rang Alexia Psaltis on the number his father had given him. "Hi, Alexia, I'm Dan Baker. I think Diana may have mentioned me?"

"G'day, Professor," came the reply. "Yes she did. She said you might want to meet me. Are you in Crete?"

"Yes I am and it would be great to meet if you have time. Would today still be possible?"

"Sure. Do you know the *Hacienda Café* in Louka Petraki Street? Say around six?"

"Six will be great. I'm sure I can find it."

"OK. Can you ring me when you're about ten minutes away? I need to do something in town first."

Dan looked at his watch and reckoned he would have just enough time to do a quick tour of the Heraklion Archaeological Museum, located a short walk from his hotel. From his previous stay he remembered it being one of the most fascinating museums he had visited, housing finds from all over Crete going back to the Neolithic period. Its pride and joy though were its Minoan treasures. Its collections included many of the finds from excavations at the nearby palace of Knossos and other sites.

Dan spent some time studying pottery and other finds from Knossos and lingered over the Phaistos Disc, a disc of fired clay found in southern Crete. The disc bore strange symbols which had been stamped on with some form of seal. The meaning and purpose of the disc remained a mystery despite attempts to decipher it.

Dan moved from room to room. In one gallery he studied the magnificent 'Bee Pendant', of which Korina often wore a replica. He could happily have spent several days there. But it was now nearly 5.15 pm and he needed to get moving to meet Alexia. He just had time to pay a quick visit to the famous Hall of the Frescoes, which housed the original wall paintings from Knossos, including the 'Bull Leaping', 'Prince of the Lilies' and 'Dolphins' frescoes. But what caught Dan's attention as he walked through the gallery were the famous 'Parisienne' and 'Ladies in Blue' paintings, depicting elegantly dressed Minoan women. What struck him were their large mesmerising eyes. He now remembered where he had seen Korina's eyes before. Was it possible that the eyes of the women in the frescoes were not just artistic licence? Could it be that they were really like that?

***

Alec Chaconas was crawling along a street in Heraklion in a stolen car. It was now 5.30 pm, and he had been following his target all day waiting for the right opportunity. She was pretty. He would really have liked to kidnap her so that he could have his way with her before killing her. But he daren't risk it. He was under strict instructions to make it look like an accident.

He had been waiting for her as she left her apartment early that afternoon. She didn't have a car and there was no underground in Heraklion. So he had decided his best bet was a hit-and-run. He had chosen a large SUV, perfect for killing pedestrians. She would be another victim of the notoriously bad driving in Greece. As a journalist her death would probably be worthy of a short report in the local press but nothing more.

After leaving her apartment in Louka Petraki Street she had walked a short distance to the *Hacienda Café* on the corner of the street. He pulled into an unoccupied space opposite the café. She stayed inside for over two hours, so long that Chaconas got out of his car several times and walked past the café to make sure she was still in there. He saw her ensconced in a corner with her laptop. Eventually she came out and entered the Kazantzaki and Chatzidaki Park. Chaconas drove round the park and caught up with her as she came out at the other side. He followed her into the old walled city. Heraklion's well preserved Venetian walls extended for about four and half kilometres, forming a triangle round the old town. At one point he lost her in the narrow, partly pedestrianised streets but then picked her up again as she came on to Leof. Kalokerinou, a main shopping street running through the middle of the city.

She then turned off into another narrow street towards the seafront.

This is not ideal, thought Chaconas. The streets in the walled town were crowded with pedestrians and the traffic was moving too slowly to build up the speed needed for his hit-and-run manoeuvre. It would also be difficult to make a quick getaway.

Chaconas saw her take a short call on her mobile lasting about a minute. Finishing the call she tucked the phone in her back pocket and abruptly turned round. The street was one way and so Chaconas turned at the first opportunity and doubled back round. He picked her up again as she went out through the city walls and entered the park she had come through earlier. He drove round the park and caught up with her as she entered Stavraki Street.

This is better, he thought, as he turned into the street. Fewer people and cars. He closed on her until he was about twenty metres behind, just enough distance to build up speed before swerving into her. He was about to floor the accelerator when she turned left.

"Dammit," murmured Chaconas, realising it was another one-way street, Andrea Papandreou. He had to turn right. He quickly doubled round with a series of right turns and re-joined the street further up. Cruising back down he saw her turning into Louka Petraki Street, where her apartment was. But instead of continuing home as he had expected, she stopped at the café she had visited earlier. She met a tall man outside and took a table on the terrace right by the road.

This is perfect, Chaconas thought, as he pulled in across the road. The café's terrace was slightly raised on a wooden platform but that wouldn't be a problem in his large SUV. He could easily build up enough speed to crash on to the terrace, hit her and then get back on to the road. She wouldn't stand a chance. And with so little traffic around, his getaway would be easy. He would wait and pick a moment when the man left her alone, but if he didn't Chaconas would do it anyway.

***

Alexia arrived at the café and saw Dan standing outside wearing the Knossos T-shirt he had mentioned on the phone.

Hmm, Diana was right. More action movie hero than academic.

"G'day, Professor, how're you doing? I'm Alexia," she said in her Sydney accent.

"Hi," said Dan, taking her hand. "Really good of you to meet me."

They took a table on the pavement outside the café. Alexia ordered a glass of white wine and was pleased when Dan asked for a beer. She always felt uncomfortable if she was the only one drinking. She particularly hated doing business lunches with people who just drank water.

"So what can I do for you, Professor?"

"Just Dan, please. I'm not sure how much Diana told you."

"Not a lot. She was in a rush, as usual."

"That sounds like Diana," said Dan smiling.

Did Alexia detect a note of sadness? Had that been the problem: Diana always rushing off somewhere?

"I'm interested in Stelios Kouklakis and the Minoan Cultural Society," said Dan, coming straight to the point.

"Do you mind if I ask why?"

"I'd prefer not to say too much right now if you don't mind. I've been invited by his daughter, Korina, to stay with them to help them decipher an ancient text. I feel a bit uneasy about them somehow."

Alexia was wondering how much to say. He wasn't exactly being open with her. But at least he was being honest about it, and Diana had emailed her to assure her he was trustworthy and she could talk freely with him.

"Okay. I'll tell you what I know or, rather, suspect. One thing though. I want your word that if there's a story in this I'll get it."

"That's a deal," said Dan smiling. "The only thing is Diana may want a piece as well."

"Don't worry about that. I'll talk to Diana."

Alexia began by telling Dan about the crime statistics and the disappearance of the foreign gangs.

"That's a pretty drastic reduction in such a short period," said Dan. "But with hardly any convictions?"

"Yeah and what's really odd is that the police don't want to talk about it. You'd think they would be trumpeting the fall in crime."

"You suspect they're hiding something? Are we talking a vigilante group?"

"I don't know but it would explain it."

There was a pause as the waiter served the drinks. Alexia took a sip of wine. "And then we have a succession of failed takeovers by foreign investors, often last minute and in mysterious circumstances."

"For example?"

"Well, the latest was the last-minute withdrawal of a bid to take over the *Energia Corporation*, a big energy company in Crete. Everything was set up.

The financial press thought it was a done deal. The stock market had already built it into the share price. Then at the very last minute the German company dropped the bid with no explanation. The financial press was mystified. I tried to get an interview with Gerhard Schaumberger, the chairman and major shareholder of the German company. He refused to speak to me."

"So you think some pressure may have been brought to bear?"

"That's my suspicion but I've no evidence. There's a lot of popular resentment in Crete to the buying up of Cretan assets by foreign investors. People think foreigners, particularly the Germans, are taking advantage of Greece's financial plight. But just how that can translate into stopping a takeover I've no idea. There's another thing though, even more worrying. Over the last few years we've had creeping control in Crete of key industry sectors by a small group of Cretan tycoons."

"Which sectors?"

"The main ones are media, including newspapers, radio and television, telecommunications, armaments and energy," said Alexia.

"Just the ones you'd want to control if you were planning a coup? Is that what you think is going on?"

Alexia took another sip of wine. "I don't know what's going on but it had crossed my mind. When I suggested it to the editor of a local paper I write for, he thought I was crazy, letting my imagination run riot. Problem is that it's all supposition, putting two and two together. I need more evidence really."

"I imagine it's difficult to get hard evidence."

"Yes. I did look into the armaments industry more closely. There are three companies producing guns and ammunition, rocket launchers, missiles and armoured vehicles. I studied their accounts. What struck me was that their stocks of unsold goods have gradually built up over the last few years."

"So they're producing more than they're selling?"

"Yes. Turnover the same but production stepped up. Effectively weapons are being stockpiled."

"That is a bit odd. I guess I see your editor's problem though. If he's going to publish he needs solid proof. In any case what's it all got to do with Stelios and the Society?"

"Stelios' companies control 70% of the industries and the remainder are controlled by the other tycoons, all members of the Society. What's more they meet regularly as they're all on its finance committee."

"Have you tried to interview Stelios or any of the members?"

"I tried but none of them were willing to give me interviews. I was referred to the Society's press officer, who just blanked me. The closest I've got to Stelios was an event that the Society was putting on, a theatre piece about the Greek myth of the Minotaur. He introduced the event. He came across to me as a bit deranged but, then again, perhaps I just wanted to think that. What's clear is that he's completely crazy about ancient Crete and the Minoans. He was going on about embracing the values of Crete's great Minoan past."

"He does sound a little eccentric!"

"I didn't actually get to speak to him because he was whisked off to talk to someone else. I did talk to his daughter Korina. A smart cookie if ever there was one. I suspect she saw straight through my cover story. Thankfully she didn't get to quiz me for long. I also spoke to Georgios Demetriou, one of the tycoons on the Society's finance committee. He'd had a few drinks and was quite talkative. I prodded him a little. I suggested the Society was a bit of a waste of space. He hinted that there was more to the Society than met the eye."

"Interesting," said Dan. "Did he explain what he meant by that?"

"No. He was shepherded away before I could ask. I was going to see whether, having got the introduction, I could follow it up with an interview. But I never got the chance. He was killed two days later in a car accident. Drove off a mountain."

"Hmm, that's a bit of a coincidence," said Dan. "Was anyone listening to your conversation?"

"Well Korina may have overheard. It could be why she abruptly whisked him off."

"Did you tell anyone about your conversation with him?"

"Yeah. I told the editor at the paper I mentioned, the *Cretan Daily News*. In fact I wrote up a piece which included a report of the conversation with Demetriou. As I say, I'd had real problems getting my editor to take me seriously on this, but when he read the piece he finally seemed to be showing some enthusiasm. That was until he showed it to his editorial board. He came back and told me he wanted me to drop it."

"Sounds like he was got at. Is the newspaper owned by members of the Society?"

"Yes. It's owned by Stelios, although the editor says he's not involved in editorial policy."

"Perhaps he doesn't need to be. He probably has someone on the board who takes care of things for him."

"Quite likely. Well that's about it. I'm sorry. A lot of it is just me joining up the dots."

"It's been really useful," said Dan. "I'm not a journalist but, for what it's worth, I suspect you're on to something."

"You will let me know if you find anything further, won't you?"

"I will. You have my word."

Alexia didn't hear Dan's reply. She was staring at a large SUV that had suddenly swerved across the road at speed and was heading straight for her. Her mouth wide open in astonishment, she heard herself scream as the SUV mounted the wooden terrace and raced towards her.

It never reached her. A hand firmly grasped her forearm and she found herself being propelled from her seat into the air with the acceleration of a fighter jet on take-off. She flew several feet before crash-landing on the table behind to the astonishment of the elderly couple sitting there.

She looked round to see Dan watching the SUV as it swerved back on to the road and accelerated down the street. He turned round and held out his hand.

"Whoops, sorry. I seem to have overdone it a little."

She took his hand and, with all the elegance she could muster, got down from the table. The waiter came out on to the terrace, asking what the commotion was. Dan asked him to sort Alexia and the elderly couple out with some more drinks as their glasses had gone flying.

"Just another coincidence?" asked Dan as Alexia sat back down at the table.

Alexia stared at him and gulped down her wine, holding the glass with both hands to disguise the fact that they were shaking.

"I think you should get out of Crete for a while," he said. "Is there anywhere you can go?"

She thought for a few seconds. "Yes. I'm sure I can go and stay with Diana."

"Perfect. I think you should get off the island tonight. Let me go back with you while you pack. Is your apartment far from here?"

"No it's in this street. But really, you don't need to. I'm sure I'll be fine."

"I don't think so. I think whoever it was will probably try again. I'd rather see you off."

"You need to take care too," said Alexia. "They may come after you now they've seen you talking to me."

"Don't worry about me," said Dan.

Alexia accepted Dan's offer and they headed back to her apartment. As soon as she got back she phoned Diana, who was upset to hear about the hit-and-run attempt but delighted that Alexia was coming to stay. Alexia managed to book a flight to Athens that evening with an overnight connection to DC. While she packed, Dan grabbed a can of beer from her fridge and poured her another glass of wine. They then got a cab to the airport.

As Alexia joined the queue for departures Dan held out his hand, but she stepped forward and gave him a tight hug.

"Thanks so much, Dan," she whispered in his ear. "Give those bastards hell. And don't forget to give me the story."

***

Korina drove into the hotel forecourt punctually at 8.30 am. Dan was waiting outside with his bags.

"Our route takes us right past the Minoan palace of Knossos," said Korina as they drove through Heraklion. "Would you like me to give you a quick tour?"

"That would be great," said Dan. Although he had been to Knossos once before he wasn't going to miss the opportunity to be guided round by a professor of Cretan archaeology.

When they arrived, the site hadn't yet opened but there was already a long queue building up at the entrance. Korina, however, was well known to the staff, who ushered them through for a private viewing.

"Perhaps I should begin by telling you a little about the excavations," said Korina. "The site at Knossos was discovered in modern times in 1878 by Minos Kalokairinos."

"A guy called Minos discovers the palace of King Minos," said Dan. "Quite a coincidence. Perhaps he was destined to find it! But I thought it was Arthur Evans?"

"Evans was the first to excavate the site of the palace about twenty years later. At the time he was curator of the Ashmolean Museum in Oxford. It was Evans who called it 'The Palace of Minos' after King Minos, who in Greek mythology lived at Knossos. The name has stuck, and of course we still refer to the civilisation as the Minoans."

Korina led Dan through the western court of the palace and past an area where remains from the pre-palatial period had been uncovered. "The site goes back to early Neolithic times, around 7000 BC, although the name 'Knossos' comes from later Greek classical texts. It's thought that at its peak, around 1700 BC, there were around a hundred thousand people living in the area. What we know as the Minoan civilisation is thought to have emerged around

2800 BC, although as you know there were different phases. The original palace at Knossos dates from around 1900 BC."

"So quite a long time after King Userkaf's reign and the marriage ceremony recorded on the disc," commented Dan.

"Yes about five hundred years later. In part that's what's so exciting about the disc. It suggests that the palace period may go back much further than we thought."

They moved on to the so-called 'Corridor of the Procession', which led to the 'South Propylaeum', the southern entrance to the palace. "This is in fact a reconstruction undertaken by Evans," said Korina. "He's a controversial character among archaeologists. Personally I think he's been judged too harshly. Archaeology was in its infancy at the time. But he did go a bit over the top when he started rebuilding parts of the site using concrete, which of course is now disintegrating. Certainly not something we would do as archaeologists these days. The 'Grand Stairway' to which we'll come shortly is another reconstruction by Evans."

"Yes. I can see why you might think he got a bit carried away."

They entered an open space in the middle of the palace. "Central courtyards like this one are a basic feature of Minoan palatial design," explained Korina. "The northern and southern entrances to the palace both lead to this courtyard. It's believed that various rituals and feasts were held here."

They climbed the 'Grand Stairway' and entered the luxurious 'Queen's Suite' with its famous 'Dolphin' fresco.

"I saw this fresco at the museum in Heraklion," said Dan.

"Yes. This is a copy. The one in the museum is the original or what passes for the original. Most of the frescoes, including this one and other famous ones, such as the 'Bull-Leaping' and 'Ladies in Blue' frescoes, are restorations. Evans commissioned an artist to recreate them from fragments of rubble strewn across the palace floor."

"Doesn't strike me as so unreasonable to try to reconstruct them. They're magnificent and give you a good idea of what the inside of the palace must have looked like."

"Yes. My favourite is definitely the 'Prince of the Lilies'," said Korina with a cheeky smile. "It depicts a hot young prince in his blue loincloth with his magnificent head gear. Of course, we don't know how accurate the reconstructions are. I suspect there may have been a fair degree of artistic licence at work. Evelyn Waugh once famously said they resembled the covers of Vogue magazine!"

They continued up the 'Grand Stairway' to the 'King's Quarters' and the 'Hall of the Double Axes'.

"I see the symbol of the double-edged axe is everywhere," said Dan. "Plutarch said the word 'labrys' was the Lydian word for a double-edged axe. I wonder whether there's any connection with the word 'labyrinth'?"

"I believe that has been suggested by some scholars," replied Korina. She led Dan into the 'Throne Room'. "This room takes its name from the high-backed alabaster seat built into the north wall of the palace."

She pointed to the beautiful wall painting surrounding the throne. "This is the famous 'Griffin' fresco. It's named after the two mythological griffins which it depicts. This fresco is actually the original."

Dan pointed to the benches made from gypsum round three sides of the room and the large basin in the middle of the room. "What was the 'Throne Room' used for?"

"We don't know for sure," replied Korina. "It may have been the court of a Priest-King or Priestess-Queen or perhaps a room reserved for a goddess, appearing in the form of a priestess. Some speculate that the throne was designed for a woman because the indentations in the seat make it more comfortable for a female!"

Korina took her place on the throne and waved her hand regally at Dan. "On your knees before your Priestess-Queen!"

"You look very much at home there," said Dan, laughing.

"Women are thought to have had an unusually high status in Minoan society," explained Korina. "The artwork depicts women more often than men, and the main deity is believed to have been a goddess."

"Did they have multiple gods?"

"We don't know for sure but they are also thought to have worshipped a Bull God and a Bird Goddess, although she may have been the mother Goddess in another form."

"Yeah, bull worship was quite common in Mediterranean and middle-eastern societies," said Dan. He walked over to inspect the central basin. "What was this used for?"

"Evans called it 'The Lustral Basin'. It was probably used for purification as part of a religious ceremony. The 'Throne Room' forms part of the palace's sanctuary complex."

"Was the palace used mainly for religious ceremonies?"

"Yes. There's a debate about whether it also served as an administrative centre. It obviously had no defensive function as there are no walls."

"Did the religious ceremonies include blood sacrifices?" asked Dan.

"Oh yes. The art and frescoes might suggest a utopian civilisation, but there is evidence of a darker side to Minoan society that some of the tourist guides play down. They certainly made blood offerings and there is even evidence of human sacrifice. That said, Crete wasn't the only place in the Mediterranean at the time where this happened. One shouldn't really judge them by our own standards."

"Well I'm pleased you guys have kicked the habit," said Dan, laughing.

Korina's eyes flashed with a cruel glint. "Careful what you say. Greeks often have two first names. My other one is Ariadne."

"Who in Greek mythology was mistress of the labyrinth, in charge of sacrifices," added Dan. "I'll bear that in mind, although she fell in love with Theseus and gave him the ball of thread to get out, didn't she?"

"She did," replied Korina, "but what you forgot to mention in your lecture is that when Theseus abandoned her on Naxos, she called upon the gods to avenge her. They took revenge by making Theseus forget to raise the white sail as he approached Athens, which was meant to be the signal for their safe return. Theseus' father, King Aegeus, threw himself off a cliff in despair."

"Another version says Theseus forgot because he was missing Ariadne."

Korina's eyes narrowed malevolently. "I much prefer the revenge version."

Dan wondered why he wasn't surprised. "Have they found any trace of the labyrinth of Greek mythology?"

"No, but some speculate that the story may have originated from the complex layout of the palace, which has over 1300 rooms interconnected by corridors. It's vast. Then of course there are the bulls depicted in the frescoes and sculptures."

They left the sanctuary area and headed to the 'North Propylaeum', the northern entrance to the palace. "This entrance is located at the end of the road from the ancient harbour. Minoan Crete was well connected with the rest of the Mediterranean. Goods from many other countries have been found in Knossos and other sites, and Cretan goods have turned up all over."

Korina spent a further half hour guiding Dan round the complex, finishing at the East Wing where Korina showed him the water and sewage drainage systems.

Dan detected a note of pride. "To think this is nearly four thousand years old," he commented. "Way ahead of its time."

"Yes. They were very advanced. It's partly why many believe the Greek myth of Atlantis to be an echo of the Minoan civilisation on Thera, which was destroyed by an eruption in the mid second millennium BC."

"Does it annoy you that Crete, with its great history, is now just an outlying region of Greece?"

Korina looked sharply at Dan, pausing a few moments before replying. "Yes it does. Crete would fare much better as an independent state. It's dragged down by Greece. Athens has no interest in Crete."

Dan would have liked to discuss the point further, but Korina abruptly announced that it was time for them to get going. They returned via the western entrance to Korina's car and drove southeast across the centre of the island towards the southern coast and Myrtos.

Dan commented on the spectacular scenery. "I just love the endless olive groves."

"Yes, Crete has some of the oldest in Europe. You should try some Cretan olive oil. I think it's the best around. Much better than the Italian or Spanish ones. But then I would say that, wouldn't I? Talking of which, I assume you're hungry by now?"

"Starving," said Dan.

"What a surprise! I've arranged for us to have lunch at a little place run by a lady who many years ago was my nanny."

"Great. I hope she has some Cretan olive oil."

"Like many Cretans she has her own olive grove!"

Ten minutes later they parked in front of a small café in the little village of Marthas. The café owner, a large middle-aged woman, appeared at the door and greeted Dan with a warm smile before smothering Korina in kisses. She led them to a vine-covered terrace behind the café, where they were presented with an appetizing selection of local specialities, including stuffed aubergines and tomatoes flavoured with oregano, goat's cheese and stuffed vine leaves. Dan took some of each, adding copious quantities of Cretan olive oil to the obvious delight of their host.

***

Vladimir Romanov and his four Russian gang members sat in a black *Porsche* SUV with tinted windows in a back street of Heraklion. They were counting the cash they had just stolen from a popular fast-food chain in Papandreou Street. It was a good haul. One of the gang had kept watch over the store for several weeks and observed the routines. The gang knew when the takings would be picked up by the armoured security van. They had noticed that the weekend takings were often not collected until Monday morning, the money being kept in a safe in the store over the weekend.

It was easy pickings. Just before the close of business on Sunday evening, the gang rushed into the store wearing balaclavas and forced the staff to hand over the takings at gunpoint. They then made their escape in the stolen car they had used for the raid, switching to the *Porsche* once they were well clear. They finished counting the cash and Vladimir began to make the split between his men, keeping the lion's share for himself of course. What he didn't know was that the raid had been watched from the very beginning.

A large *Range Rover* pulled up beside them and five men wearing black combat gear and balaclavas surrounded the car. Vladimir's men received bullets in the head through the windows before they could react. Vladimir flung his door open to try to escape, but found himself looking down the barrels of three guns. He was handcuffed and a black bag placed over his head. He was then bundled into the *Range Rover* and driven off.

***

After lunch with the former nanny, Dan and Korina headed farther south to Myrtos and her father's villa.

"What a place," said Dan as they drove up to it. "As they say, location, location, location!"

The residence lay by the sea and was surrounded on three sides by hills covered in olive groves and Mediterranean pine trees. Two armed guards waved to Korina as they approached and opened the gates. Dan spotted four more guards on patrol in the grounds.

Entering the villa, he realised that it was based on a Minoan palace. The large entrance hall was magnificent, its walls covered in frescoes even larger and more colourful than those he had seen at the museum in Heraklion. Mounted over a doorway opposite the entrance, so as to catch the eye as one walked in, was a sculpture of a bull's head with gold-coloured horns. Dan stepped over to inspect it.

"Do you recognise it?" asked Korina.

"It looks like the Bull's Head Rhyton from Knossos."

"Yes, although this isn't a Rhyton, it's a sculpture and its horns are made of solid gold," said Korina. "They're pretty sharp too!"

Dan inspected the frescoes on the walls of the room. "You said your father was obsessed by things Minoan but this is another level. It's magnificent. Eat your heart out Arthur Evans. Who needs Knossos?"

"Actually the villa is based loosely on the floor plan of Phaistos," said a voice from behind.

Dan turned to face a distinguished-looking man in his late fifties or early sixties. A little shorter than Dan, he was sturdily built but didn't have the paunch that so many men of his age group develop, doubtless the result of careful diet and hours spent in the gym. His dark hair, although greying slightly in parts, was full and thick.

"I'm Korina's father, Stelios. Welcome to my humble home."

Stelios held out his hand, which Dan took.

"It's magnificent," said Dan. "I've never seen anything remotely like it."

"I'm sure Korina will be happy to show you around on the way to your room. You may wish to freshen up after your journey. Then perhaps I can invite you for an aperitif?"

"That would be great," said Dan.

The entrance hall led out to a large stone-paved courtyard surrounded on two sides by porticos supported by columns and pillars.

"The villa doesn't actually replicate Phaistos," said Korina. "It's more inspired by it. The decoration is very different. It's much closer to Knossos in fact. Phaistos didn't have the frescoes that were found in Knossos. The decoration was more alabaster and gypsum. What this villa does share with Phaistos though are the various courtyards on different levels to fit in with the terrain. This central courtyard is the largest but there are several smaller ones to the east and west, again with porticos and rooms going off them."

"Wow! That is some view," said Dan.

"Yes. The courtyard looks out on to the sea. You have even better sea views from the balconies of the bedrooms over there on the north side. I'll take you there now. You'll be staying in one of them."

"So where do you store the olive oil?"

Korina smiled. "Are you thinking of sneaking down in the middle of the night to feed your new addiction?"

She pointed over to the eastern side of the courtyard. "There's a vast cellar that runs under that side of the villa. The steps down to it are in the corner under the portico over there. There are dozens of rooms down there, which are mainly used for storage. But even without those there must be about fifty rooms in all. Not quite Knossos-size but my father could easily run it as a hotel. He does in a way when he holds meetings of his Society here."

"I'm beginning to see why the myth of the labyrinth arose. You must need your famous navigation app just to find your way around the villa."

Korina raised her eyebrows. "Who said it was a myth?"

"Well, Ariadne, as long as there isn't a Minotaur! I guess I haven't stopped worrying since I learned your other name."

"My father does keep cattle in the fields behind the north wing of the villa, including some pretty ferocious bulls. You can take a look at them if you like. You have a second balcony on that side of your room. It might remind you of your uncle's ranch in Arizona."

"So did you have to do bull leaping as well as martial arts?"

"No, I drew the line at that!"

Chapter 13

Southeastern Crete 2483 BC

Ten long years had passed since Queen Hemite had been carried through the palace gates. She looked back nostalgically to the day when she had first met her husband, the King. He had been so handsome, so charming. That happy day now seemed a long time ago.

At first everything had gone well. She had quickly fallen in love with him. He was not only handsome but had genuine charm. He was also caring. He went out of his way to make her feel at home in this foreign land. She appreciated the fact that, despite being busy with affairs of state, he took time to show her things and explain them to her. She soon realised that this was not the closed island backwater she thought it might be. This was an advanced and cultured people with a keen interest in nature and the world around them. They were a peaceful race who, despite their powerful fleet, were more interested in trade than war. Their links with neighbouring countries meant there was a constant succession of foreign merchants and other visitors passing through the palace and a rich variety of food, spices, jewellery and other goods.

The palace Hemite lived in was magnificent, built by the King's father from local stone cut from a nearby mine. The King took her down to the site of the mine, close to the sea, and showed her the labyrinth of tunnels that had been hewn from the rock. The mining of the stone had led to the discovery of silver, copper and gold ore which had made the King's father extremely wealthy. When his father died and he assumed the throne, the popular young King decided to share a large part of the wealth with the people, including slaves whom he freed in gratitude for their labours in the mine.

It soon became obvious to her that in Crete, as in Egypt, women commanded respect, and this showed in the behaviour of the King and his entourage. While most Egyptians had only one wife, pharaohs had lesser wives and concubines in addition to the royal queen. But as Queen in Crete she was the King's only wife. The people's respect for her grew even greater when she quickly bore the King two handsome sons, heirs to the throne.

There were some aspects of her new country that she found strange though. For one thing the bulls. The bull was an important symbol in Egypt too, the Apis bull being worshipped as a deity in the area round Memphis. But here they took it to another level. They were completely obsessed. Bulls were everywhere. They were depicted in frescoes, in sculptures mounted on the walls and on coins and vases. That said, she secretly enjoyed watching the daring young men athletically leap over the ferocious beasts for the entertainment of spectators in the central courtyard of the palace.

What really horrified her though was the discovery that the stories she had heard of human sacrifice were true. Again the practice was not unknown in Egypt, but these days it was confined to criminals and prisoners of war. The practice of retainer sacrifices when a pharaoh passed into the afterlife had long gone. But here human sacrifice, particularly the sacrifice of children, was still practised. She struggled to accept it even though it was their tradition, and as her authority grew she sought to wean them off it.

As Queen in her new kingdom she enjoyed far greater status than she had ever had as the daughter of a minor wife of the pharaoh, albeit an exceptionally beautiful one. Her status back home in Egypt had also been enhanced by the important alliance that she had helped forge. Her father, King Userkaf, had placed great importance on renewing and developing trading alliances with Egypt's Mediterranean neighbours. Close links with the kingdoms of Crete, with their powerful naval and merchant fleets, were of particular importance. She regularly received envoys from Egypt bearing gifts from her father. The gifts continued even after her father died. His successor, King Sahure, was her half-brother, the son of King Userkaf's royal wife. Despite the rivalry between their mothers, Hemite had always got on well with him. And like his father, King Sahure saw the importance of expanding Egypt's trading links with its neighbours. Hemite's favourite gift though remained the one her father had given her on the occasion of her marriage, the golden necklace she had worn the day when she first met her husband. She still wore it almost every day.

But then the earthquakes started. Not just isolated earthquakes but repeated ones which grew more and more violent. The climate also changed abruptly, becoming much drier. The drought lasted a number of years, turning the lush countryside into an arid desert. Crops failed, and this was quickly followed by famine and pestilence.

The Priestess demanded that, despite the Queen's objections, the King resume making human sacrifices in the hope of appeasing the Mother Goddess. But even this didn't seem to work. The Priestess herself was killed when the temple on the mountaintop overlooking the palace collapsed during a sacrificial ceremony. The people became increasingly restless and began to blame their King. They also blamed his Queen. Her loyal handmaidens reported that there were whispers that the woes being suffered were the Goddess' revenge on the King for marrying a foreign princess. The King was having none of it and tried to shield her from it. But he couldn't.

She felt less and less welcome. She sent word to Egypt, begging King Sahure to allow her to return home, at least for a while. But she got no reply. Whether his courtiers ever told him of her messages she never found out. King Sahure doubtless had more pressing problems as Egypt itself sought to cope with a prolonged drought after the Nile had failed to flood for several years. Queen Hemite now felt isolated and unhappy in this foreign land.

Then one day a violent earthquake struck the palace complex itself. The King was out on a hunting trip and had taken their two sons, leaving the Queen at home. The quake was so violent that the roof of the palace crashed down, trapping all inside it. The Queen found herself pinned under a heavy stone seat that had become detached from the wall. She was alone. Her handmaidens lay crushed to death beneath two large pillars that had crashed down. The Queen was unable to move. At first she lay waiting, confident that her husband would soon come to save her. But he didn't. As she lay alone dying she thought of her two handsome sons and the happy day when she had first met her husband. Clutching the necklace her father had given her, her eyes dimmed. Her last thoughts were of her homeland Egypt, the land of her happy childhood to which she would never return.

***

Dan grabbed a shower and joined Korina and her father in the courtyard. They were sitting with another man whom Stelios introduced as the Head of Security.

"Ah, also known as the Tutor," said Dan. "I've heard a lot about you."

"Good things I hope," said the Tutor.

Dan guessed the Tutor, who wore his longish dark brown hair in a short ponytail, was a little older than him. Early to mid-forties maybe? He looked very fit though, doubtless the result of daily work-outs and martial art exercises.

"Of course, Korina has nothing but praise for you. You certainly taught her well," said Dan, referring obliquely to the sore neck she had given him in Spain.

The Tutor smiled grimly. Dan took an instinctive dislike to him, but couldn't put his finger on why.

While Dan was served a drink Korina disappeared into one of the rooms adjoining the courtyard. She returned with the golden disc. Placing it carefully on the table in front of Dan, she addressed him with exaggerated formality. "Now, Professor Baker, give me your first impressions if you'd be so kind. What language are these Minoan hieroglyphs? I've printed a large photo of the other side of the disc with the Egyptian hieroglyphs so you can compare the two scripts."

Dan began by reading the Egyptian hieroglyphs. "So the inscription starts on the outer circle of the disc. 'This golden disc bears witness that Great King Titiku, who rules in the southeastern region of Keftiu, took as his wife and queen, Princess Hemite, daughter of Great King Userkaf of Egypt'. Interesting. Titiku had the status of a Great King, of equal rank to the King of Egypt."

"Yes," commented Korina. "We see immediately the importance which Egypt attached to its alliance with Minoan Crete."

"Hardly surprising I guess," said Dan, "given their powerful fleet. The Egyptians would doubtless want to keep on good terms with them."

"Userkaf is known to have been keen to develop alliances with neighbouring Mediterranean countries," said Korina. "I would think cementing alliances with the kings of Keftiu would be high on the list."

Dan continued to read the Egyptian symbols. "The text goes on to talk about the exploits of both kings and their bond of common friendship. It talks of the arrival of the Princess in Crete from her home at King Userkaf's palace at Ineb-hedj. That's interesting in itself. It confirms recent archaeological evidence. For a long time it was thought that the Fifth Dynasty Kings ruled from Elephantine."

Dan finished reading the Egyptian script and turned to the Cretan text. He fell silent for about ten minutes as he traced his fingers along the strange symbols, comparing them with the Egyptian hieroglyphics. The Tutor, looking a little bored, wandered off to attend to other matters. Stelios and Korina in contrast looked on with eager anticipation.

"I think it's an Anatolian language," he said finally. "It came from what we now know as Turkey."

Stelios frowned. "You're not saying the Minoans spoke Turkish?"

Dan smiled, aware of the Greek sensitivity to Turkish influence. "No, this is far older. Long before Turkey. I need more time to work it out. But my guess is that it developed from an ancestor of the Luwic branch of Anatolian languages."

"Can you explain what you mean by the Luwic branch?" asked Stelios.

"Yes of course. There were three main branches of the Anatolian language: Hittite, Palaic and Luwic. The Luwic branch included Luwian, Carian, Lycian, Lydian and Milyan. These are very old languages that died out long ago. I think this could be even older though. As you would expect given Minoan Crete's connections with the rest of the Mediterranean, there are other influences too. I wouldn't be surprised if there was some proto-Greek chucked into the mix. But I think this is probably a language that came to Crete from Anatolia early, quite possibly during the Neolithic period, and developed locally. The Minoans had their own language."

Korina looked at her father, who gave a satisfied smile.

"That's precisely what Korina thought. And it fits. Recent DNA evidence suggests that the Minoans were indigenous, having probably come across from Anatolia during the Neolithic period. There are still people today in Crete with a DNA that closely matches that of the early Cretans."

"Yes of course, I'd forgotten. Korina told me that she and her mother are among them. Pure Cretan blood."

The Tutor, who had just re-joined them, glared at Korina.

"In short," said Korina, seemingly oblivious, "it's likely that the main alternative theory that Minoans came from Africa is wrong."

"Almost certainly I would say," said Dan. "I suspect with more time we'll be able to pin the origin of the language down more precisely, although as I say it's likely to have had influences from other sources over the years."

"But what matters," said Stelios, "is that the Minoan civilisation developed independently and had its own language."

"I guess so," said Dan, wondering why exactly it mattered.

"Ah, Kassandra," said Stelios, looking behind Dan. "Do join us."

Dan stood and turned to greet Kassandra.

"Professor Baker," she said. "So pleased to meet you finally. I'm Kassandra, Korina's mother. I've heard a lot about you."

"Very good to meet you too," said Dan.

Kassandra really needed no introduction. He would have recognised her as Korina's mother if he had met her in the street. It wasn't just that she had the same penetrating eyes; she was basically just an older version of Korina. Tall, trim and elegant with long dark hair, she wore a pleated, light blue skirt cut just above the knee with matching jacket.

Wow, if this is what Korina's going to look like when she's older she needn't have any worries, thought Dan.

"Professor Baker, I was wondering whether Stelios and I might invite Korina and yourself to join us for dinner tomorrow evening," she said. "I would have loved to invite you this evening but unfortunately we are busy entertaining some business guests."

"I'd be delighted."

"Excellent. I'll have a word with the staff. Perhaps Korina could take you to her favourite taverna tonight?"

"Good idea," said Korina. "It's right up Dan's street. A simple place with great local dishes."

"Perfect," said Dan. "Before we go I'll check whether my old friend Charles from Oxford has come back to me. He specialises in satellite imaging. I mailed him last night to see whether he can help us with the site of the palace. It's an outside chance but if anyone can find it he can."

***

Dan had just got back to his room when Charles rang. He had met Charles while teaching at Oxford University. A professor of archaeology, Charles was very British, very old school. Somewhat incongruously, he was also a leading expert in the use of modern satellite imaging to investigate archaeological sites.

"So, old chap, I've analysed the satellite images for the area around Myrtos. If you have your laptop handy I can send them to you now. I'll talk you through them."

A few moments later Dan received Charles' email. "OK, got them."

"Now, at first I got nowhere," said Charles. "I really thought I was flogging a dead horse. But then I tried using a fancy new technique borrowed from a dear friend of mine in the States. She's been experimenting with something called 'false colour imaging' to detect subtle differences on the ground. The first time I saw it I thought 'Bloody hell, Charles,' if you'll pardon the French, 'what have you been missing all these years?' Anyway, to cut a long story short, I tried out the technique on the images for the area round Myrtos. The results are quite splendid. I'll show you what I mean. Click on the image on the left."

"I don't see anything," said Dan.

"Precisely, old chap. That's because there is nothing. But click now on the next image along, same location but using the new technique."

"Wow! I can't believe it's the same place."

"One and the same. It's quite a big site and there are features that to me look very much like walls. There's something odd about the site though. The geology looks strange to me. Anyway you should definitely pop up there and give it the once over."

***

Dan and Korina strolled about twenty minutes along the coast to the local taverna which, as Korina had said, was a modest affair serving unpretentious, yet delicious, local fare. It was another warm July evening and they sat beside the sea under a vine-covered terrace, wafted by gentle breezes and entertained by a local musician playing a Cretan lyra.

"Have you heard from Charles yet?"

"Yes. He called me. He found something interesting near Pirgos. I've brought my laptop with me to show you."

Dan showed Korina the images, demonstrating the effect of using the false colour imaging technique Charles had learned from his American friend.

"That looks promising," said Korina, "and we know there were early Minoan settlements around that area. We should go up there tomorrow and have a look."

***

Two men armed with guns walked along the rows of dimly lit prison cells. The men walked past the male prisoners, who were being held separately, and unlocked the gate of one of the cells confining the women and children. They selected four attractive young women and a young boy, forcing them out at gunpoint. Locking the cell they dragged them out of the chamber, ignoring their pleas and those of the other prisoners.

After being led down a long passage the women were taken into a series of sparsely furnished rooms containing little more than beds. The guards ordered them to undress and lie down on the beds. The boy was taken to another room where he was awaited by a man, who ordered him to kneel. When the men had finished, the women and the boy were led back to their cells in tears.

The following morning Dan and Korina drove up to the location near Pirgos that Charles had directed them to. Korina had enlisted some volunteers from the local archaeological society to help them carry out a preliminary survey. They started by inspecting the site, which was on the lower slopes of a mountain, for obvious features and surface pottery. It wasn't long before they discovered a number of fragments of pottery that Korina identified as early Minoan.

"The whole site is on a slope," commented Korina. "The palace at Phaistos was built to take advantage of the sloping ground but this is really steep. And there's no sign of any terracing."

"Yes. I know I'm a layman, but I can't see someone choosing to build a palace here. Charles was right in saying the geology is strange. If you look up the mountainside there's a massive cavity near the top, a sort of crater or crevasse."

"There must have been a landslide at some point. The upper part of the slope has slipped down to where we're standing."

"An earthquake maybe?"

"Quite possibly," said Korina. "Earthquakes are very common in this part of the world. The palace at Phaistos was damaged several times by quakes. If there is a structure here it was probably buried by the landslide and lies many metres beneath our feet. Perhaps we should go down to the bottom of the slope and see whether we can spot anything down there. The landslide may have run out of steam by the time it got lower down. Any remains would be at a shallower depth."

They did as Korina suggested. Noticing a long protrusion in the earth, Korina set the volunteers to work exploring it. They found that it was caused by masonry just under the surface. They began clearing the earth around it and started finding more early Minoan pottery. After an hour or so one of the diggers asked Korina to come over. The earth had suddenly collapsed inwards as she dug, revealing a gaping hole beneath the masonry, like the entrance to a tunnel.

Korina inspected it. "I think it's the lintel over the top of a doorway or an entrance."

Dan picked up a torch. "Let's have a look, shall we?"

He tried to crawl into the hole but it was too small for him.

"Let me try," said Korina.

"OK, but be careful. It may be unstable."

Grabbing the torch Korina squeezed herself through the hole and disappeared. There followed a few minutes of silence.

"Are you OK?" shouted Dan.

"I'm fine," came back a muted reply.

About ten minutes later Korina re-emerged, her eyes gleaming through the layer of chalky dust that covered her face.

"Well, we've found our Minoan palace. I was right. This piece of masonry is the lintel over an entrance. Once you get through the hole it's less clogged with earth and opens out into a large entrance hall. Then, as we guessed, the palace extends back into the slope created by the landslide. The entrance hall leads into a courtyard, which is largely buried, but you can squeeze through into a portico that ran along the eastern side of the palace."

"Sounds similar to your parents' place," said Dan.

"The design's very similar. Many of the pillars supporting the portico have held or have become lodged against the walls of the palace when they fell. It's a bit of struggle but you can make your way through. Some of the rooms off the portico are completely intact and accessible. Others will need to be excavated. The entire palace is decorated with alabaster and gypsum and there are frescoes galore. It's stunning. I took some photos with my phone."

Everyone excitedly crowded round, gasping in amazement as they saw the photos.

"There was something else though," added Korina. "I saw two skeletons in the portico trapped under a pillar. They still had traces of items of clothing they were wearing."

"That must mean that no one came to help them or recover the bodies," said Dan.

"Looks like it. If the palace was consumed by a landslide, I guess rescuers might not have been able to get in to help survivors, if there were any. And the landslide would also explain why the palace was never rebuilt. The site was just abandoned. It may be that they rebuilt it somewhere else. Perhaps we have another palace nearby?"

Dan laughed. "Let's not get greedy! I would like to get in there to have a look."

"Once you're through the hole, you'll be fine. Why don't we try to widen it? We'll have to be careful not to overdo it though as the lintel might collapse."

After half an hour's careful digging the hole had been widened enough for

Dan to squeeze through.

"It may be better to go feet first," said Korina. "Then you can just jump down once you get through the hole. I had to do a kind of cartwheel."

Dan didn't fancy imitating Korina's acrobatics and took her advice. Squeezing through feet first he dropped down into the large entrance hall Korina had mentioned. She followed him in. The floor was strewn with rubble but large sections of the stone paving on the floor were still visible. Korina shone her torch at the walls to reveal the stunning frescoes that she had photographed. Not dissimilar to those at Knossos and the Heraklion Museum, their condition was amazing considering their age. The brightly coloured figures depicted in the paintings were still vivid and sharp.

Korina led Dan out of the entrance hall and into the courtyard. As she had said, the courtyard soon ran into a mass of solid earth that had slid down on to it. They began to make their way along a section of the portico. In places some of the pillars supporting it had collapsed and they had to scramble over or under them. They reached the two skeletons Korina had mentioned, trapped under fallen pillars. The skulls were badly damaged but their torsos still bore fragments of the garments they had been wearing.

"Clearly these poor people had no idea what was about to happen," said Dan.

"No. We'll have to get the geologists to take a look, but an earthquake does seem the most likely explanation."

Korina led Dan into a room adjoining the portico and shone her torch into the corner. "I noticed some fragments of clay tablet on the floor over there."

They walked over to them and knelt down. Dan picked up one of the pieces. "Minoan hieroglyphs."

Korina removed a leather bag from her shoulder and opened it. "I shouldn't do this, but I want to take advantage of your expertise while you're here." She recorded the precise location of the fragments and placed them carefully in the bag.

They went back into the portico and entered another room. Dan's torch revealed something on the floor by the wall. He walked over and knelt by it. "It's another skeleton. And I think it may have been a woman. She's wearing a magnificent necklace."

"Probably, although men often wore necklaces too."

The skeleton was less badly damaged than the two that were trapped under the pillars in the portico. The abdomen and skull were intact.

Korina knelt down beside it and carefully picked up the necklace. "Pure gold. And look, one of the gold pieces has an inscription."

The script, in ancient Egyptian hieroglyphs, was clearly visible. Dan read it aloud. "From King Userkaf to his beautiful daughter Hemite on the occasion of her marriage."

"My God," said Korina. "We've found Princess Hemite. This was the palace of King Titiku mentioned on the disc."

Dan was about to say that archaeology wasn't meant to be this easy, but was dissuaded by the memory of the sore neck he got when he last uttered the words.

"Her legs are trapped," said Korina, pointing to a large stone chair that had fallen on its side. "I fear she lay here unable to move and may have taken some time to…"

Korina rose from the skeleton, staring at Dan. "Oh God! I'm so sorry. I didn't…"

"It's OK," gasped Dan, his chest tightening as the images of his recurring nightmare about Aliah flooded his brain. "I think we had better go now."

Having scrambled back out Korina allowed the volunteers to see the interior for themselves, cautioning them to take great care. She then swore them to secrecy while promising to make sure they were involved in the excavation of the site.

"I'll ask my father to send one of his guards here until the site is secured," she said.

***

When Dan and Korina got back to the villa they went to their rooms to shower. Dan came down to find Korina sitting at a table in the courtyard, piecing together the fragments of tablet in what looked like an incomplete jigsaw.

"I think we may have fragments of several tablets," she said, looking up at Dan. "I bet you're thirsty after scrambling around the site. Let me get you a beer while we look at them."

"That'd be great. It may be an idea to fetch the disc so we can compare the hieroglyphs. I doubt we're familiar enough yet with the Minoan script to read it unaided."

They worked intensively, using the Egyptian script on the disc to decipher the Minoan symbols. Many passages came to an abrupt end where the tablets had shattered and others were hard to read. Even with the help of the disc there were numerous symbols they couldn't understand. But after an hour or so, with a fair amount of guesswork, they had a rough translation of some of the fragments.

"This is a significant find," said Korina. "Not the usual inventories you get in the later Linear B tablets. It's an account of a king's reign and deeds. More the sort of thing you get in Egyptian texts. This bit records a conversation between the King and the Priestess."

She began to read aloud.

"*And the Priestess said to the King, 'Have no fear, Great King. Your reign will be long and prosperous. The Mother Goddess will be appeased and these difficult times will pass. The kingdom will enjoy many seasons of plenty and endure long after your reign. But be warned. In your lifetime you will suffer a tragedy'.*

"*The King was greatly concerned. 'What tragedy, my Priestess?' he asked.*"

"It looks as though the land was going through a rough time," commented Dan. "So the King decided to consult the Priestess on what the future held."

"There's a bit missing. So we don't have the Priestess' reply to the King's question." Korina continued reading.

"'*There will come a time, long after your reign, when the kingdom will fall to kings from the north with fearsome weapons. They will burn and plunder the land for its gold. But just as the moon waxes and wanes their time will come and go and the land will pass to other conquerors from neighbouring lands'.*

"*The King was horrified. 'Is that the fate of my land', he asked, 'to be a vassal state?'*

"'*No', said the Priestess. 'After many moons the kingdom will rise again and be greater than ever before'.*

"'*Tell me, Priestess. How will that come to pass?'*

"'*A Great Queen of pure blood shall arise and unite the whole land. She shall set her foreign enemies against each other. Their great ships shall be destroyed as they cower in their harbour'.*"

"There's more here we couldn't work out," said Korina. "We then go back to the King.

"'*And what will be the sign of her coming, Priestess?'*

"'*I see a time of great unrest where nations are torn apart and there is displacement of peoples. The moon shall grow to a size seldom seen before and turn immediately to blood. Five times the moon shall wax and wane before it turns to blood again. I see a stranger of many tongues from a place far beyond the setting sun who shall come to our land. He shall come as a friend, but shall betray the Queen, who shall suffer a great loss. It is then that the Queen shall rise up against the foreign conquerors and banish them from the land forever. But first she shall sacrifice the stranger to the Bull God to obtain his blessing for her endeavours'."*

"Great stuff," said Dan, "although a lot of it is pretty general as you might expect. The Priestess no doubt wanted to give herself some wriggle room! To be fair though she was right about the kings from the north. The Mycenaean Greeks who took over Crete later in the second millennium were basically heavily armed thugs."

"Yes, and although the moon turning to blood is common in ancient prophecies, she adds a fair amount of detail. What she's describing sounds like a full eclipse of a super moon. An unusual event. Funnily enough there was one in January this year. The moon seen from Crete was gigantic and then turned blood red. It was very dramatic. So much so you had the inevitable predictions about the end of the world."

"But she then goes further and predicts a second blood moon five moons later," said Dan. "Probably even more unusual."

***

It was a warm evening and dinner was served in the courtyard. The staff served a delicious first course of fish baked in olive oil and lemon, which was accompanied by a delightful local white wine. Dan began to wolf it down but, seeing Korina's amused look, made a conscious effort to slow down.

Stelios asked about Dan's naval background and his interest in boats. Kassandra was intrigued by his Syrian connection and quizzed him about his stepmother. As soon as he decently could, he steered the conversation away from himself and his family. He asked about Stelios' passion for things Minoan.

"I wouldn't say passion. I'd say obsession," said Kassandra. "He's President and founder of the Cretan Society for Minoan Culture."

"Korina has told me a little about the Society, but I'd be interested to hear more."

"Well its aim," explained Stelios, "is to promote research into Crete's Minoan history and provide a forum for people to share their common interest."

"Does the Society promote archaeological digs?"

"Yes. Korina supervises the Society's archaeological activities. It provides substantial funding for digs and makes donations to the university and to museums. It also has good connections with government and helps overcome red tape. Greece is a very bureaucratic country."

In other words, it finds the right person to bribe, thought Dan. "Korina mentioned it also puts on theatre pieces and re-enactments of Minoan rituals?"

"Yes. Stelios is a great fan of those," said Kassandra. "Korina too. She often takes part, playing the role of a priestess."

Korina's eyes lit up. "I really enjoy it. I love the acting and wearing the fabulous costumes and jewellery. And there's no better way to bring the past to life. I often invite my students to attend as it helps them visualise how the Minoan finds were used."

"So what do the re-enactments entail? Bull-leaping?"

Kassandra smiled. "Not so far! The scenes are often set in a royal court or palace sanctuary."

"I thought Korina looked at home in the Knossos Throne Room! So do the enactments include offerings and sacrifice?"

"The ones in the sanctuaries, yes," said Korina.

"Not human ones I hope!"

Korina laughed. "Only if we can't get bull's blood!"

Kassandra gave Korina a disapproving look. "Now, now, don't be naughty!"

Korina smiled. "Ever since I told Dan my other name was Ariadne, he's been worried he might end up being sacrificed to the Bull God!"

"Especially after reading the Priestess' prophecy," said Dan.

Stelios leant back from the table in laughter. "It's true that the Minoans made human sacrifices, particularly in troubled times. There was one particularly disturbing find in the temple of Anemospilia, not far from Knossos. Archaeologists found the remains of a teenage boy on a sacrificial table. Analysis of the bones showed that the blood had been drained from the upper part of his body. They think his throat was cut with a bronze dagger engraved with a boar's head that lay beside him. The interesting thing is that the bodies of three people were found near him. It's thought that an earthquake struck just after the boy was sacrificed, killing the Priestess and a temple servant. We're talking 1700 BC. So it was probably the same earthquake that destroyed the palace at Knossos. Archaeologists think the sacrifice was probably a response to earlier earthquakes. They were hoping to appease the Mother Goddess."

"So maybe it's best not to visit Crete right after an earthquake," said Dan with a cheeky grin.

"I hate to disappoint you, Dan," said Stelios laughing, "but our sacrifices are rather more mundane. For the most part, in fact, Minoan sacrifices didn't involve the shedding of blood. Their offerings were mainly of produce such as wheat, oats, olive oil and wine. We do, as Korina said, stretch to bull's blood on a special occasion when we've had to cull one of our bulls!"

"Well that's a relief," said Dan. "Where do these re-enactments take place?"

"We have a replica of a Greek theatre in one of the courtyards," explained Kassandra. "The Society also puts on theatre pieces for the general public. The last one, a few weeks ago, was a play based on the story of Theseus and the Minotaur at a theatre in Heraklion. It was a sort of amateur theatrical version of the Minotaur Opera performed at the London Royal Opera House a few years ago."

"Ah yes. I saw it while I was teaching at Oxford. Who played the Minotaur?"

"A local thespian," said Korina. "He was far too fit for the part really."

Kassandra frowned at Korina.

"Well he was," insisted Korina. "But he was well disguised by his bull mask."

"And Korina played Priestess Ariadne, mistress of the labyrinth," said Kassandra.

"Of course, and you wonder why I worry," said Dan, drawing more laughter.

Dan was surprised how much he was enjoying Stelios' company. He found his eccentricity entertaining and, unless Stelios was disguising it well, he wasn't the hard bitten Cretan businessman wary of foreigners that Dan had expected. He was welcoming and ebullient.

The staff brought out the main course of lamb kleftiko. Cooked in parchment paper with vegetables, olive oil, oregano and rosemary, it smelt and looked delicious. Stelios poured Dan a glass of red wine to accompany the lamb.

"This wine is delightful," said Dan. "Where's it from?"

"It's a local wine called Liatiko," said Kassandra. "I prefer to serve local Cretan produce wherever possible."

Dan decided to risk steering the conversation round to politics. "Stelios, the prophecy talks about Crete rising again and being stronger than ever. Do you think Crete will ever regain the stature it had during the Minoan period?"

"Well it would have to become independent first," said Stelios.

"Is there an independence movement in Crete?"

"Not really. Not one worthy of the name. Most people are happy being part of Greece, or at least they were until recently. The financial problems in Greece have led some to call for independence."

"Could Crete survive on its own?"

"Of course it could," said Korina. "Crete is one of the mainstays of the Greek economy. It's one of the few Greek islands that is self-sufficient when it comes to food, and it has highly profitable agriculture and tourism sectors."

Stelios frowned. "I should explain that Korina is an enthusiastic supporter of Cretan independence. But she's young and idealistic. It is true that economically Crete would be fine. But the bigger concern is security. Older people are conscious of the fact that our island has been repeatedly overrun by invaders, even in recent times. Cretans on the whole are happy to have the large Greek and US naval bases in Souda Bay. It makes them feel secure."

"Crete should have its own security, its own navy," insisted Korina. "It can't rely on other countries. They have their own agendas."

Stelios smiled. "What do you think, Dan? As an American do you have any views on whether Crete would be better off as an independent country?"

Dan thought it wise not to take sides. "Well I certainly wouldn't want to see the US splintering. But I guess we have our own history. I was wondering how important independence is for regions that are part of the EU. Ultimately Cretans and Greeks are all EU citizens and many of your laws are made in Brussels. Wouldn't Crete have to reapply for EU membership if it were no longer part of Greece?"

"I think the EU would want Crete to remain a member," said Korina. "Whether Cretans would want to is another matter. There are arguments for keeping more control and just having a trading arrangement with the EU. The point is that it should be for Cretans to decide."

"How do Cretans feel about foreigners coming to Crete?" asked Dan. "I understand that in the UK Brexit debate immigration and control of borders were major issues. I think there's been a backlash against immigrants in other EU countries as well, for example Germany. My friend Antonio in Mallorca was telling us there had even been hostility towards foreign tourism, with tourists being attacked."

The conversation was interrupted briefly as the staff topped up their wine and water glasses.

"There is a feeling," said Stelios, "that Greece, including Crete, has been overrun by foreign criminal gangs in recent years and that the police are struggling to cope. I think tourists are welcome, although Cretan people do struggle with the drunken louts you get in some of the resorts. The British in particular have a reputation for getting drunk and causing trouble. As you see, Cretans drink a lot of wine but they don't get drunk and misbehave, not in public anyway!"

"What about the Germans? I understand there's some anti-German sentiment," said Dan.

"Yes. There is. It's over fifty years since the Nazis were here but Cretans still haven't forgotten the Nazi occupation. The Nazis committed some terrible atrocities, wiping out entire villages. It hasn't been helped of course by the EU's hard line, forcing austerity on Greece. Many people blame Angela Merkel, the German Chancellor. There's also concern about the Germans buying up assets in Crete and Greece more generally. So all in all there is some simmering resentment. I don't think you would notice it as a tourist though, and certainly not as an American."

Kassandra interrupted the discussion, perhaps worried that the conversation had taken too serious a turn. "It's getting late. We should talk about arrangements for tomorrow."

"Yes. I have to run over to Chania for a faculty meeting," said Korina. "Dan, you're welcome to come with me but you may prefer to stay here and have a look around the area."

"Well I could do with catching up on emails and making a few calls," said Dan.

"If you wish," said Stelios, "I'd be happy to show you round our shipyard in Ierapetra. It may be of interest to you."

"That would be great," said Dan. "I'd love to have a look round some of your vessels if that's possible?"

"Well, that's settled then. I have a meeting of one of the Society's committees tomorrow, the finance committee. But that's not until the evening. So shall we plan to head off mid-morning?"

"Perfect," said Dan.

"I think it's time for Kassandra and myself to leave you two young people to enjoy the rest of your evening."

Stelios and Kassandra stood up and withdrew from the table. Dan and Korina lingered for a while finishing the red wine. Korina insisted on Dan trying some *Raki*, a local grape-based Cretan spirit.

"This is excellent. Well, your father didn't seem at all bothered about having an American in his home."

"No I told you he wouldn't. I think perhaps I gave you the wrong impression of him when we were on the yacht."

And maybe Alexia is barking up the wrong tree, thought Dan, *and Stelios is just a benign eccentric*.

They talked about the golden disc, the ancient Minoan palace and the clay tablets containing the prophecy. Any one of those would have been a major find in itself, but to find all three in such a short period of time was amazing.

"It's getting late and I have a long drive tomorrow," said Korina finally. "But before we retire let me show you the stage where the latter-day Minoans act out their plays."

***

Priestess Ariadne, mistress of the labyrinth, sat on her alabaster throne wearing a multi-coloured layered skirt. The long lapels of her tight-fitting red top gradually parted as they led from a purple waist band to her shoulders, partly exposing her breasts. On her head she wore a golden crown and around her neck a golden pendant depicting two bees with their wings outstretched, clasping a honeycomb.

The prisoner was brought by the guards into the Throne Room in chains and thrown on to the floor before her. Five men knelt before the Priestess.

"Who is it that accuses this man?" the Priestess asked.

"It is I, Priestess," said one of the five men.

"Of what crime is he accused?"

"He is accused of robbery."

"What evidence is there that he committed this crime?"

"There are statements by witnesses to his crime."

"Show them to me."

The man stood up and handed the Priestess three scrolls. He then returned to his knees. The Priestess read the scrolls and asked,

"Does the prisoner have anything to say in his defence?"

The prisoner, who was gagged, made some unintelligible muffled sounds.

"Very well," said the Priestess. "The prisoner has nothing to say. I find him guilty of the crime of which he is charged."

The Priestess then fell silent as if in a trance.

"The Bull God accepts the sacrifice," she said finally. "Take the prisoner away. He shall be cast into the labyrinth."

The prisoner was dragged to his feet and led down a long passage. The Priestess followed. The passage led to a sturdy wooden gate held shut by large iron bolts.

"Open the gate and cast him in. May the Gods have mercy upon him," said the Priestess.

The prisoner's hands were untied and he was thrown through the gate, which closed behind him. He heard it being bolted from the other side. The prisoner had been told about the labyrinth. His captors had enjoyed taunting him with stories about the Minotaur, the ferocious monster that dwelled in this underground maze of tunnels. Half man half bull, it relentlessly pursued any prey that entered its lair. It had the stealth of a man and the strength of a bull. It enjoyed toying with, and terrifying, its prey.

The prisoner didn't really believe the story. He had heard rumours, but surely no such beast could exist. Despite that he was petrified. He stood by the gate for a while trying to calm himself. Then he tiptoed farther in, listening intently. He soon lost any sense of direction. But to his relief he heard nothing. Perhaps whatever it was that inhabited these tunnels was asleep? Or was it just lurking in a nearby passage waiting to leap on him? He realised his legs were shaking.

Then suddenly he heard something. The sounds were faint at first. The noises of a bull. Grunts, snorts, bellowing. *My God*, he thought, *they were telling the truth!* Gradually the sounds grew louder, echoing round the interconnected passages.

He began to run but didn't know which way to go. The noises were all around him, in front one moment then behind the next. They were becoming deafening. The creature was nearly upon him. Running in blind panic he tripped and fell. Turning his head, he watched in horror as a huge beast came thundering down the dimly lit passage, its lowered head and large horns pointing towards him. A split second later the horns ripped agonisingly into his body. He screamed as the creature shook him like a rag doll before finally dropping him to the floor.

In his final moments Russian gang-leader Vladimir Romanov stared up at the closed circuit cameras that had filmed his every move. His eyes dimmed and he passed into blackness. His last thoughts were of his childhood in Moscow.

Chapter 14

Stelios drove Dan along the coast from the villa to the port at Ierapetra, passing through Gra Lygia and Potami. The road was relatively flat and uninteresting, but Stelios was in a talkative mood and spent the journey telling Dan about the local history. Ierapetra, he explained, had been a Roman port and then a Venetian stronghold. Dan noted he omitted any reference to the Ottoman Turkish period.

"So this is our local shipyard," said Stelios as they arrived in Ierapetra and drove through the gates. "It's quite small by comparison with our others, for example in Heraklion and Piraeus on the Greek mainland."

Dan noticed the gates were guarded by armed men with large dogs. "Is security here a problem?"

"Security has been a problem everywhere in Crete in recent years. As I was saying last night, there's been an influx of foreign criminal elements. We've given up relying on the police. The Tutor has expanded our security staff substantially at all our sites, not just the shipyards. It's made a huge difference. Talk of the devil, here he is."

"Welcome to the engine room, Professor Baker," said the Tutor. "I fear your timing isn't ideal. We've a large shipment due shortly."

"Fair enough," said Dan, feeling decidedly unwelcome. "Let's keep it short. What I'd really be interested in is a quick look round one or two of your ships. How about that freighter over there, the *Princess Ariadne*? It looks great. Almost like an old fashioned tramp steamer."

"Well I'd prefer you to have a look round another one if you don't mind. The Ariadne's currently being fitted with some new electrics. There's another freighter over there that's almost identical."

"Good idea," said Stelios. "Let's have a look at that one."

Dan and Stelios went over to the other freighter and walked up the gangway on to the deck. The bridge of the vessel ran amidships with steps going up on either side. Fore and aft were two large decks with stairwells leading below.

"What do you carry?" asked Dan.

"All sorts really," said Stelios. "The outbound trips are usually agricultural produce, the return trips almost anything. It occurs to me there's something I forgot to say to the Tutor. Do you mind if I leave you to look around on your own for a few minutes?"

"Not at all. I'll just wander around."

Dan saw Stelios and the Tutor disappear into a large warehouse on the quayside. He seized the moment and headed over to the *Princess Ariadne*. He couldn't see anyone on deck and no one seemed to be paying much attention to him, so he climbed up the gangway.

As the Tutor had said, the layout was very similar to that of the other vessel. Again two stairwells on deck led down below. The bridge, accessible by flights of steps either side, was located amidships with deck cabins immediately behind. Dan spotted two men in overalls standing by the bridge smoking. He climbed up the steps to speak to them.

"So what are you guys up to?" he asked nonchalantly.

"Who are you? Where's your badge?" asked one of the men.

"Oh I'm with Stelios," said Dan. "He suggested I have a look round. So what's the upgrade for?"

"You're not allowed on the ship without a badge," the other man said.

Dan realised he was getting nowhere. "OK. Sorry. I'll head back down then. I don't suppose I could beg a cigarette off you?"

They looked at him suspiciously, but one of the men opened a pack of cigarettes, handed one to Dan and gave him a light.

"You have to go now, otherwise we'll be in trouble for not reporting you."

Dan walked back down the steps and headed towards the gangway. He paused at the top to draw on the cigarette and began to cough after inhaling the cheap tobacco smoke. Out of the corner of his eye he saw the two men laugh as they headed back into the bridge after their cigarette break. As soon as they had disappeared Dan stubbed the cigarette out and dived down the stairwell on the starboard side of the deck.

Finding himself in a long corridor, he walked towards the stern of the vessel, passing through two open hatches before coming to one that was closed. Dan opened the hatch to find a large hold. It was almost completely dark, the only light coming from two small portholes at the rear. Dan stepped in and immediately caught a strong smell of excrement. Quickly covering his nose and mouth with his hand, he turned around to get out, but as he did the hatch door closed behind him. Dan tried the door but it had been locked from the outside. The smell and fumes were so strong Dan could barely breathe. He turned round and promptly trod in something soft and squishy. Switching on his phone torch he shone it down at his feet. The floor was covered in small piles of dark brown gunge.

"Holy crap," murmured Dan. "I've heard of cattle class but this is ridiculous."

He needed to act quickly before he was overcome by the fumes. Switching off the torch to allow his eyes to adjust to the darkness, he began scanning the hold for a way out. There was no other exit, only the two portholes towards the rear. He doubted he could squeeze through them, but if he could open them at least he would be able to breathe. He looked round to see the best way of navigating the sea of gunge. He was about to set off towards the portholes when the hatch door opened.

"Professor Baker," said the Tutor. "How terrible! How in God's name did you manage to get yourself locked in here?"

Behind the Tutor stood the two workmen he had spoken to on the bridge. They were both smirking, one of them pretending to hold his nose.

"What on Earth were you carrying in here?" asked Dan.

"Manure and farm products," said the Tutor. "That's partly why I didn't want you coming on board this ship. Apart from the electrical work we haven't cleaned and disinfected the holds yet after the previous trip."

"Oh sorry. Did I come back on board the wrong ship? They look so alike."

"We really should leave. It could be dangerous for your health in here," said the Tutor menacingly.

He led Dan off the ship and took him back to Stelios, who was waiting on the quayside. Stelios didn't appear to be amused. "I think we'd better go now. Please take your shoes off before you get in the car." He hardly said a word on the return trip to the villa, Dan's attempts to engage him in conversation prompting no response.

***

When Dan got back to the villa he had a long cleansing shower and then rang his father. "Hi, Dad, how're you doing?"

"I'm doing OK, son, in the circumstances. Anything to report?"

"Not really. Met Kouklakis over dinner last night and today had a look round the dockyard and a couple of freighters, including the *Princess Ariadne*."

"So what's your next move?"

"Not sure. My instincts tell me there's something going on here. But I'm not sure what."

***

Dan had barely finished his call to his father when his Oxford friend Charles rang.

"Hello again, old boy. After our call I continued poking around and I spotted something else. It's really rather odd. Could be a complete red herring of course, something modern, but the images show an unusual underground feature. The only thing I can compare it to is the maze at Leeds Castle."

"Leeds Castle?"

"Sorry, perhaps you didn't get south of the river when you were here. It's a heritage site just south of the Thames in Kent. The castle is nothing special really as it largely dates from the nineteenth century. Nice location though and it has a spectacular maze created using several thousand yew trees. Once you get to the centre you get back to civilisation through an underground grotto complete with macabre forms and mythical beasts. You should go sometime. You'd like it. But the feature here on the satellite images is entirely underground and is on a much grander scale. The odd thing is that it seems to run straight from a modern villa, going into the hillside behind."

"Can you give me the precise location?" asked Dan.

"Certainly, old chap. You're right there. The villa is the one where you're staying."

***

"I was wondering whether you fancy going out for dinner," said Korina when she got back from her faculty meeting in Chania. "I feel like celebrating. You probably don't want to do 'Meet the Parents' again anyway."

Dan feared that Stelios' hospitality might have run out after the trip to the dockyard. "It was a fun evening but I'd love to go to that little taverna again."

It was another beautiful evening and they dined at the same table as before under the covered terrace by the sea. As it became dusk the full moon rose above the horizon, casting its rays over the darkening sea. Korina talked excitedly about her plans for excavating the palace, and in what seemed no time at all it was midnight.

They were getting ready to leave when, for the first time that evening, Korina stopped talking. She pointed up at the moon, which had taken on an orangey hue. They stood watching as it slowly turned red like a blood orange.

Dan looked at Korina and smiled. "Perhaps the prophecy is about to be fulfilled! What did the Priestess say? Was it five moons after the super moon eclipse there would be another blood moon? How many have there been?"

Korina thought for a few moments. "The super moon was at the end of January. It's now late July. So five, I think!"

***

Dan was keen to explore the underground feature which, according to the images Charles had sent, extended from the north wall of the villa into the hillside behind. He slept until about 2 am and then lay awake waiting until all was quiet in the rooms and corridors around him and the courtyard below.

At around 3 am he slipped quietly from his room and descended the stairs to the ground floor. Seeing no one about, he crossed the central courtyard to the portico running along its eastern side. He had just reached it when two guards emerged from the steps that came up from the cellar. Dan darted behind one of the wide pillars supporting the portico. The guards stood at the top of the steps and lit cigarettes. Dan took the opportunity to look for a better hiding place, trying the door of a nearby room. It was locked. He realised it was the room from which Korina had fetched the golden disc, probably Stelios' office.

Dan returned to his hiding place, such as it was, behind the pillar. After lighting their cigarettes the guards began walking down the portico towards him. They were busy talking and joking. He quickly assessed his options. He could either stay behind the pillar and hope the guards didn't see him or nonchalantly emerge into the portico, pretending he had been unable to sleep and was having a stroll round. He decided to risk remaining hidden. He waited until the guards came close and then, holding his breath and with his back to the pillar, gradually eased himself round on the courtyard-side as they passed by.

Thank God for Minoan over-engineering, he thought, patting the massive pillar after they had passed by.

As soon as the guards had disappeared, Dan walked over to the steps leading down to the cellar. When he reached the bottom it was pitch black. He switched on his phone torch and found he was in a long corridor running north to south, with rooms leading off on either side. Dan turned left, heading under the north wing of the villa towards the hillside behind it. As he walked along the corridor he shone his torch into several of the rooms leading off and saw they contained large storage vessels mounted on wooden racks.

After about a hundred metres the corridor led into a large room. Dan reckoned that the underground feature spotted by Charles emanated from somewhere around here. He began inspecting the walls to see whether he could find a hidden door. There was nothing obvious. The walls were all fitted with floor-to-ceiling wooden racks holding bottles of wine and spirits.

After about ten minutes he had found nothing. He was about to give up when he heard faint voices. He realised they were coming from the other side of one of the walls. The voices grew louder and then he heard a click. A section of the wall, together with the wine rack mounted on it, began to open. Dan shut off his torch and darted behind a large storage vessel.

Light flooded through the open door, casting the shadows of two figures which disappeared as the cellar light went on.

"I'm sure I saw a light over there in the corner," said a male voice.

Dan cursed himself for not switching his torch off sooner. Hearing footsteps approaching his hiding place, he crouched down and made himself as small as he could. The footsteps stopped. The man was presumably looking around searching. Dan tried not to cough as he inhaled tobacco smoke from the man's cheap cigarette.

"Oh come on," said another male voice. "You're just imagining it. You're getting jumpy."

"Hang on a minute," said the voice close to Dan. "I've just spotted something."

This time Dan had no choice. There was no way a midnight stroll would have taken him here. He was just about to spring out from his hiding place when an arm reached past him and grabbed a bottle of *Raki* from the rack on the wall.

"I think we've earned some of this," said the voice.

"Yeah. Better keep it quiet though."

The light went off and the two men disappeared into the corridor leading to the villa. Flicking his torch back on, Dan went to the section of the wall from which the men had emerged, searching for a hidden switch or handle between the bottles of wine on the enormous rack. After a minute or so he found a switch. He pressed it and the wall opened.

"Open sesame. Welcome to Stelios' secret underworld," he muttered.

He passed through the door to find himself in a whitewashed subterranean passage lit by security lights. The passage stretched out in front of him for about a hundred metres. After walking about halfway along he came to a junction where a corridor branched off to his right. He ignored it and continued straight on towards the hillside behind the villa. After another fifty metres or so the passage led into a large chamber with gypsum benches running along two walls. At the far end of the room, opposite the entrance, was a sturdy wooden gate with padlocked iron bolts. Dan shook the gate but it was firmly shut. He walked back towards the villa and turned left into the side passage he had passed, concluding that it led towards the hill on the eastern side of the villa. After about eighty metres it began to curve round gradually to the south towards the sea.

A number of rooms led off the corridor. He peered inside the first one and discovered it was a huge armoury, with storage cabinets full of weapons and ammunition.

"My God! There's enough here to equip a small army," murmured Dan.

Next to the armoury was a series of simply furnished bedrooms, equipped with beds, wash basins and little else. Moving farther down the passage, he came to another room which was an almost exact replica of the Throne Room in Knossos, complete with a high-backed alabaster throne seat, gypsum benches and a replica of the Lustral Basin. The wall was adorned with a copy of the Griffin Fresco.

"Funny that no one mentioned this at dinner the other night. It would be perfect for Stelios' plays and re-enactments."

Next to the Throne Room was a further room, lavishly furnished with leather sofas and four large HD TV screens mounted on the wall.

"Hmm, not sure what happened to the Minoan theme."

The only Minoan influence in the room was a sculpture of a bull's head mounted on one of the walls. Like the one in the villa's entrance hall, it had fearsome golden horns.

Dan heard voices from the passageway and stepped behind the door, his back pressed hard against the wall. The voices carried on past down the corridor. Dan peered round the door and saw two guards pushing trolleys laden with food and drink.

"Is someone throwing a party I haven't been invited to?"

Dan gave it thirty seconds and followed the guards, remaining far enough behind for the gradual curvature of the passage to keep him from view. Several corridors branched off to the left and right but Dan ignored them and carried straight on. He began to smell the sea and felt a fresh breeze coming towards him. A couple of minutes later he emerged into a large cavern. Along the right hand side was a quay, with several motor launches moored alongside. Across the mouth of the cavern were two massive sea gates, presumably intended to keep out unwanted visitors.

There was no sign of the men with the trolley. Dan assumed they must have turned off down one of the side passages. He began looking round the cavern but, hearing voices approaching, darted behind a row of four large crates stacked on pallets on the quayside. Three men whom Dan recognised as guards entered the cavern. One of them was smoking. Another man angrily grabbed the cigarette from his mouth and stubbed it out on the floor.

"You idiot! Do you want to blow us all up?"

Puzzled, Dan inspected the crate on the pallet in front of him. It bore the word *Semtex*.

"So what is Stelios doing storing high explosives beneath the grounds of his villa?" he whispered.

One of the guards climbed on to a fork-lift truck on the quayside and advanced towards the row of crates. Dan quietly moved back behind the last of the crates and peered through a gap. The driver picked up the first pallet, reversed back down the quay and dropped it under a small crane. In the meantime another guard had gone down the steps to the motor launch, started the engine and positioned the boat under the crane. A third man climbed on to the crane and lifted the pallet off the quayside, dropping it carefully on to the launch. The same operation was repeated twice.

The crate hiding Dan from view was now the last one left on the quayside. The driver steered towards it, slipping the prongs of the fork-lift truck under the pallet. Dan looked round but there was nowhere else for him to hide. He would be spotted the moment the crate was removed, stranded in the middle of the quay. The driver pulled a lever and started lifting the pallet.

Suddenly a voice from the motor launch below shouted,

"Stop, you idiot. Can't you see we're full? Do you want to sink us?"

To Dan's relief the driver lowered the pallet, removed the prongs and reversed back down the quay. He jumped off the fork-lift truck and boarded the launch. The crane operator ran to the end of the quay and flicked a switch opening the sea gates. He joined the others on the motor launch and they headed out of the cavern, the gates closing behind them.

"What on Earth," Dan murmured, "are they doing taking *Semtex* out to sea in a motor launch at this time of night?"

He left the cavern and walked back down the main passage. As he was passing one of the side corridors he heard faint voices. Venturing cautiously towards them, he recognised the language as Arabic. He entered a large chamber, one which was very different from the plush screen room he had discovered earlier. It was a prison. On each side of the chamber were cells with bars, occupied by men, women and children.

Dan walked slowly along the overcrowded cells, looking at the gaunt and frightened faces of the prisoners. Their soiled clothes little more than rags, they watched him in silence. Then a male voice spoke to him in Arabic.

"Praise be to Allah. My brother!"

"Houmam," said Dan, embracing his Syrian stepbrother through the bars of the cell. "How long have you been here?"

"I've lost track of time in this place but about three weeks I think. We were hijacked after we left Turkey. They killed the people smugglers and brought us here."

"Is Milana with you?"

"Yes. She is. And so is your niece," he said, pointing over to another cell.

"How were you brought here?"

"We were transported on a ship and then moved on to motor launches, which brought us into a cave. We were then led here through a tunnel."

"What was the ship called?" asked Dan.

"The *Princess* something."

"*Ariadne*?"

"Yes it may have been."

Dan got the picture.

"Are you all OK?"

"Yes, we're OK. But many are weak and tired. The guards bring us food but they are cruel. They taunt us with stories of a labyrinth inhabited by a monster which is half bull and half man. They call it the Minotaur. There was another prisoner here, a Russian. They took him away and he didn't come back. They told us he was sacrificed to the Minotaur and threatened to do the same to any of us who disobeyed them."

"There's no such thing as the Minotaur," said Dan. "It's a myth. They're just trying to frighten you."

"They also take our women and children away and rape them. The one with the ponytail who seems to be in charge likes young boys. They've raped your niece twice."

Dan broke from his embrace. He fell silent for a few moments, struggling to control his anger and think clearly. "I swear they will pay for this. I can't free you tonight, but have faith, brother. I'll be back tomorrow night. Get everyone ready. Until then not a word."

It was hard to leave the hostages, but Dan knew it didn't make sense to try to free them tonight. With the Tutor and the guards, not to mention Korina with her martial arts skills, it would be better to wait for back up. He headed back down the underground passages and out through the hidden door into the cellar, hiding at one point in a room as more guards came past. He went back up the steps to the central courtyard, where he bumped straight into the Tutor. Dan was still seething with anger but fought to control it. "An early morning stroll?" he asked conversationally.

"I rarely sleep well," replied the Tutor. "What are you doing up?"

"Too much Cretan *Raki*, I guess."

"Well there are worse fates," said the Tutor. He somehow made the innocuous remark sound intimidating.

But all Dan felt was rage. "There are indeed," he said.

***

Dan made a call as soon as he got back to his bedroom. "Dad, I've found them. They're alive."

"Thank God. How are they?"

"They're OK but they've had a tough time. They were kidnapped and are locked in a cell beneath the villa. Dad, Jana has been raped several times by the guards."

The Admiral was silent for a few moments and then asked, "Have you any idea why they were kidnapped?"

"No, but I also discovered they've been storing crates of *Semtex* beneath the villa. They were taking them out to sea tonight in motor launches."

"So what's the plan, son?"

"Can you arrange a Navy SEAL team?"

"I'll try. I'll ring you back," said the Admiral, ending the call.

***

Five minutes later Dan's father rang back. "Son, they're willing to help but the nearest SEAL team is on active duty in Syria. Realistically it's going to be a couple of days before they can mount a rescue operation."

"That's too long, Dad. Stelios is up to something and I don't want to leave Houmam and his family down there any longer."

"How about I ring the commander at Souda Bay and ask him to contact the

Cretan police or army?"

"Too risky, Dad. If Alexia is right they have some key figures in the police and army in their pockets."

"OK. So what do you want me to do?"

"Get the SEAL team back as soon as possible. Put the guys at Souda Bay on notice we'll need transport. In the meantime time I'll handle it myself."

"Shall I see whether I can get Antje to help you?"

"Good idea. I'll ring her. Can you arrange transport? I'll need her here by tonight."

"I'll see to it. Take care, son."

***

"The moment has come," said the Leader of the Inner Sanctum. "It is not by chance that the prophecy has been discovered at this time. It confirms we were right to think January's blood supermoon marked the beginning of a momentous year. This second prophesied blood moon is a sign we cannot ignore. It is time to act. I seek your approval to put our plan into operation with immediate effect."

The members of the Inner Sanctum unanimously agreed.

***

Antje's mobile rang. She saw it was Dan. It was 4 am.

"What time do you call this to be ringing a young lady? Have you no respect?"

"I need you here by tonight."

"What? I was going to have my hair done. Oh this is going to cost you," she said.

"Not now, Antje. I'm not in the mood. Get yourself here."

With that Dan abruptly ended the call. He had only ever spoken to her this way once before. It was a long time ago. He had just lost a man from his command in SEAL Team Six. That day he made the terrorists who were responsible pay.

"I'll be there," she murmured.

Chapter 15

Dan went for an early morning run. He was still pretty slim but depressingly was finding it harder and harder to stay fit. This morning though the conditions were perfect for running: dry, bright and cool before the heat of the day; and his mind was racing, which somehow quickened his pace. He had brought his binoculars with him because he was still trying to figure out where the motor launch had been going in the middle of the night. Then he saw a freighter anchored just off the coast near the sea cave he had discovered earlier that morning. He stopped and examined it through his binoculars. Realising it looked familiar, he trained them on the bow of the ship, looking for the name.

"Well I never, the *Princess Ariadne*, freshly refitted with new electrics. I hope they've got rid of the smell."

There was a hive of activity around the ship, with crates being lifted from motor launches that had pulled alongside.

"So that's where they were going with the explosives," he murmured. "They must have had more *Semtex* stored somewhere. What the hell are they up to?"

He resumed his run and headed back to the villa. The guards recognised him and let him into the grounds. He was stretching his hamstrings on a wall in front of the villa when the Tutor appeared.

"A morning jog, Professor?"

"Yeah. Have to try and combat the onset of old age."

"Indeed," said the Tutor. "But do you normally take binoculars with you when you go running?"

***

Dan got back to his room and rang his father in Boston, which was seven hours behind Cretan time.

"Dad, sorry to ring you in the middle of the night."

"Don't worry, son. Your stepmother and I haven't slept much recently."

"I've just found out where they were taking the explosives. The *Princess Ariadne* is anchored off shore. I've still no idea what they're up to though. I think you should get someone to track her."

"Will do, son. I arranged transport for Antje. She'll be with you by this evening."

***

Korina suggested they go back to the palace site to have another look round. Dan agreed as there was nothing more he could do until Antje arrived. He kept wondering what Korina knew of her father's dark activities. Was she part of them? He wanted to believe she knew nothing about them. But was that really possible?

They spent the afternoon exploring the palace and collected more fragments of clay tablet, Korina once again painstakingly recording their location. When they got back to the villa Dan made the excuse that he wasn't feeling well and went to his room. Preoccupied by the discovery of the hostages locked away beneath the villa's grounds, he hadn't been able to concentrate on the palace site. He had struggled in vain to banish the thought of the further abuse to which they might be subject during the day.

And then, as he lay awake in his room, his mind went back to Princess Hemite, whose tragic end had evoked the memory of Aliah's death. He kept telling himself that he had no reason to believe that Aliah was not killed instantly; his dreams were just the product of his out-of-control imagination while asleep. But it was no use. The parallel was too close. Unable to sleep he lay wide awake, waiting for the villa to fall quiet.

It was now 3 am. Dan's initial rage on finding the hostages in the early hours of the previous day had gradually subsided and given way to a steely determination to free them. He checked his phone. There was a text from Antje, saying she had arrived and was in position outside the villa.

He crept out on to the balcony of his bedroom and peered into the central courtyard below. Seeing no one he went downstairs, crossed the courtyard and descended into the cellar. He stood at the bottom of the steps for a few seconds and listened. Hearing nothing, he headed towards the room with the hidden door he had found the previous night. Flicking the disguised switch, he opened the door and crept along the secret subterranean passage behind the villa.

Dan planned to pick up some equipment from the armoury and then head to the prison chamber to free the hostages and lead them out of the villa. The plan began to go wrong almost immediately. Stopping at the armoury he found the cabinets were empty. Not a single weapon left.

"Hmm. OK. I guess we'll have to do it the hard way then."

But when he entered the prison chamber he knew for sure that his plan would have to change. The male prisoners were gone. Only women and children remained.

Dan walked along the cells.

"Dan, praise be to Allah," said a tearful female voice. It was Houmam's wife.

"Milana. Thank God, but where is Houmam?"

"They took him away during the day. They took all the men away," she said, bursting into tears.

"Did they say where they were going?"

"No. Houmam asked but they just pushed a rifle into his back and told him to move on."

Dammit, thought Dan, trying to banish his regret at not acting sooner. He began to form a new plan of action.

"Milana," he said, holding her head between his hands and looking into her eyes. "I have to go now. I'll find out where they've gone. I swear I won't let any harm come to Houmam. I shall be back very soon to get you. Stay strong."

With that he ran back into the main passage and headed towards the sea cave where he had been the previous night. When he got there he found it deserted. He wasn't surprised as he suspected the *Princess Ariadne* was long gone. He raced back down the subterranean passages, through the hidden door and up into the villa. Walking swiftly along the portico adjoining the courtyard, he heard voices coming from Stelios' office. The door was slightly ajar. Standing with his back to the wall he peered in as discreetly as he could.

"Come in, Professor Baker," said Stelios. "We've been expecting you."

***

Six hours earlier Antje had assumed a strategic position on the hillside behind the villa. Completely hidden, she had an excellent view of the whole complex. Dan had told her there was no reception in the subterranean passages beneath the grounds and not to expect messages from him. If he didn't appear with the hostages she was to presume he had been killed or captured. It would then be her call.

If it came to that, she knew what she would do. But she didn't believe it would. Most people knew Dan as a gentle academic, but Antje had seen what he was capable of. He was calmer under pressure than anyone she knew and seemed completely unfazed by physical danger. And when he got angry he was deadly. For many anger got in the way. It stopped them thinking rationally and caused them to make mistakes. But anger had a different effect on Dan. It made him more focused and determined. It also brought out a ruthless streak, a killer instinct, known only to those who had served with him. She knew Dan hated that side to his character, but sometimes it was necessary.

That said, he was older now. It was over ten years since he had left the Navy. Antje hoped he hadn't lost too much of his edge. There had been a close bond between them ever since their first meeting when their teams conducted a joint operation. They would never be together – it wouldn't work for either of them. But she couldn't bear it if something happened to him.

Antje dismissed the thought. He would be fine. She needed to focus on the part she had to play. Dan was depending on her to deal with the guards who were patrolling outside the villa and protect the hostages when he led them out. Using her night glasses she surveyed the grounds and the surrounding hillside. She counted two guards on the gate and four more patrolling the grounds, all heavily armed. She also spotted a lookout hidden behind bushes on the hillside to the east.

"Hmm, I think you'll be my first date tonight." She quietly moved round the valley side and crept up close behind him.

***

Korina had hardly slept. She was still excited about discovering the palace and the remains of Princess Hemite. The tablets had also turned out to be a terrific find. It was the highlight of her career so far, what she had got into archaeology for. But at the same time it made her feel sad. It was a tragic story. The princess whose wedding was preserved for posterity on the magnificent golden disc had ended up dying slowly and alone in this foreign land.

She was cross with herself for her lack of sensitivity. She had uttered the words about Hemite's lingering death without thinking of Dan's recurring nightmare in which Aliah lay trapped in the wreckage of the MSF centre. She had been so excited about the find that she had just blurted them out. He had seemed OK about it though and had been fully engaged in helping her decipher the tablets.

But yesterday, when they visited the site again, he seemed subdued the whole day, his mood similar to how he was on the yacht after speaking to Antonio. His normal passion and energy were somehow missing. When they got back he said he wasn't feeling well and went to his room. She wondered whether it was an excuse. Was he still suffering after her careless comments? Or did it run deeper? Was he still angry with her for what she did to him in Spain?

She'd had no choice but to surprise him. She couldn't let him hand the disc over to the Spanish authorities. It was too important. And she'd taken great care not to hurt him. But she still felt guilty about it, particularly after Dan had done his best not to worry her and to shield her from the Italian gang. He didn't need to of course. She knew all about them. When her father had heard she was going after the disc, he had despatched the Tutor to protect her. He had been with them in Mallorca and had flown on to mainland Spain in the company jet.

Tossing and turning, she decided to get up. She tucked her phone into the back pocket of her pyjama shorts and went downstairs. She headed for the kitchen and poured herself a glass of water. On her way back to bed she spotted Dan walking along the portico at the side of the courtyard.

Odd, she thought. *What's he doing wandering around at this time of night?* She followed him and saw him linger outside the door to her father's office and peer in. He then disappeared through the door.

***

Dan walked into Stelios' office to find him standing there with the Tutor, Kassandra and four middle-aged men.

"You were expecting me?"

"Yes," said Stelios. "The Tutor saw you wandering around last night and decided to check the video footage. So, not satisfied with snooping round the *Princess Ariadne*, you decided to explore the cellar, and tonight you thought you would snoop around my office. Are you going to tell me what you were doing? Are you some form of thief or industrial spy?"

Interesting, thought Dan. *No mention of my little foray into their subterranean wonder world.*

"Well yes I admit it. I'm a thief. I'll let you into my guilty little secret. Ever since I tasted the nanny's olive oil I've become addicted. I really can't get enough of it. I was hoping to sneak some. I couldn't find any last night and thought I might have better luck tonight."

Stelios smiled. "We don't keep the olive oil in my office, Professor Baker."

Dan slapped the side of his head. "Dammit! Of course. How could I be so stupid?"

Sadly, unlike Stelios, the Tutor didn't have a sense of humour.

"Who are you?" he asked menacingly. "Who are you working for?"

"Oh sorry. I thought Korina had introduced me. I'm Professor Dan Baker. I work for Harvard University."

The Tutor didn't give even a flicker of a smile. Instead he took out a pistol and whipped it across Dan's face.

"On your knees," he said.

Dan did as he was told, wiping a trickle of blood from his cheek.

"Let me ask you again," said the Tutor. "Who are you working for?"

Dan remained silent.

"Oh dear," said Stelios. "It's such a shame. Korina and I really liked you and hoped, with your expertise, we might be able to work together. I must confess though the Tutor was suspicious of you from the start. Please don't make us get rough with you. I really don't like that sort of thing."

Funny, thought Dan, *he's almost pleading with me.*

The Tutor wasn't pleading though. "This is your last chance," he warned, pointing the pistol at Dan's forehead. "I shall count to two. There won't be a three. Tell me who you are and what you're doing here."

"One…"

Dan remained silent.

"Two…"

The Tutor's finger tightened on the trigger.

"I was looking for the refugees."

Stelios looked puzzled. "What are you talking about? What refugees?"

Dan was astonished. Unless Stelios was a good actor he genuinely knew nothing about the refugees.

"Ask the Tutor," said Dan realising that there must have been things going on behind Stelios' back. "He'll tell you all about them. Perhaps he'll tell you why he decided to kidnap them."

Dan feared the Tutor would feign ignorance but he didn't.

"You'll find out soon enough," he said with a cruel smile.

Stelios was visibly shocked. "Kassandra, would you mind leaving us," he said after a few moments.

"I'd prefer to stay," she replied. "I want to hear what has been going on."

"As you wish. I demand to know what you have been doing," said Stelios to the Tutor.

The Tutor remained silent for several moments, looking intently at Stelios. "Very well, I'll tell you," he said finally. "For many years I worked loyally for you. I did so because I thought you were a man of vision, someone who would do great things for Crete. But you've disappointed me. You talk endlessly of embracing the ideals of the great Minoan kingdom and uniting the people behind its shared values. But you've shown yourself to be a dreamer. You're all talk and no action. All the Society does is hear boring lectures on Minoan history and watch pathetic charades and theatre pieces. If it were left to you nothing would happen. Nothing would improve. It's become obvious that you're too weak. It's been left to the Society's Inner Sanctum to take the action needed to protect Crete's interests."

"What Inner Sanctum?" asked Stelios. "I know of no Inner Sanctum."

Whoops, thought Dan.

"No, Stelios you don't. It was better that way."

"I am President of the Society," said Stelios. "I demand to know about this Inner Sanctum."

"All right, I will tell you. Do you think it's by accident that crime has fallen so dramatically in the last few years? How do you think it is that our businesses are no longer attacked?"

"Tell me," said Stelios.

"It's because the Inner Sanctum has taken action to catch the foreign criminal scum that has invaded our country and has brought them to justice."

"What do you mean by 'brought them to justice'? This Sanctum has been working with the police?"

"No. The Inner Sanctum has been doing the police's job. The police have given the Sanctum information and left it to deal with the criminals."

"What do you mean by 'deal with the criminals'?"

"I mean catch them, try them and put them to death."

Stelios looked stunned. "So what else has the Sanctum done?"

"Do you think it's just by chance that Crete has retained control of its industries and that we've not been overrun by foreign investors?"

"And how has the Sanctum achieved that?"

"By dissuading the foreign scum from taking over our businesses. But that's just the start. The ultimate aim of the Sanctum is one which I originally thought you shared, to restore Crete to the great independent state it once was. For too long Crete has been dominated by other countries. The Greeks, the Romans, the Venetians, the Ottomans, the Nazis. The list goes on. A once great power humiliated by foreign occupiers. Crete is the oldest civilisation in Europe. It was once the most advanced and greatest power in the Mediterranean. The Minoan fleet was universally feared, even by great powers such as Egypt. The golden disc that Korina found bears witness to that. The King of Egypt bowed before the Cretan King by sending his favourite and most beautiful daughter to be his queen. It's time that Crete reasserted itself as the great power it once was."

Something's not right here, thought Dan. The Tutor might be a master of ancient Greek martial arts but Dan had seen no evidence of any real interest in Minoan history. He had looked utterly bored when Dan had been deciphering the hieroglyphs on the disc. He sounded almost like a parrot mimicking sounds he had heard.

"This is total madness," said Stelios. "Crete is too small to stand alone in the modern world. The people would never support it."

"There you are again being weak and feeble. There's no reason why Crete can't become the great power it once was. You make me sick, you and other Cretans who are so fearful. You worry about our security, about the Russians, the Turks and the Arabs. You're like weak children hiding behind the skirts of the Americans and NATO with their naval base in Souda Bay."

"I may be a little eccentric, but I'm not crazy," said Stelios in a steely voice. "Having a grip on reality is not being weak."

"Where you're right," said the Tutor, "is that, as long as the Americans are here and the people are so fearful, the time will not be right. We need to shatter the illusion of security. And that's what we are about to do. The American base in Souda Bay will be attacked by Syrian suicide bombers."

"What?" exclaimed Stelios.

"A vessel carrying the refugees and packed with explosives will sail into the Naval Pier. The disruption and devastation will be massive. Cretans will then see the truth: the Americans don't make Crete safe, they make us a target. They don't care about Crete. They're too busy with their operations in Afghanistan and Iraq. Our control of the media will ensure that the people get the right messages. They'll be told that the only way for Crete to be secure is to regain its independence and look after its own security. Then the moment will come, and it's the moment we have been preparing for. The members of the Inner Sanctum are the most powerful people in Crete. Using the influence they have inside government, the police and the army, and with the help of the armed force and armaments we have built up, the Sanctum will gain control of the island and restore the great civilisation that Crete once was."

Dan could scarcely believe the drama playing out in front of him. It was of course no coincidence that he was there in Stelios' villa. Dan wasn't there just for the disc and the Cretan King's palace, fascinating though they were. The intelligence his father had got from the NSA had led them to suspect that the *Princess Ariadne*, one of Stelios' ships, had been involved in kidnapping his stepbrother. But beyond that he really had no idea what was going on. He didn't know why Stelios would want to kidnap a boat load of refugees. He realised now that his assumption that Stelios was behind things was completely wrong. He had begun to have his doubts when they had dinner together. He found that he liked him. Stelios was a bit pompous and certainly eccentric, but a killer, a maniac and a kidnapper of refugees? Dan struggled to believe it; and there was no way Stelios would be involved in the rape of women and children.

He had, on the other hand, taken an instant dislike to the Tutor. There was something slippery and untrustworthy about him. But it seemed inconceivable that the Tutor, a hired help, could be undertaking something on this scale and controlling a group of powerful Cretans. Yet it explained everything: the secret subterranean world, the explosives that Dan had seen being loaded on to the freighter, the new electrics on the *Princess Ariadne*, the lingering smell of human excrement in the hold and the sudden disappearance of the male refugees, who were unwittingly to take on the role of suicide bombers.

"So when will this spectacular event occur?" asked Stelios.

Good question, thought Dan. *Just what I wanted to ask.*

"It's already under way," said the Tutor. "The refugees were transported to the freighter yesterday. It will reach Souda Bay later this morning."

Oh, just great, thought Dan. *What's the hurry?*

As if responding to Dan's silent question, the Tutor added,

"The timing is pre-ordained. It shall be as prophesied in the tablet. The Arab Spring has led to great unrest and widespread displacement of peoples across the Mediterranean. And now the moon has turned to blood for a second time, five moons after the super moon eclipse in January. The foreigners shall be set against each other, and their great warships shall be destroyed as they cower in their harbour. There are two frigates and a large US aircraft carrier moored in Souda Bay which have been supporting operations against ISIS."

Oh, come on, thought Dan. *You surely don't believe that crap?*

"Nonsense," said Stelios, echoing Dan's thoughts. "But in any case, people will know it's one of our freighters."

"Do you really think I haven't thought of that? My men will leave the freighter shortly before the detonation and steer the ship remotely. A report will be filed that the vessel has been hijacked. There will be little left of the ship other than the charred bodies of its Syrian crew."

Of course, stupid, that's why they only took the men. Terrorists would hardly take their women and children with them, would they?

"I won't allow this," said Stelios. "Who are the members of this Inner Sanctum who have sanctioned this outrage? Who is their leader? Surely not you?"

It was then that the final piece of the jigsaw slipped into place. Kassandra stepped over and put her arm around the Tutor's waist. She gazed at Stelios with her penetrating eyes. "I am the Leader of the Inner Sanctum. It is I who founded it. Its other members are those around you in this room. You know them as the Society's finance committee. Sadly the Tutor is right. You are a disappointment, Stelios, a dreamer. Like the Tutor, my father also thought you a great man. It's why he left you half of the business. I never forgave him for that. I recognised long ago that you were weak. I needed someone stronger to help me do what has to be done. The Tutor has been carrying out my wishes and those of my fellow members of the Sanctum."

Ah, thought Dan, *now I get it. It's not just the hired help going off on a frolic of his own. It was Kassandra's words he was parroting. It's she who has pulled the strings all along, and she has used her toy boy, the hired help, to do it. He is her enforcer. You just couldn't make this up!*

"The Tutor is right," Kassandra continued. "It will be as prophesied. Upon the second blood moon a Great Queen shall arise and banish the foreigners from the land. But first she shall suffer a great loss."

The Tutor smiled smugly and raised his gun. He shot Stelios who collapsed on the floor clutching his chest, a look of astonishment on his face.

Oh great. Just great. I really hadn't seen that one coming.

With the drama that had unfolded it was almost as if the Tutor and Kassandra had forgotten about Dan. But now they turned their attention to him. The Tutor trained his gun on him.

"And now for the treacherous foreigner of many tongues from a land beyond the setting sun," said Kassandra smiling. "It is time you fulfilled your part of the prophecy."

"I wondered when you'd get round to that," said Dan. "Isn't there something a little circular about this? You murder your husband, thereby suffering a great loss, and then murder me to fulfil the rest of the prophecy."

Kassandra smiled. "Yes. An interesting conundrum. Sadly, one you will have no time to solve."

Dan tried a more prosaic line of argument. "You won't get away with this. Stelios is an important figure. The police will ask questions about his death. They'll want to turn this place over." It was a bit lame, he knew, but to be fair it was the best he could do on the spur of the moment.

Kassandra was unimpressed. "Professor Baker, you disappoint me. I thought you to be more intelligent than that. Don't you see? You've presented us with the perfect opportunity. Stelios finds you snooping in his office looking for the disc and you shoot him. You're killed as you try to escape. Your fingerprints will be found on the gun that killed Stelios. The police will look no further when your guilt is confirmed by our honourable Inner Sanctum member, the Heraklion Chief of Police, who by the way is standing right behind you. Why do you think I wanted you to stay here?"

Oh, just perfect. The pair have actually planned this. They get rid of Stelios and pin it on me. These guys could have written the script for Dallas.

Dan tried another tack. "You do know the game is up? The NSA and CIA have been monitoring your so-called 'Inner Sanctum' for a while. They know all about you."

"They know nothing," said Kassandra confidently. "If they did you wouldn't be here on your own."

Fair point, thought Dan. *So that one didn't work either. OK last roll of the dice.*

"Tell me about the Minotaur and the labyrinth," he said, guessing a little as to what went on. "Tell me about how you send your victims to their grisly deaths without trial and how you watch them die on the TV screens. Is that what the new Minoan Crete will be like?"

Kassandra flashed her eyes accusingly at the Tutor before turning her gaze back to Dan. "Be quiet, American. So you know about the labyrinth. I assume the guards must have spoken about it to the hostages. It makes no difference. The people in the Cretan police who matter already know about it. They're grateful to us and tip us off so we can deal with the criminals for them. You Americans are the ultimate hypocrites. You can hardly take the moral high ground. You shut people up without trial in Guantanamo Bay and torture them.

You send drones into foreign countries to kill anyone your military leaders deem fit to murder. You send in planes knowing that innocent people will lose their lives, dismissing it as collateral damage. You even target medical facilities and kill doctors, nurses and patients."

Dan felt as though he had just received a punch in the gut. He wondered whether Korina had told Kassandra about the US air strike on the MSF centre that had killed Aliah.

"In any case," continued Kassandra, "criminals are sentenced to the labyrinth after a fair trial on the evidence. I fear you've run out of reasons for me to keep you alive."

She gave a signal to the Tutor, who raised his gun and pressed his finger on the trigger. Kassandra was right. Dan had now run out of ideas and time.

***

At that moment Korina entered her father's office. Seeing Stelios on the floor, she ran over to him and knelt by his body. The Tutor lowered the gun. Kassandra walked over to Korina, knelt beside her and put her arm round her.

"I'm sorry you had to see this, Korina. This evil man has betrayed you and killed your father. He was caught trying to steal the disc."

Korina continued to kneel by her father's side for several minutes. Then she slowly stood, turned towards Dan and stared at him with a look of sheer hatred.

So much for the poker face, thought Dan.

"Shooting him will be too quick, too merciful," she said. "I demand revenge. I want to see him die slowly and painfully for killing my father."

Oh, this just gets better. What is it with this family?

Kassandra smiled, evidently pleased by her daughter's reaction. "You're worthy of the name Ariadne, my daughter. It is perhaps no coincidence I gave you that name. We have both been betrayed and suffered a great loss as prophesied by the Priestess. But perhaps it is you, not I, who is the Great Queen mentioned in the prophecy. Professor Baker shall die in the labyrinth. You shall sentence him yourself. 'The Great Queen shall sacrifice the stranger to secure the Bull God's blessing for her endeavours'."

What did I tell you? I just knew this was going to happen, thought Dan.

The Tutor smiled, plainly relishing the prospect.

"Yes," said Korina. "It shall be as foretold in the tablet. I, Priestess Ariadne, shall condemn him."

Not you as well! You were my last hope for sanity.

"But tell me about the labyrinth," said Korina.

"I shall explain," said her mother. "When the excavations were done for the villa we uncovered an ancient labyrinth of tunnels that goes under the hillside behind the villa. There are kilometres of interconnected passages. When you enter you quickly lose your way, just as in the labyrinth of Greek mythology. We had assumed the tunnels were a Neolithic silver or copper mine but couldn't understand why they were so large. We now think the site may also have been mined for stone for the construction of the palace complex you discovered. For many years we did nothing with it. Then the Tutor realised what its use should be. Over the last ten years foreign criminal elements have gained control of Crete. The situation is out of control. The police struggle to catch them. So we had to take action. Our businesses were being raided constantly, our staff threatened, assaulted and even killed. So the Tutor began to build an independent security force. When the criminals raid our businesses we catch them and ensure that justice is administered. The labyrinth is a fitting way of doing that. They spend their lives terrorising innocent victims. It's only fair and just that they should spend their last moments enduring the same terror."

And, of course, it's in the best possible Minoan taste, thought Dan.

"But the Minotaur is just a myth," said Korina.

"Yes. The Minotaur is a story we tell the prisoners, many of whom are uneducated. There is of course no Minotaur."

Phew! Best news I've had all day.

"But your father's prize bulls do the job equally well."

Hmm, maybe not!

"So my father knew about this?"

"No. I wanted to spare him the worry. He had enough on his plate running the business. These actions have been carried out by a small group of trusted members of the Society, the Inner Sanctum, over which I preside."

"I think it'll be the perfect way for this American to die," said Korina. "It's just a shame I can't watch."

"Oh, but you can," said her mother. "And you can take part. Criminals are sentenced after a fair trial with witness evidence. I think it's only right that we should follow the same process with Professor Baker. We can't sink to the low standards of the Americans. We are after all a civilised society. So far I've presided over the trials and passed sentence. I think it's now time for you to join the Inner Sanctum and assume that role. After all, your name is Ariadne."

"Yes. And I shall start with this bastard," said Korina.

"On this occasion I shall forgive your language, my dear. I shall explain the procedure. Perhaps you should put on the outfit you wore for the theatre piece."

The Tutor called in two of the guards, who bound Dan's hands behind his back and gagged him. He was dragged to his feet and led down into the cellar, through the hidden door and along the passageway to the Throne Room.

***

Dan lay prostrate before Priestess Ariadne, his hands and feet tightly bound and mouth gagged. Korina had changed for the part into a magnificent gold-coloured skirt, but Dan's view was mainly of her open sandals and brightly painted toenails.

"Who accuses this man?" asked the Priestess.

"I do, my Priestess," replied the Tutor, kneeling before her.

"What are his crimes?"

"He is guilty of murder in cold blood."

"What evidence is there that he committed this crime?"

"He committed the crime in the presence of myself, four members of the Inner Sanctum and your mother, Priestess."

"May the witnesses come forward and give their testimony."

Kassandra and the other members of the Inner Sanctum stepped forward in turn. The Priestess asked each witness,

"Did you see this man kill Stelios Kouklakis?"

"Yes, Priestess, I did," came the reply from each witness.

The Priestess then addressed Dan. "Does the prisoner have anything to say in his defence?"

Dan didn't give them the satisfaction of trying to speak through his gag.

"Very well," said the Priestess. "The prisoner has nothing to say. I find him guilty. I shall consult the Bull God on his fate."

The Priestess fell into a trance-like state for several minutes. She then said,

"The Bull God accepts the sacrifice. Take the prisoner to the labyrinth."

***

Dan's ankles were untied and the gag removed. He was then taken by the Tutor and the guards down the long passage to the room with the padlocked wooden gate that Dan had discovered earlier. Priestess Ariadne walked behind them. Kassandra and the members of the Inner Sanctum took their places in the room with the TV screens.

"Professor Baker, we shall accord you the honour of meeting our finest and fiercest bull," announced the Tutor.

"What? Just one? Oh come on. I'd have thought I was good for at least three."

"Sadly," said the Tutor, "we can only let one bull into the labyrinth at once. They have the unfortunate habit of fighting each other. This particular bull would soon kill any others."

"So what should I call him? Bertie, Angus or how about Big Mac? Yes. Mac the Minotaur has a certain ring to it, don't you think?"

Dan could see by the Tutor's expression he was irritating the hell out of him. He thought he was about to get whacked by his pistol again. Instead Priestess Ariadne stepped forward until her face almost touched Dan's. Her mesmerising eyes looked directly into his.

"Enough," she said. Putting one hand around his waist, she grabbed him by the balls and squeezed.

Dan grimaced. *That's not very priestess-like*, he thought.

"You try to hide it but I sense your fear. I look forward to watching you run in terror through the labyrinth."

Slipping her hand down on to his butt, she drew him closer and squeezed even harder. She held him there helpless in her grasp for a good five seconds.

"Ariadne's revenge, you bastard," she whispered.

Antje, you could learn a thing or two from this girl, he thought as he doubled up in pain.

Ariadne released her grip and stepped back.

Dan saw a satisfied cruel smile on the Tutor's face.

"Untie his hands and cast him in," ordered the Priestess.

The guards opened the gate and threw Dan into the labyrinth. The gate closed behind him.

***

The lookout on the hillside behind the villa was lying flat on his stomach, scanning the perimeter of the grounds with night vision binoculars. The villa guards had a rota for lookout duty and it was his turn tonight. He had been there about three hours and had seen nothing. He didn't expect to. There had never been any trouble. He was thinking it was about time to have the food he had brought with him. Before doing so he checked in as he was required to do every hour. He had no sooner done that than someone jumped on his back and wrapped a cord tightly round his neck. Unable to move he choked until he blacked out.

When he came round he found himself laying hogtied and gagged. A tall blonde woman was sitting on a boulder next to him, eating his food.

"This isn't bad," she said. "My compliments to whoever made it. I hope for your sake you can speak English. I have some questions for you." She removed the gag.

"Fuck off bitch. You'll pay for this."

"Oh dear. No manners," she said, replacing his gag. "But at least we've established that you speak English."

She wrapped her leopard-skin covered thighs around his head and squeezed. He screamed through the gag at the unbelievable pain that shot through his brain as she crushed his skull between her legs. Relaxing the hold slightly she said, "Now, you can begin by telling me about the people in the villa."

He tried to speak through the gag but no words came out.

"I'm sorry, I can't hear you," she said, squeezing again. "Ooh, I'd like to do this all night really. Such a great workout!"

She eventually removed the gag and asked, "Shall I do it again? Please say yes!"

"No. Please," cried the lookout. "I'll tell you anything you want to know."

The woman took out her phone and recorded everything he said. She then released her grip, replaced the gag and dragged him over to a ditch.

"Well thank you for a very satisfying evening. I'll send someone round for you later. Why don't you have a snooze now?"

He blacked out as he received a whack across the head with the butt of her rifle.

***

Struggling after Priestess Ariadne's fond farewell, Dan forced himself forward into the labyrinth. He was in a subterranean tunnel network, presumably the one that Charles had seen on the satellite images running into the hillside behind the villa. Peering at the roof of the tunnel he saw there were multiple cameras mounted on long rails running along the roof.

So I guessed right, thought Dan. *That's what the HD screens in the TV room are for.* The cameras, which were doubtless fitted with motion sensors and sound, would run along the rails following the action so the spectators could enjoy the sport. These were not nice people.

Dan waved to the nearest camera, gave a cheeky smile and headed off humming to himself. He walked for about five minutes, turning constantly to the left and right in the maze of passages. He heard the cameras whirring back and forth above his head along the rails attached to the roof of the tunnel, keeping him in view. He suspected he was now well into the hillside behind the villa. Although he had a good sense of direction, he realised that finding his way out was going to be really hard. The passages curved round, making it difficult to keep his bearings.

At least it's lit, he thought, noticing the cables running along the walls of the passages. He wondered whether at some point they might switch off the lights. For the moment though they doubtless preferred the tunnels to be lit so they could watch him on the screens.

The only sound he could hear was from his shoes treading on the loose, gravelly surface. The smells were familiar enough though. They reminded him of his uncle's ranch in Arizona where he loved to go to as a boy. He remembered sitting round the campfires after a long day on the range, enthralled by the stories of bravado told by the cattlemen. For Dan they were heroes, and he longed to be one of them when he grew up. Looking back of course many of their stories were far-fetched to say the least. But they did give him some practical advice in case a bull started to be aggressive.

Always take care if a bull walks sideways in front of you. It's his way of threatening you. He's showing you how big and powerful he is. If you can, back away slowly to show you're not a threat. But never take your eyes off him until you're in a safe place. Never turn your back.

They also told him what to do if the bull charged.

Whatever you do, don't run. You won't make it. He has a bigger stride and he has four legs. He can hit three times your speed at least. Stand your ground. Don't lie down. That may work for a horse. It won't work for a bull. He'll as likely trample you. You don't want to be trampled by a 2000 pound plus animal doing thirty miles an hour.

Take off your jacket or your shirt. Anything. Keep your eye on him and wait until he gets close. Then throw the shirt to distract him and jump the other way. If you're lucky he'll follow the shirt.

That's just great, thought Dan. *That was in an open field. Here I am stuck with a bull in a cave system.* Then he had a thought. Maybe that could work to his advantage. Dan hadn't liked to challenge the cattlemen but he thought he saw a major flaw in their advice. If you were performing the clothes trick in an open field, what the hell did you do when the bull realised he had been tricked and came at you again? You couldn't just keep picking up your clothes and repeating the same trick over again. Surely, sooner or later he would wise up or you would just get it wrong and end up being speared.

But in a tunnel network…?

Oh well, I don't have any better ideas, he thought, *so I may as well give it a try.* At least he had a plan. He knew what he had to look for. After a few minutes he found it. Ahead of him was a fork where the passage split into two, the two branches gradually diverging. He walked up to it and stopped. Then he began to shout.

"Big Mac? Where are you? Here I am. Come and get me!"

His voice echoed round the cavern.

Silence.

He repeated his taunt.

Still nothing.

He shouted out again. This time he heard something. A low-pitched bellowing and snorting, followed by the sound of hooves. Big Mac was on his way. The sounds seemed distant at first but they soon grew louder, echoing round the interconnected passages of the labyrinth. Dan stood still, listening intently. He was banking on Mac coming up the main passage in front of him. If he didn't, Dan's plan could still work, but it would be harder to execute. It wasn't going to be easy anyway. He stood with his back to the fork where the passage split into two and watched the main passage in front of him.

The sounds were much louder now, filling the whole cave system around him. Then just as suddenly they stopped. It went completely silent. Mac was nearby but had stopped moving or was moving very slowly. He was doubtless listening and smelling. He remembered the cattlemen saying that bulls had a surprisingly good sense of smell. Dan was feeling the tension rise within him. But he still played to the camera. He took off his shirt and held it to his nose.

"Sorry, Mac, I seem to have forgotten to shower. I hope I'm not putting you off."

He hadn't. The bull was now there, at the end of the passage in front of him as he had hoped. The cameras above them went into overdrive, whirring back and forth to capture the action.

"Well someone's getting excited. You're obviously quite a celebrity, Mac."

The bull remained at the end of the passage staring at Dan for a few moments. Dan stared back.

Always keep your eyes on it. Never turn your back.

As the cattlemen had predicted the bull turned sideways to deliver a broadside threat.

"Ooh, Big Mac. You're such a magnificent beastie. So strong. So manly. Such lovely big horns. I think I could fall in love with you."

Dan's flattery didn't work. The bull turned towards him and lowered its horns. It stomped on the ground several times and snorted. And then it charged.

Dan was not playing to the gallery now. He was focusing on what he had to do. He stood stock-still, his feet slightly apart, holding his shirt in front of him. Timing was going to be everything. Get it wrong and he would be impaled on those enormous horns or just pummelled against the cave wall.

Wait. Wait. Wait. Now…

***

Everyone except Dan had now gathered in the TV room. The members of the Inner Sanctum sat with drinks watching events on the HD screens. The sophisticated camera and sound system in the labyrinth and multiple screens allowed them to view the live action from different angles as it happened. There was also the facility to show slow motion replays of the best bits if they wanted.

The members of the Sanctum were impressed by Dan's bravado as he spoke to the camera. He appeared composed and was clearly playing to the gallery.

"He'll end up running for his life, just like the other criminals before him," predicted the Tutor with a cruel smile. "And it will be all the more satisfying to see his arrogance crumble and be replaced by abject fear."

The spectators cheered and clapped as another screen showed the bull slowly making its way through the labyrinth. It would not be long now before they would enjoy watching Professor Baker being torn apart on the bull's horns. This was Kassandra's finest bull. It had won many prizes. It had also notched up several kills, administering justice in the labyrinth to the foreign scum who had raided their businesses. The last one had been Vladimir Romanov. He had provided great sport. It had been so satisfying to see the Russian hard man run for his life in terror. But it wasn't long before the bull had caught him and shaken his punctured body in the air. Even more satisfyingly, it had taken him a whole ten minutes to die in agony.

They watched as Dan walked swiftly and purposefully deeper into the labyrinth, humming away.

"That's odd," said one Sanctum member. "He appears to be looking for something."

"Well he'll find it soon enough," said another, laughing.

Then Dan stopped at a junction in the cave network. He began shouting, almost as if he were taunting the bull, telling it where he was. This was very odd behaviour. Other victims had cowered, creeping around quietly in the hope of not attracting the Minotaur. Then even more oddly he took his shirt off. He started smelling it and apologising to the bull for not taking a shower. Was he being serious? Perhaps he was insane?

Then even when the bull appeared at the end of the passage he continued to stand still and wait. He was talking to the bull, telling it how handsome it was!

"The idiot isn't running," said one spectator. "Doesn't he know the bull is about to charge him?"

"Perhaps he thinks he's Dr Doolittle," said another.

"Or a Bull Whisperer perhaps," said the first, snorting at his own joke.

"Or perhaps I overestimated his intelligence," said the Tutor with a grim smile.

Then finally the bull began to thunder down the long passage, moving faster and faster until it was at top speed. Dan continued to stand at the other end of the passage, dangling his shirt in front of him.

"He thinks he's a Spanish toreador with a cape," said another Sanctum member. "But shouldn't it be red?"

Dan still didn't move. The spectators prepared themselves for the satisfying climax.

***

Dan got the timing spot on, leaving the shirt in place but sidestepping just before the bull struck. As predicted by the cattlemen on his uncle's ranch, the bull charged straight through Dan's shirt, its head colliding with the corner where the passages intersected. The bull collapsed, temporarily stunned, the tip of one of its horns lying on the floor.

"Sorry about the horn, Mac. But don't worry, it'll give you a dashing heroic look. I'll borrow the tip if you don't mind? Might come in handy."

Dan knew he had to act quickly. The bull would not be comatose for long. And there was no way he was going to kill such a magnificent beast. He went close to one of the cameras and said,

"I'm sorry. But Mac seems to have had an accident. He's no more. He's a dead Mac. He's joined those ex Big Macs in the sky."

Dan paused, feigning surprise.

"What? Not even a flicker? Oh I give up. Anyway, you only have yourselves to blame. It's your fuck up. I said you needed three."

Now the tricky bit, thought Dan. *How the hell do I get out of here?*

Dan had absolutely no idea where he was and in which direction to head to get to the entrance. He put his badly torn shirt back on.

"I'll send you the bill later, Mac."

As he tucked the shirt into his pants Dan felt something in his back pocket. He slipped his hand in and pulled out a phone. It wasn't his. It was Korina's, or should he say Priestess Ariadne's? She had obviously slipped it into his pocket while squeezing his balls.

And there I was flattering myself she just had to feel my butt before letting me go.

Korina's phone was open at the navigation app she had told Dan about on the yacht. "Oh well, sorry, Theseus, but technology has moved on from the ball of thread."

He went to the drop down menu and selected *Retrace Steps*. The phone instantly displayed a route similar to that on a Sat Nav. "Wow! I must get one of these in case I make a habit of this."

For once in his life Dan followed instructions; at least he did for a while. After a few minutes he began to hear voices ahead. The voices came closer and closer. He decided to disobey the app and took a right turn, crouching down behind an outcrop in the cave wall. Six armed guards went by.

Dan re-joined the route. Behind him he heard faint sounds of the bull coming round. The sounds grew louder. They were excruciating to hear. Big Mac was clearly in pain and very, very angry.

"And that's before he sees himself in a mirror," murmured Dan.

He speeded up, following the app back to the entrance to the labyrinth. The gate was closed but not bolted or padlocked.

"Well, Mac, they have guns and you don't. That's pretty unfair. Time to even things up a bit."

He took the broken tip of the bull's horn and drove it into the cables, killing off the cameras and the lights. "They're all yours, Mac."

Stepping out of the labyrinth he bolted the gate from the outside, leaving the guards in darkness with the bull. He had hardly stepped out when he heard screams from inside.

After dealing with the look-out, Antje returned to her position on the adjoining slope. The look-out had been talkative. She now knew everything about the villa, the people in it and what had been going on. He had professed his innocence when it came to the rape of the women and children, saying he had been no part of it. It was nonsense of course, but she had played along to encourage him to tell her what the guards and members of the Inner Sanctum had been up to. If she'd had any hesitation about killing these guys before, she had none now.

"Bert," she murmured, thinking of her promise to her boyfriend, "these are mean bastards and deserve what's coming to them."

She needed to deal with the guards before it was time for the look-out to check in again. She began by shooting the four guards patrolling the grounds. They operated in pairs but it didn't help them. Her Russian-made sniper's rifle was virtually silent and she took each pair out in less than a second. Finally she shot the two guards on the gate. Then she sat and waited.

***

Dan ran down the subterranean passages behind the villa. He reckoned he had trapped all the guards who were inside the villa in the labyrinth with Big Mac. Assuming everyone else would have retired to watch the live action, he headed to the screen room. He walked in to find the Tutor, Kassandra and Korina, still dressed as Priestess Ariadne, waiting for him with the members of the Inner Sanctum. They stood by the HD screens with the sculpture of the bull's head behind them.

"I underestimated you," said the Tutor, pointing a gun at Dan. "I won't do it again. On your knees."

Dan knelt before the Tutor.

"Korina, please secure his hands."

She stepped behind Dan, took his hands and tied them behind his back.

Dan needed to buy time. "I kind of get the whole Cretan independence thing. Really I do. Not sure it's a great idea, but I do get it. You're not the only ones. There are independence movements the world over, and there have been throughout history."

They listened to him in silence. The ropes on his hands were loosening but he needed more time. He had to keep their attention.

"I also get why you decided to take law enforcement into your own hands.

You couldn't just let your businesses be raided."

He noticed Kassandra nod almost imperceptibly in agreement. His hands were still not free.

"What I don't quite get, though, is why you had to install cameras so you could watch the action on screen. That's a bit over the top, isn't it?"

"Justice must not just be done, but be seen to be done," replied the Tutor with a pomposity worthy of Stelios.

Dan's hands were now free. But he needed a distraction as he was on his knees and the Tutor had a gun trained on him.

"OK. Fair enough. I get that too. Well sort of. But what I will never get," he continued, "is the rape and abuse of the refugees' women and children. I hear you, Tutor, particularly like young boys."

As Dan had hoped, Kassandra plainly had no idea her toy boy was into young boys. Her face showed that she was unimpressed by the news. She looked at the Tutor in disgust. The Tutor turned towards her and was about to say something. It was the moment Dan had been waiting for. He prepared to jump up and drive his head into the Tutor's abdomen.

Korina got there first. Still wearing her long priestess' skirt, she launched a vicious kick at the Tutor's stomach, knocking him backwards. He crashed into Kassandra, who fell and banged her head against the wall. She lay still. Korina glared at the Tutor, the anger in her face surpassing anything Dan had seen before.

The members of the Inner Sanctum had evidently seen enough. They rushed for the exit to the room.

The Tutor gave a grim smile. "I knew it would eventually come to this, Korina," he hissed. "Your mother hoped that one day you would succeed her and lead the Inner Sanctum. As Priestess Ariadne you would be the figurehead of the new independent Crete. But you don't have your mother's strength and courage. You are weak just like your father. As your tutor I knew this. But she wouldn't listen."

Korina stepped forward to face him.

"Yes. Come on," said the Tutor, dropping his gun on the floor. "I don't need the gun. It is time. If you can't fulfil your destiny then you must meet your fate. You can't defeat me. You have never defeated me."

***

After watching Dan disappear into her father's office, Korina had crept quietly along to the door. Hearing voices from within, she had stood outside and listened. She was stunned to hear the conversation between her father, Dan and the Tutor. There were plainly things going on that her father knew nothing about. She was shocked to learn of the activities of the Inner Sanctum and the planned attack on Souda Bay using the Syrian refugees. How could all of this be happening in her home without her knowing? How could the Tutor be doing this behind her father's back? She knew the Tutor, like herself, was a keen supporter of Cretan independence. They had often talked about it while she was growing up. But the discussion had always been about achieving their goal by political means.

Korina could scarcely believe it when she heard her mother say that she led the Inner Sanctum and had ordered the attack on Souda Bay. She was still reeling from her mother's revelation when she heard a gunshot. Listening in stunned silence, she hoped against all the odds that what she thought had just happened had not. But it had. She heard her mother telling Dan that they planned to set him up for her father's murder. Korina was now crouching on the floor outside the door, choking and feeling nauseous. Scarcely able to breathe, she continued to listen. She then realised from what was being said that the Tutor was about to execute Dan. She took a deep breath and walked into the room.

She saw her father on the floor and rushed over to him. Kneeling by his body, she fought to hold back the tears but couldn't. She rested her forehead on his chest and quietly wept. Her mother came over and put her arm round her to console her. Korina tried to stop herself flinching. She could hardly bear her mother touching her. But with her mother's embrace her tears stopped and she felt her grief giving way to anger. She harnessed the inner strength that had come from her years of training and began to focus. How could she stop the Tutor murdering Dan? She rejected the thought of demanding they ask the police to arrest him. There was no way they were going to let Dan stand trial. Then she had another idea. While she had been listening by the door, there had been talk of criminals being sent into the labyrinth. She knew of no labyrinth but could guess what it might be. She couldn't ask about it directly without giving away that she had been listening in. So, drawing on her acting skills, she announced in a hard voice that Dan should die slowly and in terror, in the hope that this would prompt her mother to cast him into the labyrinth to meet his fate. Her ploy worked and, even better, her mother gave her material to work with by speaking of the prophecy. She wasn't sure whether her mother truly believed herself to be the prophesied Great Queen, but she plainly had a strong belief in her destiny.

Korina was horrified when her mother told her the grisly details of what happened in the labyrinth, but she was gambling that Dan would know how to deal with a bull. She remembered what he had said about spending time on his uncle's farm in Arizona and hoped he wouldn't be as terrified as the other victims. It was all she could think of to provide a stay of execution. At least this way he would have a chance, and it would give her more time to work out how to deal with the situation.

They then went through the ridiculous charade of the mock trial. She rejected the thought of asking for his gag to be removed. If Dan professed his innocence it would just complicate things.

As they headed down towards the labyrinth she was wondering whether there was anything more she could do to help him. Then she thought of the navigation app on her phone. She had told Dan about it and hoped he would remember. If she could quietly give him her phone, the app should help him find his way out. Korina walked behind the procession to the gates of the labyrinth, allowing her to retrieve her phone from the pyjama shorts she was still wearing under her priestess' outfit. But how to give it to Dan without being noticed? She then had the idea of slipping it into his back pocket while publicly squeezing his balls to distract everyone. She wasn't sure whether he had noticed though as she had squeezed harder than intended. He seemed to be in quite a lot of pain.

Once Dan had been cast into the labyrinth, everyone gathered in the screen room. Korina suppressed a smile as Dan played to the gallery. The spectators were unsettled at his defiance. The Tutor looked more and more irritated that Dan was spoiling his show. There was scoffing as Dan talked to the bull and performed his Spanish toreador trick, but the scoffing stopped as the bull charged into the wall. The Tutor was now beside himself with rage as Dan stood in front of the camera and mocked them. He was so angry that he was no longer thinking rationally, which doubtless was what Dan was hoping for. The Tutor ordered the guards into the labyrinth to hunt Dan down. Then the cameras went blank. Dan had obviously managed to shut them down.

A little later he appeared in the screen room. Korina complied with the Tutor's request to secure Dan's hands, but tied them loosely enough for him to free himself. She also retrieved her phone from his back pocket.

She could see that he was playing for time when he said he understood the logic of what they were doing. Then he asked about the rape of the women and children and spoke of the Tutor's perverted penchant for young boys. It was obvious from her mother's reaction that she knew nothing of this and was horrified.

At that point Korina exploded, unable to contain herself any further. She launched a kick at the Tutor, who was taken by surprise and fell back against her mother, knocking her over. But the Tutor quickly recovered from her assault. He was grinning cruelly at her, saying she was weak like her father and could never defeat him. He had probably secretly been hoping it would turn out like this. She was Stelios' child, not his. And he was right of course. She had never defeated him. He would almost certainly kill her but she was past caring. It no longer mattered whether she lived or died.

***

As the Tutor advanced to confront Korina, Dan stepped between them, his hands now free. "Why don't you try me for size, you pervert?"

"Dan. No," said Korina, "you don't stand a chance. He'll kill you."

"She's right," said the Tutor, "and I'll enjoy..."

The boast he was about to utter cost him his life. It gave Dan the advantage he needed from the start. Before the Tutor had finished the sentence Dan struck with a punch to the face so powerful that it broke the Tutor's nose, blood splattering all over his face. It had been a while since the Navy SEALS but the training had stuck. He remembered what the instructor had said.

Aggression. So much of martial arts is about defence. But in a real fight defence and blocking gets you killed. The best form of defence is attack. Be aggressive. Incapacitate your opponent. Go for the most vulnerable parts. However big he is, if he can't breathe or you've injured his spinal cord he can't function.

The Tutor, still reeling from the surprise punch, tried to strike back. But he never recovered.

Dan had remembered something else the instructor had said.

Footwork, movement and balance.

Dan stood perfectly balanced, neatly side-stepping the incoming strike. He was no longer there when it arrived. Instead he was in again, throwing vicious punches at the Tutor's head and throat. The Tutor staggered back, stunned and struggling for breath. Keeping up the momentum Dan bent his left knee and thrust his right boot into the centre of the Tutor's chest. The Tutor was propelled backwards up against the wall of the chamber. Dan advanced, preparing to land further blows. But the Tutor didn't move. He remained suspended on the wall, blood seeping from his mouth and stomach. Dan's kick had impaled him on one of the sharp golden horns of the bull's head sculpture mounted on the wall. The Tutor groaned and twitched in his death throes for several minutes and then went still.

"That one's for you, Big Mac," murmured Dan.

He turned towards Korina, who stared at him in silence.

"Korina! I…"

She didn't wait to hear what Dan had to say. Bolting out of the screen room she ran down the passageway.

He rushed after her. "No! Korina, come back."

Chasing her along the subterranean passageways, he followed her through the hidden door back into the cellar. He had to reach her before she got out of the villa. But Korina was too fast for him. He couldn't catch her. As he came up from the cellar he saw her disappear into the entrance hall at the other side of the central courtyard. He was still about twenty metres behind her as she went through the front door. He sprinted to the door and rushed outside, shouting and waving his arms in the air.

"Antje. No. Don't shoot!"

But he was too late. A shot rang out.

***

After disposing of the guards Antje had remained in position and waited. About an hour later four middle-aged men rushed out of the building, heading for their cars.

"So you bastards must be the Inner Sanctum?"

They stopped dead in their tracks when they saw the two guards lying motionless on the ground near the gates. In a matter of seconds Antje had gunned the four of them down. Then she waited.

About ten minutes later Korina came running out of the villa.

"Oh no, dear God! Please no," whispered Antje.

She looked through the scope of her rifle and aimed, but didn't pull the trigger. Something held her back. Seconds later Dan emerged, screaming at her not to shoot. But as Antje kept looking through the scope, a woman appeared at the door of the villa. She was aiming a gun at Dan's back.

***

It took a split second after the gunshot for Dan to realise that Korina was unharmed.

Thank God, he thought, incredibly Antje had missed.

But she hadn't. Dan saw Korina staring past him back to the entrance of the villa. He turned to see Kassandra clutch her chest and slump to the floor.

Korina ran over to where her mother lay. She knelt beside her and held her head in her hands.

Kassandra stared up at her, grimacing in pain. "The prophecy will be fulfilled, Korina."

"Mother. Don't try to speak. I'll get help."

Her mother spluttered and slowly shook her head. Her voice lowered to a barely audible gasp. "He has betrayed you and he will betray you again. But fear not, one day you will become the leader of an independent Crete."

Kassandra died before Korina had the chance to reply. She lingered for a while by her mother's body. She then stood and walked past Dan as if in a trance. Without looking back, she got into her car and drove out of the gates.

Chapter 16

Dan's mobile rang. It was his father.

"Hi, son. Well they may have been reluctant to do anything before but we have their attention now. They're sending a Navy warplane, a Super Hornet, to destroy the freighter. They don't want it getting anywhere near the Naval Pier in Souda Bay. There are two US warships plus a carrier moored there."

"Where's the *Princess Ariadne* now?"

"It left your location yesterday afternoon and is now located twenty-five miles east of Souda Bay."

"Where's the SEAL team? Have they got back yet?"

"They're trying but probably won't get there in time."

"Get me a chopper, Dad."

"Already done, son. It should be with you any minute. At Antje's suggestion I also took the liberty of contacting two of your old command. They were flown in last night."

***

Dan had hardly finished the call when a Navy Seahawk helicopter came fast and low over the hill and landed in front of the villa. Dan and Antje ran over to the chopper to be met by the beaming faces of Joe and Ed, two of Dan's former command in SEAL Team Six. Joe, a big muscular black guy, almost filled the chopper door. Ed, who looked like the archetypal mad professor, was no weakling either but seemed small at the side of Joe.

"Well if it ain't the professor and Antje babe," said Joe in his southern drawl.

Ed pointed to the gash on Dan's face from the Tutor's pistol-whipping. "Cut yourself shaving, did you?"

"Quit the crap and get this crate in the air," ordered Dan.

"Yes, sir," said Joe with a big grin.

Dan jumped aboard and immediately clutched his knee, causing Antje to shake her head in dismay. She climbed in and sat by the Navy pilot who, she was delighted to see, was a woman.

"Where's the freighter?" she asked as soon as they were airborne.

The pilot pointed to the screen. "Intercept in forty minutes."

They flew north over the mountains in the eastern part of the island, crossing the northern coast just east of Malia. As they headed out to sea the pilot took a left turn heading west along the coast towards Heraklion, Rethymnon and Souda Bay, which lay just east of Chania.

Dan took stock of the weapons and gear on board. "OK. We don't have much time for subtlety. I've seen the freighter. It's like an old tramp steamer. It has decks fore and aft with the bridge across the middle. We'll go in from behind the stern and drop down on to the rear deck. The bridge has deck cabins behind it, so we'll be obscured from view. With a bit of luck it should give us a few extra seconds. We'll need to avoid the crane rig on the rear deck. Antje, Ed, you guys stay on the chopper and provide cover. Joe and I will fast-rope down on to the deck."

"Sounds like a good plan to me," said Joe.

Antje glanced at Joe's massive frame. She wasn't so sure, but said nothing.

Dan and Joe chose submachine guns and handguns, Ed opting for an assault rifle. Antje preferred to stick with her own Russian-made equipment and just grabbed a vest and headset. After passing Rethymnon the pilot took the chopper down almost to sea level. They hurtled along just above the waves, hugging the coastline so that the cliffs would hide them from the freighter's radar.

"If we go any lower we're gonna get our feet wet," shouted Joe, grinning from ear to ear.

Antje sighed. "Just get yourself ready to go. You haven't got your vest on yet."

A few minutes later they skirted the headland east of Souda Bay and passed the Drepano lighthouse, which marked the entrance to the bay. They saw the freighter in front of them, heading towards the Marathi NATO Pier Facility on the prohibited north side of the bay.

"We're running out of time," said Dan. "We need to go."

The pilot raced towards the freighter, positioning the chopper so that it was directly behind the freighter's stern. Just as it seemed they were going to smash into it she pulled back on the stick...

Houmam sat with the other male hostages on the rear deck of the freighter. They were guarded by five armed crew members and had been told to put their hands on their heads and remain quiet. They had not been informed of the kidnappers' plan, but Houmam knew it couldn't be good news after seeing the large quantity of explosives loaded on board.

He felt desperately sad as he reflected on how it had all turned out. But most of all he had an acute sense of guilt. He had let his family down badly. His gamble had not paid off. He had brought them all the way from Syria, just for this. They had been herded like cattle into the disgusting dark hold on the freighter, where they had been starved and forced to wallow in their own excrement for three days. And then they had been locked away in windowless underground cells for several weeks, his daughter repeatedly raped by the cruel guards.

His only consolation was that he knew Dan would keep his word and return to free his wife and daughter. He would never see them again but at least they would be able to start a new life. They would have to do it without him though, which would be hard for them. But he was sure his mother's family would do what they could to help. Houmam was now close to tears. He wished he had never…

His thoughts were interrupted when a large helicopter came low over the stern of the freighter as if from nowhere, slowing quickly into a hover above their heads.

***

"Wow, this girl can fly," said Antje to Ed.

"I think I'm in love," replied Ed.

Dan's plan worked well. The male refugees were sitting on the deck behind the bridge. The five armed crew members surrounding them were caught by surprise by the sudden appearance of the chopper. In less than a second its large side door was open. Dan and Joe threw out the ropes to drop down to the deck. Antje and Ed took their firing positions in the open chopper door.

The execution was perfect, or it would have been perfect if Joe and his rope had not parted company halfway down. Joe dropped like a stone for the remaining ten feet, landing on top of Dan who was already on deck.

"Whoops! Sorry. Always struggled with the rope thing," shouted Joe.

The crew members on the rear deck were just recovering from the shock of seeing the chopper when they witnessed Dan's and Joe's grand entrée. They couldn't help but laugh.

It was their last. Antje and Ed picked off four of them from the chopper. The remaining guard was about to fire when Houmam jumped up from the deck and clattered into him, knocking him off his feet. Joe got up, feeling perfectly fine after his soft landing on Dan, and made sure the guard never got to his feet again.

"Good distraction, guys," said Ed, laughing. "I now know why it's called fast-roping!"

Antje just sighed. "My God, is this SEAL Team Six or Sixty-Six?"

Dan was still struggling a little after being squashed by two hundred and thirty pounds of solid muscle.

"Don't worry," he said. "We'll get better."

"I sincerely hope so," said Antje quietly to Ed.

Dan stepped gingerly over to Houmam, feeling his rib cage.

"How many more?"

"Three more plus the commander," replied Houmam. "They're on the bridge."

"Stay here and tell everyone to keep down low."

As Dan had predicted, the chopper was obscured from the bridge by the deck cabins behind it. Hearing the noise of the rotors and gunfire, the freighter commander rushed out of the bridge on to the platform on the starboard side. An experienced commander, he recovered quickly from the surprise assault. He beckoned his men out on to the platform, ordering them to fire down at the deck. Dan and Joe dived for cover behind a motor launch stored on deck, Dan's agonised grimaces betraying the damage done to his ribs by Joe's fall. They sheltered behind the launch as the crew fired a hail of bullets into it.

"Fire at the hostages," shouted the commander. "That should smoke them out."

The men did as ordered, switching their fire to the refugees.

"Dammit," said Joe. "Why don't those sons of bitches pick on someone who can shoot back?"

As the commander had anticipated, Dan and Joe were not going to let the hostages be slaughtered. They broke cover and made a bolt for the steps leading up to the starboard side of the bridge, firing as they ran.

"Kill them," shouted the commander.

Dan and Joe were sitting ducks. Or they would have been if Antje hadn't seen it coming. She had asked the pilot to manoeuvre the chopper to the front of the bridge. The pilot slipped the chopper down over the port side of the freighter and skimmed along the waves below the bridge, bringing the chopper back up over the front deck. She then turned the chopper sideways, giving Antje and Ed a clear shot at the starboard platform where the commander and his crew were standing.

"Smart girl," murmured Antje. The pilot's manoeuvre had kept them out of view until they popped back up over the front deck. Hearing the chopper behind them, the crew stopped firing down at Dan and Joe and turned to aim at it. But before they had the chance to fire Antje and Ed started spraying the platform with bullets. The commander reacted quickly and ordered his men to hit the deck and crawl back inside the bridge.

Dan and Joe reached the bottom of the steps leading up to the bridge.

"Heading up to the bridge," said Dan.

"The Hornet pilot has ordered us to abort," said the chopper pilot. "We're getting too near the Naval Pier. He's gotta launch."

"Can you patch him?" asked Dan.

"Wilco," said the chopper pilot, doing as Dan requested.

"Two minutes," said Dan.

"Affirm," said the Hornet pilot. "No more."

Dan and Joe rushed up the steps to the bridge.

"Holy shit," said Joe, catching his breath. "I'm sure there are more steps on these freighters than there used to be."

Dan was visibly struggling for breath with his damaged ribs.

"You OK?" asked Joe. "You look like you just ate some of Ed's cooking?"

"Not that bad, surely?" said Dan, grinning.

"Oh, thanks a bunch, guys," said Ed.

"One minute," announced the Hornet pilot.

"Wow! Doesn't time fly when you're having fun," said Joe.

"Come on, class! Focus please," said Antje in a schoolmistress tone.

"Yes, ma'am," said Joe.

Dan and Joe were focusing, and they knew there was no time for caution. Opening the starboard door to the bridge, they dived in to find the commander and the three remaining crew members crouching on the floor, still alive and functioning.

The commander fired at Dan, knocking his weapon out of his hand. Then he jumped up and launched himself towards a large console. Lifting a protective cover, he turned a key and pressed down on a red button. A digital timer on the console began counting down. Joe fired at the commander, hitting him squarely in the chest. He slumped down against the helm motionless. Dan lunged towards the console, but one of the crew fired at him catching him on the side of his upper thigh. Joe shot the crew member in the head. The two remaining men scurried behind a bulkhead on the far side of the bridge and started firing, forcing Joe and Dan to dive for cover.

"I'm too old for this," murmured Dan, trying to stretch his rib cage to stop the pain. Dan and Joe were now pinned down again and time was running out.

"Thirty seconds. Abort. Abort," said the Hornet pilot.

Despite the pain Dan was on the point of attempting a further, and probably suicidal, lunge at the console.

"Cover me," he said, looking round at Joe.

"No need," replied Joe, pointing across the bridge.

Dan looked across to see the two crew members behind the bulkhead tip sideways on to the deck, blood pouring from their mouths and necks, their eyes wide open in stunned disbelief. A few moments later Antje stepped out, brandishing a knife dripping with blood.

"Dammit," she said, inspecting her nails. "Can't I leave you guys on your own for a minute?"

Dan rushed over to the console and stopped the countdown. "Pilot. We have the ship."

"Roger that," said the Hornet pilot. "Can I assist?"

"Request Navy vessel, bomb disposal and medical assistance."

"Wilco," said the pilot, "and congratulations!"

***

Within an hour the refugees had all been taken aboard the *USS San Diego*, a Navy crew taking charge of the freighter. They were temporarily accommodated in the naval base at Souda Bay. Although several had received bullet wounds when the commander ordered his men to fire on them, none were seriously injured. Dan's leg wound was superficial and was soon patched up by the medical staff. He was told he had broken several ribs but there was nothing they could do for him other than give him painkillers. The ribs hadn't punctured his lungs and would heal on their own within a few weeks.

The SEAL team who had been on duty in Syria arrived. Dan was despatched with them to secure the villa and ensure that the refugees' women and children were safe pending the arrival of a Navy ship to pick them up. Dan took the opportunity to pick up his things and to collect the golden disc from Stelios' office, planning to drop it off at the Heraklion Archaeological Museum.

When the Navy ship with the women and children reached Souda Bay there followed an emotional reunion with the male refugees. A number of the hostages were in a bad way physically and psychologically after their terrifying experiences. Medical assistance and counselling were provided, particularly for the women and children who had been subject to abuse by the guards. Dan was pleased to see his niece was holding up well despite the appalling treatment she had received. She was strong just like her parents. He was proud of them all.

Dan and Antje were debriefed and Antje's recording of her interrogation of the guard passed over. The Commander at Souda Bay took responsibility for liaising with the Cretan and Greek authorities and was invited by the security and police forces to attend an emergency meeting.

Chapter 17

Dan's father was asked by the Chief of Naval Operations or CNO to attend a hastily convened meeting of the Joint Chiefs of Staff at the Pentagon. He was then asked to join the CNO at a meeting of the National Security Council at the White House. The CNO suggested he wear his naval uniform but he declined.

The President as usual cut to the chase. He wasn't interested in listening to the military apparatchiks. He wanted it from the horse's mouth. The CNO decided to hand over to Dan's father. The President questioned him for a whole hour. Dan's father was polite but frank and to the point. He'd had a reputation for straight talking in the Navy and retirement had done nothing to change that.

"So, for Christ's sake, how come a retired four star admiral and his ex-Navy SEAL son, a Harvard professor, end up running a covert foreign operation to rescue a member of their family? Isn't that what the CIA are for?"

Dan's father explained that he had approached the CIA, but they said their job was to stop terrorists using the refugee crisis to infiltrate the West, not to help refugees.

"What? Even a member of an American family?"

"No, Mr President, particularly not a Muslim."

"What are you saying? Are you saying it's down to my administration?"

"No, Mr President. You asked me to tell you what happened. That's what I'm doing."

Dan's father had been warned before the meeting that the President was allergic to criticism, but somehow the chemistry between them was good. The President seemed to like his straight talking.

"What about the Navy? Wouldn't they help? You're an ex-admiral for God's sake?"

Dan's father saw the CNO, who was sitting next to him, shift uncomfortably in his seat.

"This wasn't really a Navy matter, Mr President, at least not at first. But they did provide technical support, satellite tracking and so forth. The NSA were helpful too. It's how we worked out where the refugees might be. And of course once we knew about the plot the Navy spun into action. They did a good job, those guys at Souda Bay. You should be proud of them."

"I am, and I'm grateful," said the President, looking at the CNO.

"Tell me about the plot. Tell me what happened. I want to know every detail."

Dan's father gave the President a blow-by-blow account, placing emphasis on the outstanding performance of the servicemen and women and the bravery of Houmam and the other hostages. The President seemed to be totally enthralled by the whole episode.

"I'm pleased it ended well," said the President, who called the meeting to an end. He asked his Communications Director to stay on.

***

"A lot of people say I'm a racist," began the President. "Let me tell you. I'm the least racist person you can imagine.

"People say I think all Muslims are terrorists and have no place in America. Guess what! This is fake news. Another lie spun by the media.

"They say I want to build a wall between America and Syria. I don't. Don't even think about it.

"Let me tell you a tale of heroism. Yesterday a bunch of Syrian refugees helped our brave servicemen and women thwart a plan to attack our naval base at Souda Bay in Crete. It was a despicable plan. I can't tell you how despicable it was. If it hadn't been for the brave and selfless acts of those refugees many American lives would have been lost. What they did was a beautiful thing.

"I'll tell you what. Never say America is not grateful to those who help her. Never say she does not value her friends.

"So today I say to those refugees and their families. If you want to come to America you are welcome. I give you my personal guarantee. Come and live in the country you have helped protect.

"God bless you all, and God bless America!"

Dan, Antje, Joe and Ed sat in a taverna in the Venetian harbour in Chania, not far from Souda Bay, listening to the President's press conference. Dan had treated them to a long lunch of local fish caught earlier the same day by the restaurant owner's brother, or so he claimed, followed by Cretan lamb, accompanied by ample quantities of beer, wine and spirits. It had been great to catch up. They hadn't met up properly for a while.

"I wonder how my dad fixed that," said Dan.

"He might have mentioned the role played by certain ex-Navy SEALS," commented Antje.

"Not to mention an ex-Norwegian special forces agent," Joe added.

"It doesn't matter," Dan replied. "All that matters is that the refugees are safe and we prevented those maniacs from killing countless US and Greek servicemen and women."

Ed asked, "So what's next?"

"Look. I'm really grateful," said Dan. "But right now I have to lick my wounds and give a final lecture in Naples next month. Then I have a boat to sail round the Med."

"And then what? Back to being a boring old professor?" asked Antje.

"Then we'll see. But at the moment I could do without more exciting adventures," said Dan wearily.

Antje peered sceptically at Dan but didn't reply.

***

Dan had no sooner left his old friends than his mobile rang.

"Professor Baker," said the familiar voice of Brigadier General Romano. "I'm sorry to trouble you again but I've been thinking further about the Ferrari matter. I could pull the gang in for questioning but, with the lawyers they have, I think that would be a high-risk strategy. I could end up with no conviction and looking very foolish. So I was wondering whether I might call on your help. To be fair I should warn you that there may be a degree of personal risk…"

Oh no, thought Dan. *Here we go again.*

Chapter 18

Dan's father called Diana. "I believe Alexia's staying with you. I thought I'd let you know that it's OK for her to return to Crete now."

"Thank you, Admiral. I don't suppose by any chance you'd have something to share with me about the President's broadcast?"

"I do. There are some bits though that I'd ask you to keep confidential for the moment."

"Why's that, Admiral?"

"I prefer not to say. What I can say is that there may be another story in it for you in due course."

"Admiral, you should be writing suspense novels. OK, deal. So enlighten me. What have you and Dan been up to?"

The Admiral gave Diana the story of Dan's quest to find his stepbrother and family, the events in the villa and the capture of the freighter as it was about to enter Souda Bay. He asked Diana to keep his and Dan's name out of the story for the moment and to make no mention of the golden disc.

"Wow," said Diana. "Thanks, Admiral. That's some story. I need to get on air with this fast before they make the movie. Shame I can't talk about Dan's role in it. Don't forget to let me know when I can tell the whole story. I'd like to interview this Antje woman as well."

"Good luck with that," said the Admiral. "You won't let me down, will you? It could endanger Dan's life if it gets out that he's been in Crete."

"No way I'd let you down, Admiral. Quite apart from the danger to Dan you'd stop giving me the stories!"

***

Hi, this is Diana Klaas on CNN News. We have some sensational news about the Souda Bay attack. CNN have discovered who was behind it. We are joined by our special correspondent Alexia Psaltis, who is just back from Crete.

Diana couldn't have wished for a better story on the first day in her anchor role at CNN. For Alexia it was her first appearance as a correspondent for CNN. Her report was to turn her instantly into a household name.

So, Alexia, I understand you've learned that a secret Cretan separatist group were behind the attack and that it was part of an orchestrated plan to bring about Cretan independence.

Yes, Diana. I've learned that behind the attack was an organisation which goes by the innocuous name of the Minoan Cultural Society. I can also tell you how the plot was foiled by a team of ex-Navy SEALS...

Diana and Alexia had carefully rehearsed the interview, making sure they kept Diana's promise to leave the Admiral's and Dan's names out of it.

***

Korina drove through the gates of the villa. The last few days had been the most testing of her life: the murder of her beloved father; the death of her mother; the shock of discovering the hideous plan to blow up the refugees in a fake suicide attack on Souda Bay; and the appalling abuse of women and children that had gone on without her or her father's knowledge in the villa.

And then there was Dan. During their voyage from Naples she had grown fond of him and in Altea she had begun to realise it was more than that. For the first time in her life she was falling in love. When Dan put his arm around her while they were walking back from the restaurant in Altea, she had hoped the feelings might be mutual. But it turned out he had just been using her. She didn't really blame him for what he had done. He'd had no choice. But that didn't make it any less hard. He had tried to call her but she couldn't bring herself to speak to him. She didn't want to listen to his apologies or explanations. It was all too raw.

She also suspected he had made off with the golden disc. She had asked a friend to pick it up from the villa, but it was nowhere to be found. She couldn't believe it. Dan knew it was precious to her and that she held it on loan from the Heraklion Museum. How could he do that to her after everything that had happened? How could he be so cruel? Perhaps her mother had been right with her dying words. He wasn't to be trusted. For the first time in her life she felt very alone.

She needed to pull herself together quickly though, or at least to give the appearance of doing so. Fortunately the police had been informed of the full story by the US commander at Souda Bay and didn't suspect her of being implicated in the Inner Sanctum's crimes. On the contrary, they showed her great sympathy and merely questioned her to see whether she could help them further. But with her parents' death she had inherited the business empire and there was an immediate crisis she had to deal with. The police had acted fast and rounded up the other members of the Inner Sanctum, including the Heraklion police chief, as well as more than a hundred of her father's employees whom they suspected of being implicated. The directors of the various business divisions were desperate for her to take the lead in dealing with the management and reputational issues. She had rung the university to inform them she needed to take indefinite leave of absence to deal with things.

As she drove through the gates for the first time since her father's death, she felt an overwhelming sense of sadness and guilt that she had failed to prevent it. She had replayed again and again in her mind the events in his office. Had she gone into the room sooner she would probably have stopped them from shooting him. They wouldn't have wanted to do it in front of her because they wouldn't have been able to pin it on Dan. But it had all happened so quickly, and as she listened outside it simply didn't occur to her that they were going to kill her father. She missed him badly. He was eccentric but she loved him dearly. She felt lost without him. He was the only man who had ever really cared for her.

The police had now finished their forensic work at the villa and told her she was free to move back in. But she had decided to put the villa up for sale. She couldn't bear the thought of living there. She could scarcely face coming back at all. But before the villa was sold she needed to return to collect her things and decide what she would keep. She took a deep breath and entered.

***

Dr Mario Lombardi, Director of the Naples Archaeological Museum, walked into his office at exactly 9 am. A creature of habit, he had arrived at the same time for the last twenty years. Taking off his white Borsalino Panama hat and white linen jacket, he sat down at his highly polished rosewood desk in his neat elegant office. He had as always assiduously cleared his desk of papers the night before. It was a practice he insisted on all his staff following. While he had been museum Director there had been a rigorously enforced clean desk policy.

"Untidy desk, untidy mind," he often told his staff.

He always followed the same morning routine. As soon as he arrived his secretary served him a cappuccino to drink while he read the newspaper. Today his routine was disturbed though. His secretary buzzed him to say that a Professor Baker was asking to speak to him. Lombardi was puzzled but took the call.

"Dr Lombardi," said the voice on the phone. "This is Dan Baker. You may not remember me but we've met a couple of times at receptions at the university."

"Professor Baker. Of course I remember. To what do I owe this honour?"

"Dr Lombardi. It's a slightly delicate matter. Is this line private? We won't be overheard?"

Lombardi assured him it was his private line and he was alone in his office.

"Thank you. I ask because I have some information about the murder of your employee, Giovanni Rossi, and the whereabouts of the golden disc mentioned in the scroll he was studying."

"Murder? I thought it was an accident. The poor man fell off the platform in a Metro station."

"I suspect it was just made to look like an accident. I believe he was pushed and I think I know who did it."

"Really?" said the Director, who was beginning to feel a little nervous. Why had Baker phoned him to tell him this? Was he going to challenge him before telling the police? Or was he planning to blackmail him?

"Yes, Dr Lombardi. I think it was his girlfriend, Korina Kouklakis."

Lombardi relaxed a little, breathing more easily.

"What leads you to that conclusion, Professor Baker?"

"Well, Rossi printed off the MSI images and passed them to her."

"I wondered how she got them."

The Director cursed himself as soon as he uttered the words. How would he know that she had the images?

"Oh, I didn't realise you knew about that," replied Dan. "But I guess the police must have told you?"

"Yes," lied the Director. He had not been interviewed yet by the police in connection with Rossi's death.

"I think she arranged to chair one of my lectures so she could get an introduction. At the conference she invited me to dinner in her capacity as chairperson and showed me the images. Rossi had worked out that the merchant acquired the disc in Alexandria and, after being shipwrecked in Spain, hid it. But they couldn't make out the entire text and wanted my help.

It's what I do, deciphering ancient texts, or at least part of what I do."

"Yes I know, Professor Baker. You are one of the world's leading experts in ancient Mediterranean texts."

"You're too kind. Anyway, she gave me the images to look at. On our way out of the restaurant we saw the TV report of Rossi falling under a Metro train the previous night. She looked stunned, although now I think she was just acting. I think she already knew he was dead. She had killed him. We went our separate ways but then she rang me to say she had been burgled. She said she was worried about whoever did it coming back and was beginning to think Rossi's death was not an accident; she thought they were after the MSI images. I invited her to stay on my boat. Looking back, I think the whole thing was a set-up. I think she'd pushed Rossi off the platform and invented the burglary."

"If you're right, she must be very devious," said the Director.

"Oh you haven't heard anything yet. She pleaded with me to take her over to Spain in my boat and help her look for the disc. I went along with it but I must say I was starting to be suspicious of her. There was something about her that made me feel very uneasy. But what really shocked me was that to persuade me to go she flirted with me outrageously and made it obvious she wanted to go to bed with me on the yacht."

"That's a bit rich just after her boyfriend had died," said Lombardi. "Had she had a lot to drink? Grief can work in funny ways."

"No. I don't think so. I guess I should have known better, but I agreed to go to Spain. Then, while we were sailing to Mallorca, she started talking about what we would do if we found the disc. She said she knew a dealer in Crete who would give us a good price and we could split the proceeds. I was horrified. I was assuming, if we found it, we would hand it over to a museum."

"Oh dear," said Lombardi. "She was just in it for the money. That must have been quite a surprise, coming from a professor of archaeology."

"Yes. It was. Anyway, and this is the main reason I'm calling you, I decided to take precautions. From Mallorca I rang a close friend of mine at Alicante University, a former girlfriend. She's a specialist in experimental archaeology. I gave her details of what the merchant had said about where he'd hidden the disc. She knows the area well because she excavated a Roman villa nearby. I made the excuse to Rossi's girlfriend of wanting to visit an old friend while we were in Mallorca. It meant spending an extra day there, which gave my friend in Alicante time to go and look for the disc. She struck lucky and found it almost straight away."

"That's amazing. So what did you tell Rossi's girlfriend?"

"My friend in Alicante had the idea of making a replica. She said she could do it within a day. She did a fantastic job. It was made of clay and tin, painted with gold. Having later seen the original I can say it looked very authentic. You wouldn't know it was a fake until you got it to the lab and inspected it closely."

"So you switched it?"

"Yes. My friend went back and buried the replica in the same spot where she'd found the original."

"It was very good of her to do all this."

"It was. But she enjoyed making the replica. She loves doing stuff like that. And we're still very close. Between you and me I wouldn't rule out our getting back together soon. She also feels indebted to me because I regularly review her scholarly articles and arrange to get them published in the States. I'm editor of a major American journal."

"As a matter of curiosity what's her name?"

"It's María. María Sanchez. Do you know her?"

"No. I just thought I might."

"My dislike of Rossi's girlfriend continued to grow. I suspect she had some accomplices in Spain. I went for a stroll one evening and caught her in a local bar talking to a man and a young blonde woman. She claimed they were just local residents she'd got chatting to, but I have my doubts. But the coup de grace was when she attacked me after we discovered the disc, or what she thought was the disc. I really didn't see that coming. I was thinking she might steal it but I didn't expect her to assault me. She obviously has some kind of martial arts training. I was lucky. There was a guy climbing nearby and he started shouting. She ran off with the replica disc and he came over to check I was OK. I think if he hadn't been there she might have finished me off."

"Yes. I'm beginning to see why you think she may have murdered Rossi. So have you told the police about it?"

"No. I haven't. I've thought about it. The problem is that it's all supposition really. I have no proof she murdered Rossi. And what are the police going to do? I've no idea where she is now. I figure they're more likely to arrest me for illegally acquiring artefacts. I could get the sack. I somehow don't think Harvard would like one of its professors to be involved in antiquities theft! Why do you ask? Do you think I should go to the police?"

"I'm not sure. Probably not," said Lombardi, "for the reasons you give. In the few dealings I've had with the police I've found them very bureaucratic. I always think they're looking for easy targets rather than catching real criminals. So your girlfriend still has the genuine disc?"

"María? No, I do. I have it here on my yacht in Spain. I've been in hospital in Benidorm for the last few days recovering from the injuries Rossi's girlfriend inflicted on me, but I'm about to head back to Naples. I'll be back there in a few days' time."

"What do you plan to do with it?"

"Well that's the reason I'm ringing you. Sorry. It's taken me a while to get round to it. I got a little side-tracked. It's all been a bit traumatic. I was wondering whether the Naples Museum would be interested in acquiring it. I wouldn't require a fee myself. I'd just ask for a little something for María for her work."

The Director thought for a moment before replying. "I think that might be difficult. Not so much the fee. It's just that these days there's a mass of bureaucracy, particularly with one-off items like this. We have to get certificates of authenticity and all sorts. EU rules. The museum has to be careful not to acquire items of questionable origin. It's stupid really, counterproductive. It's partly why so many pieces end up on the black market."

"Oh that's a shame," said Dan. "I guess other museums will have the same problem?"

"Yes I fear so."

"Oh well, thanks for your time and thoughts. We must have lunch by the way one day when I get back," said Dan.

The Director was silent for a few moments.

"Dr Lombardi, are you still there?"

"Yes. Sorry. I was just thinking. I'm wondering whether there might be a way I can help you. I've had this problem in the past with one-off items. I have a contact, an old friend in fact, who is a reputable dealer, well as reputable as any antiquities dealer!"

"But would he be able to guarantee that the disc would be put on public display and be available for scholars and students to study? That's the point really. That's why I'd like to give it to a museum."

"I don't know but I can ask him if you wish?"

"Thank you. It's not exactly what I was hoping for but I'd be grateful. It looks like my best bet."

***

Ferrari was having breakfast with his wife on his yacht in the Santa Lucia marina when the museum Director rang.

"I've just had a call from Professor Baker. He says he has the golden disc."

"Now that is a surprise. I thought it was long gone. Him too actually. How does he come to have it?"

The Director told Ferrari what Dan had said.

"Do you think he's telling the truth? I always struggle to relate to guys who aren't motivated by money," said Ferrari.

"I don't know but he sounded genuine enough. I think he's found himself mixed up in something and is out of his depth. He was very worried about his reputation as a Harvard professor. He seemed very disappointed when I told him the museum couldn't take it."

"How did he get your name? Does he know you?"

"Yes. We've met a few times. He knows me well enough to ring me."

"Well it does fit," said Ferrari. "We know Rossi's girlfriend did something to him over there in Spain while they were up the mountain. My men told me she came down alone with a large bag and made off. And he's right about her being a martial arts expert. She overpowered a couple of my men here in Naples. I'm sure she'd have had no difficulty taking care of the professor. What he says about her meeting a man and a woman makes sense too. I think they were her accomplices. The woman in particular was a nasty piece of work. She enjoyed interrogating one of my men, repeatedly stamping on his wounded leg."

The Director sounded alarmed. "What did your man tell her? Did he say anything about me?"

"No," lied Ferrari. "Don't worry, my old friend. He doesn't know about your involvement. I work on a need-to-know basis with my men. I can see why the professor thinks it was Rossi's girlfriend who pushed him off the platform. Why wouldn't he? She was ruthless enough, and he has no idea that we were involved."

The Director stopped him. "I'd rather not know too much about that side of things if you don't mind. I still don't quite get why you needed to kill him."

"He was too talkative for his own good I fear, as you pointed out. So you're sure Baker hasn't spoken to the police?"

"Again I don't know for certain," said the Director. "But I'm not sure I would in his position. As he says, there's a strong possibility the police might be more interested in charging him with antiquities theft than exploring his theories about Rossi's death."

"I guess that's right," said Ferrari, "and, as you say, he wanted the museum to take the piece. It was you who came up with the idea of involving me."

"Yes. He was reluctant to deal with you. But he saw he had little choice. I told him that no museum would touch it."

"Good work, my old friend. And he says this friend of his at Alicante University managed to make up a replica disc in a day. Is that possible?"

"Oh yes. It would become apparent it wasn't genuine once you inspected it closely. But I'm sure she'd have been able to make something that looked convincing enough to fool whoever found it for a while."

"Do you know her, this María…?"

"Sanchez," said Lombardi. "No. I checked her on the university website though. She's listed there. And I saw she had a whole series of articles published in an American journal that Baker edits."

"OK," said Ferrari. "What's there to lose? Let's arrange a meet but we'll do it somewhere where we can watch him for a while first."

"He says he'll be arriving back at the Santa Lucia marina in two days' time."

"Perfect. Let's meet him there."

"Shall I ask him to contact you when he arrives?"

"Yes. But not on this number. I'll give you a mobile number that can't be traced back. Just one thought. I don't suppose you'd like to come along and check the disc is genuine? It might make him more comfortable if you're there."

The Director thought for a moment. "You're right that it might help give him the reassurance needed to clinch the deal, but I'd rather not. I don't mind slipping you bits of information but I really don't want to get involved in your business."

"OK. Fair enough," said Ferrari. "You've done enough already, old friend. I'm very grateful. If he mentions it, why don't you say you'll be there and then, when we meet him, I can just say you got stuck in traffic. So as regards payment he just wants something for his girlfriend?"

"Yes. As I say he isn't very motivated by money. He's very concerned though that the disc should be available for the public and scholars to view. Can I say you'll meet that condition? I think it would be a deal-breaker if not. He's not very happy doing business with a dealer in the first place. He may even have changed his mind when I ring him back."

"Well we wouldn't want that. Tell him the condition is fine, even though it will restrict possible buyers."

"And what shall I say about the compensation for the girlfriend? He may not ask but I should have a figure in mind just in case."

"Shall we say 50 000 euros?"

"I think that's too much," replied the Director. "Perversely if it's too generous he might get worried. Let's say 30 000."

***

Lombardi rang Dan back and told him that his old friend would be interested.

"So who is this person exactly?"

"I prefer not to give you his name," said Lombardi, "but he's an old friend and I trust him."

"I'm sure he's fine, but I'm still a bit concerned. I'd have preferred you to take it for the museum really."

"As I said, sadly that's not possible," replied Lombardi. "He's agreed though to meet your condition that the acquirer should put the piece on display. It's likely to restrict possible buyers but he's happy to go along with it. Oh yes, and he's happy to compensate your girlfriend for her work."

"Former girlfriend, for the moment. What would you suggest I ask?"

"I don't know really. I didn't discuss it. 30 000 euros?"

"That's more than enough. It's really just a thank you for the work she put in. I'm still a little worried about meeting some dealer I don't know though."

"Well, as I say, I can vouch for him. If it helps I suppose I could come along if we can arrange a convenient time."

"If you could it would make me feel much more comfortable," said Dan. "You'll get to see it yourself then. You may change your mind and want it for the museum!"

"I'd love to have it for the museum," replied the Director. "But it would just be too complicated."

"OK. But I think whoever acquires it should really make a donation to the museum. Anyway, if the weather holds I should get to Naples around 6 pm the day after tomorrow. We can discuss it then. Shall I phone when I arrive?"

"Perfect," said the Director. "Let me give you a mobile number."

***

Alexia had hit the headlines with her first appearance on CNN, and she was immediately offered a full-time role as CNN's southern Europe correspondent. Diana suggested she stay on in Washington for a while and look for a flat there. But Alexia thought that in her new job she really needed to be based in Europe, otherwise she would end up spending all her time flying across the Atlantic. She would give some thought as to where to live. She loved Crete but liked the idea of spending time elsewhere, for example Rome or Naples. CNN didn't really care where she was based as long as she was near a major airport.

A couple of days after getting back to Crete she got a call from Korina's secretary.

"Ms Psaltis, I've been asked by Ms Kouklakis to inquire whether you'd be interested in meeting her."

"That'd be great," said Alexia, scarcely believing her luck but feeling a little apprehensive after her subterfuge at the theatre. "When and where?"

"Just one moment. I'll put you through to Ms Kouklakis."

Alexia's apprehension evaporated as a relaxed Korina came on the phone.

"Hi, Alexia. How about a café somewhere in Heraklion in about an hour?"

"Great," said Alexia. "I often go to the *Hacienda Café* on…"

"I know it. See you there."

Alexia took a table on the terrace outside the café, carefully avoiding one too close to the street. It would be a while before she sat right by a road again.

"Sheila, back from Sydney so soon?" said Korina, smiling and holding out her hand as she walked up to the table.

"Sorry about that, Ms Kouklakis," said Alexia taking her hand. "I don't think you were fooled though."

"No worries," said Korina, imitating a Sydney accent. "Please call me Korina. As it turned out you were right to take precautions."

"What can I do for you, Korina?"

"Let me begin by saying how impressed I was by your report on CNN. I've had a lot of contact with the media in the last week or so and I think your report stood out from the crowd. You obviously got the inside story from somewhere. I think I know where. But that's not what impressed me. What I liked was the fairness and accuracy of the report. You struck me as a person of integrity, someone who wants to get to the truth."

Alexia had never thought of herself in those terms. She wondered what Korina wanted. "You must have been through a tough few days?"

"I have," said Korina. "You're wondering what I want. So let me get straight to the point. I'd like to do a deal with you."

Alexia frowned slightly. "What sort of deal?"

"Since my father's death I've spent a lot of time on the phone assuring everyone, including the media, business partners and investors, that the business is fine despite the recent events. An interview with you on CNN would allow me to talk to an audience right across the world in one go."

"So you're thinking of a story about the business?"

"I don't really mind how you pitch it. It could even be a human interest story if you wished: how I am coping after my parents' death. All I ask is that you give me the opportunity to get a few messages across."

"What sort of messages?"

"Mainly the message that it's business as usual and I have things under control. I'm not asking you to sacrifice your principles. I'd just ask you to be as fair and accurate as you were in your report. I am not scared of probing questions. In fact I'd welcome them."

Alexia had little doubt that things would be under control if Korina had taken charge. The story would be a great follow up to the reports she had done about the Souda Bay attack.

"You mentioned a deal?"

"Yes," said Korina. "Without being too dramatic, the Souda Bay episode has eclipsed one of the most exciting archaeological discoveries of this millennium."

"You mean the golden disc with the Minoan script?"

"How much do you know about that? You didn't mention it in your report on CNN."

"Only so much," admitted Alexia. "I know an ancient disc has been found that is a sort of modern-day Rosetta Stone but with Minoan and Egyptian script."

"And do you know the story that the disc tells?"

"It's something to do with the wedding of a princess? To be honest I thought I'd follow it up later. CNN wanted to get the Souda Bay story out quickly before anyone else broke it."

"That's understandable," said Korina. "The discovery of the disc would have been major news but for the Souda Bay incident. There's been nothing at all about it, even in the local media. There's more to it than just the disc though. Do you know about the discovery of the Minoan palace?"

"No," said Alexia. "Is it connected with the disc?"

Korina explained how the inscription on the disc had led to the discovery of the ancient palace. "It's a major find, much older than the palaces at Knossos and Phaistos and in much better condition. The frescoes are fabulous. And then of course we have the human-interest story with the remains of the Egyptian princess mentioned in the disc. Quite a sad story. She died alone in the palace after it was destroyed by an earthquake."

"I've never done an archaeological story before but I'd love to cover this one," said Alexia.

"If you're happy to do the interview about the business, I'll take you down to the site myself so you can do an exclusive first report on it. It's on my father's, sorry my, company's land. It's guarded so no one has been near it yet. With all the other stuff I've had to deal with, I haven't had time to talk to the authorities about getting permission to excavate it."

"Can you give me one minute? I need to call someone," said Alexia.

Alexia walked out of earshot and phoned Diana, who thought it a great idea and told Alexia to grab it. Diana said she would sort things out with the producer. She pointed out that they might need to postpone the broadcast about the palace until the Admiral was happy for them to give the full story of Dan's involvement and the disc, but that was a detail that could be sorted out later. Alexia should go ahead and film both interviews straight away. Alexia doubted Korina would mind postponing the broadcast about the palace. Korina was more concerned about getting the interview about the business on air quickly.

"OK," said Alexia returning to the table, "that's all arranged. We'll do both interviews together if you don't mind. I'll arrange a camera crew. When would suit?"

"Great. Next day or two would be fine. We'll probably need a separate day for the palace as the site is down near Myrtos. You may need some special lighting if you want to film inside. It's pretty dark in there."

***

Dan had just finished speaking to the museum Director when he received a call from the Brigadier General.

"Excellently done, Professor Baker, if I may say so. You should be an actor. I don't suppose you'd be interested in freelancing for my undercover antiquities squad?"

"I'll pass on that one if you don't mind," said Dan, ignoring the compliment. "So you were listening in?"

"Oh yes," said the Brigadier, "and we also recorded every word of his conversation with Ferrari. Your associate's interview with Ferrari's man gave me enough detail to justify a phone tap. I think with these recordings I should have no difficulty getting a search warrant for Ferrari's boat. Now, you'll shortly be receiving a call from someone in the Italian consulate in Heraklion. We're sending a plane to transport you and the disc to your yacht in Spain. I'll be in touch again to finalise arrangements. Good luck."

***

Ferrari's men had been waiting near the entrance to the Santa Lucia marina for several hours, looking out for Dan's yacht. It was early evening when it entered the marina. They saw Dan standing at the controls as the yacht made its way slowly to its berth, reversing in alongside two similarly sized vessels. They called Ferrari, who joined them.

Dan took a few minutes to secure the yacht, after which he disappeared below. Before long he re-emerged and stretched out on a sun lounger with a beer. He then picked up his phone. Luigi's mobile rang.

"Hi. This is Dan Baker. I was given this number to ring."

"Hello, Professor Baker."

"I'm here in the marina."

"Thank you. Where exactly?"

Luigi had been told to ask so that Baker didn't suspect they were watching him.

Dan explained where his yacht was berthed.

"Very well. We'll be along shortly."

Ferrari and his men watched Dan for a while as he continued drinking his beer. He then went below deck and came back up with a large bag and another beer. He resumed his position on the sun lounger.

"Well it looks OK," said Ferrari. "Let's go."

Ferrari and three of his men walked over to Dan's yacht. Luigi was still recovering from the knee injury inflicted by Antje. With his tightly strapped leg he was doing an excellent impression of Robert Louis Stevenson's Long John Silver in *Treasure Island*.

They reached the yacht and requested permission to come aboard.

"Granted," said Dan. "Would you guys like a beer?"

Ferrari never drank anything as common as beer. In any case he just wanted to get it over with. "That's very kind of you to offer but no thank you, Professor Baker. Perhaps we should get straight down to business and then you can enjoy your evening."

"Are we not going to wait for Dr Lombardi? He said he would join us."

"Oh, apologies," said Ferrari. "I should have said. The Director just phoned me to say he's stuck in traffic. He said to carry on and he'd join us as soon as he can."

"OK," said Dan. "I guess we should start without him then. So here it is."

He slid the golden disc out from the large bag. "Feel free to inspect it, gentlemen."

Ferrari studied the disc closely for several minutes. He picked it up and felt the weight. He examined the markings. He was no expert but after years of experience of antiquities dealing he was confident he could spot a fake a mile off.

"Congratulations, Professor Baker," he said finally. "A wonderful piece. It's such a shame the Director can't take it for the museum."

"Yes. He may have told you I'd much prefer that. I asked him several times though. He was quite clear that he couldn't."

"So, Professor Baker, I understand you want me to find a collector who will be willing to display the piece?"

"Yes. That's very important. I think scholars from the world over and the public will want to view it. For my part I've already taken some high resolution photos of the hieroglyphs to allow me to continue to study them. I still haven't quite fathomed out the Minoan symbols yet."

Ferrari frowned. "I'm afraid I'll have to ask for those as well. I don't think a collector would want to have photos of the find floating around."

"Oh no, I need those. Why should the purchaser be bothered if he's putting it on display anyway?"

At that point Ferrari ended the charade and produced a gun, which he pointed at Dan. "Where are they, Baker?"

Dan looked very nervous and started visibly shaking. He seemed to be frozen to the spot.

"Professor Baker," said Ferrari in as soothing a voice as he could muster. "There's really no need to be alarmed. I won't harm you if you do as I say. Would you please go and get the photos."

"I... erm... I..."

"This is hopeless," said Ferrari to his men. "Take him to the farmhouse. We'll arrange an accident later but we need him to help us with the disc first. And be discreet please. Remember to watch out for the CCTV cameras. Luigi, go below and find the photos."

Luigi hobbled over with his peg leg but never reached the steps. His path was blocked by the massive figure of the Brigadier General emerging from below deck. Simultaneously eight armed Carabinieri officers, who had been hiding all afternoon on the two boats moored alongside, stood up and jumped on to the deck. Within a split second Ferrari and his men were disarmed and found themselves face down on the deck being handcuffed.

"I'm arresting you," the Brigadier said, "on, among other charges, suspicion of murder, conspiracy to murder, attempted kidnapping and antiquities theft. Take them away."

***

The gang were bundled into a Carabinieri prison van that had drawn up in front of the yacht. The Brigadier spoke to his second-in-command.

"Make sure you do it by the book. Keep them separate. I think some of his men may talk. How are the other team doing?"

"They're still searching Ferrari's yacht but they've phoned to say it's like picking lemons off a tree."

"Excellent. Oh yes, and take Ferrari's wife in for questioning. I suspect she may talk if we handle her properly. No handcuffs or rough treatment please."

"Yes, sir."

"So, Professor Baker," said the big man, turning to Dan, "excellent acting again. You really should be on Broadway."

"I think I'll stick to my day job if you don't mind! Do you think you'll be able to make the charges stick?"

"Oh yes," said the Brigadier. "We have more than enough. The recordings of the phone conversations and what we are finding on Ferrari's yacht would probably be enough in themselves, but catching them red-handed is the icing on the cake. I'm pretty sure that with what we have now his men will talk. His wife too I think. She has even more to gain than his men by co-operating with us as she might escape without charges. I'm also hoping I might get enough to convict Ferrari of the murder of my officer. Thank you again for your help. That really was beyond the call of duty, Professor Baker. Shall I arrange for the return of the disc to Crete?"

"If you wouldn't mind," said Dan. "I fear Korina will think I've stolen it. I don't think I'm her favourite person anyway. She's not taking my calls."

"I understand. I fear my omniscience doesn't extend to your relations with Ms Kouklakis. What I will do is ensure the consulate return the disc."

***

It was 9.03 am and Dr Mario Lombardi, Director of the Naples Archaeological Museum, had just arrived at the office, taken off his Panama hat and white linen jacket and sat down at his neat paperless desk in his neat paperless office. He was following his morning cappuccino and newspaper routine when his secretary buzzed to say there were two Carabinieri officers to see him. He was puzzled as they had not made an appointment.

"Well, I suppose you'd better show them in," he said.

A very large, middle-aged Carabinieri officer entered. He was accompanied by a smaller, younger officer also in uniform.

"Gentlemen, what can I do for you?"

"Good morning. I'm Brigadier General Romano. I'll get straight to the point. I am arresting you on charges of corruption, conspiracy to murder and aiding and abetting illegal antiquities trading."

The Director was humiliatingly led out through the museum in hand cuffs, to the gasps of the museum staff.

***

Korina sat in her father's old office at the headquarters of the shipping business in Heraklion. It was now a month since her father's death but she still thought of it as his office. She had replaced the photos of herself which her father had always kept on his desk with ones of him. It was hard at first to see his smiling face, but gradually the photos were becoming a source of strength and inspiration. She had certainly needed all the strength she could muster. For the first few weeks after her father's death, she had attended wall-to-wall meetings with worried customers, business partners and investors as well as television and newspaper journalists hunting for a story. It had been gruelling but at the same time had kept her occupied and had prevented her from dwelling on the dreadful events at the villa.

Meeting Alexia had been a godsend. Korina's interview with her on CNN had been demanding and Alexia had also asked to talk in private off camera to a number of Korina's employees. It had been a bit of a gamble but it had worked. Alexia's report had been as fair and accurate as Korina had hoped. It had been broadcast later the same day and Korina had immediately received calls from business partners and investors all over the world congratulating her on the interview. She even received a call from a newly formed Cretan political party asking whether she had considered entering politics. They were looking for an influential figure to lead the party and help them campaign for Cretan independence. She replied that for the moment she needed to focus on the business, but might consider it in the future. They agreed to speak again in a few months.

The day after the interview, Korina had driven Alexia down to the south coast and the site of the palace, the camera crew travelling separately. Alexia had made it clear she was temporarily off duty and Korina should feel she could speak freely. Korina had still been wary about being too open but had found Alexia to be great company. They had since met up several times for coffee and drinks and were rapidly becoming friends.

Korina had found the visit to the site hard, not because of Alexia's questions but because of the memories it evoked of her time with Dan in Spain and Crete. However hard she tried to banish him from her thoughts, he was never far away. He had phoned her numerous times. Somehow he had found out that she was working at her father's company, perhaps through the CNN interview. But she had refused to take his calls. She just couldn't get over his cruelty in walking off with the disc. She had checked with the museum, hoping to hear that he had dropped it off there, but they hadn't heard from him and didn't have the disc. She realised from the events at the villa that Dan had a ruthless streak, but she had never imagined that he would stoop so low. She thought of taking his last call just to give him a piece of her mind, but she was now finally beginning to surface and didn't want to set herself back by hearing his voice.

She had accomplished a lot over the last few weeks. She had managed to avoid any lasting damage to the business and, with the help of her directors, had restructured things a little to make it run more smoothly. She had finally seen the advantages of the MBA degree that her father had made her do, and the weeks she had spent working at the business each year meant that it wasn't completely new to her. She had a pretty good idea how each business division worked and she had met most of the key staff. Her father's secretary, a close friend of Korina, had agreed to stay on as her secretary, which had been a major boon. She had quietly told Korina that the staff loved having her there and that the working atmosphere was better than ever.

She was beginning to realise though that she was desperately in need of a break. The emotional stress and sheer hard graft of getting the business back on track had taken its toll. She was thinking she might take a couple of weeks to go and relax somewhere on a beach.

Her thoughts were interrupted by her secretary, who buzzed her to say that a Brigadier General Romano of the Naples Carabinieri was on the line and wanted to speak to her.

"I think not," said Korina. "Can you make some excuse please?"

"I think you might want to take this call," she replied. "He says he wants to make arrangements for the return of the golden disc."

***

As usual Emilio Ricciardelli arrived at his office at the Naples Carabinieri headquarters at 9.30 am. Unlike many of his colleagues who started work much earlier, he had never been an early riser even when he was young and keen. And now there was no point. He had reached a stage in his career when he knew he would be promoted no further and was now just serving time until he collected his pension. Although not huge, his pension would be enough to allow him to live comfortably, particularly with the extras he had been able to earn quietly on the side.

Observing his regular routine, he hung his jacket on the stand in the corner of his office and went into the office kitchen to make himself a coffee using one of the excellent expresso machines that his boss, the Brigadier General, had bought for the staff. He came back with his coffee and placed it on his desk. He turned on his computer and entered his user name and password. A message flashed up: *USER NAME or PASSWORD INVALID.*

Gosh, I must be tired this morning, he thought, re-entering both. The computer showed the same message again. *Something must be wrong with the system*, he concluded. He was about to switch off the computer and try again when a colleague entered his office.

"The Big Man would like to see you," he said, referring to the Brigadier General by his nickname.

"OK. I'll go along as soon as I've managed to log in," said Emilio.

"I think you should go now. He said it was very urgent."

Sighing, Emilio walked over to the stand and retrieved his jacket. The Brigadier General, although relaxed in many ways, insisted that jackets be worn for all meetings. Walking down the corridor he knocked on the Brigadier General's door.

"Come in," he heard him say.

Emilio entered and found the Brigadier General sitting at the large conference table in his office flanked by two senior officers whom Emilio didn't recognise.

"Signor Ricciardelli," said the Brigadier General with unusual formality, "please sit down."

Suddenly feeling very nervous, Emilio sat down opposite the three senior officers.

"Permit me to introduce to you Brigadiers General De Luca and Moretti from the Milan Force. I should put you on notice that this is a formal interview. It will be recorded in full and anything you say may be used as evidence in any disciplinary or criminal inquiry."

The Brigadier General produced four documents which he placed in front of Emilio. "Would you be so kind as to read these statements?"

Emilio spent twenty minutes reading them. He found, to his horror, that they were sworn statements by three of Ferrari's men and Ferrari's wife implicating him with the gang. They gave detailed descriptions of information that Emilio had passed on to the gang, including details of the Carabinieri's investigation and Emilio's call to Ferrari saying the investigation had been dropped.

"Do you have anything to say?" asked the Brigadier General when Emilio had finished.

"No, except that this evidence is hearsay. These witnesses are just saying what they claim Ferrari told them. They would say anything to save their skins."

Encouragingly, Emilio noticed the senior Milan officers nod almost imperceptibly.

"In that case perhaps you would be kind enough to listen to these recordings," said the Brigadier General, switching on a machine.

For ten minutes they listened to a series of telephone conversations between Ferrari and Emilio confirming everything in the witness evidence given by Ferrari's men. When the recording ended the Brigadier General said,

"There are a number of other similar conversations. For your information I took the precaution of obtaining proper authorisation for all the phone taps. Do you have anything further to say?"

"I want a lawyer," said Emilio, who was now struggling to breathe let alone speak.

"You shall have one," said the Brigadier General.

He passed Emilio a further document. "I formally charge you with the offences listed therein, which include corruption, conspiracy to interfere with the course of justice and knowingly endangering the life of a police officer. Take the list with you. You'll have plenty of time to read it. As you see, I have taken the precaution of involving two senior officers from another Force in this interview. I have done this partly for your own protection. I've asked them to bring officers with them to ensure you are safely escorted out of the building.

You will be taken to Milan to await trial. Gentlemen, would you be kind enough to remove this officer from my sight before I do something I regret?"

Two Carabinieri officers from Milan entered and led Emilio away in handcuffs.

Chapter 19

Over a month had passed since the events in Crete. Dan had been occupied straight afterwards helping the Brigadier General with his sting. At first he had felt a sense of elation at the way things had worked out. He had freed his family and the other hostages and averted a major tragedy at Souda Bay. His father had acted quickly to seize the moment and had managed to arrange fast-track visas for the refugees. Houmam's family were temporarily staying with Dan's father and stepmother until they got themselves sorted. His daughter was doing well in the circumstances, although what happened to her in Crete would doubtless stay with her for the rest of her life. But she was strong and Dan had no doubt they would all do well in America.

It had also been great to catch up with Antje, Joe and Ed. They had done a great job and he felt lucky to have them as friends. The Brigadier General phoned to tell him that Luigi Carbone and two other men from Ferrari's gang had given full confessions. Ferrari's wife had been particularly helpful as she had told the police everything she knew about Ferrari's activities over a number of years. The Brigadier General had been able, as he had hoped, to add the murder of his undercover officer, Federico Mancini, to the list of charges. Having seen the evidence, the Prosecutor had ordered that the accused be remanded in custody pending trial. The Brigadier General had also arrested the museum Director and an officer at the Carabinieri headquarters in Naples who had been passing information to Ferrari. Dan was pleased he had helped bring them all to justice.

And then, almost a lifetime ago it seemed, there had been the discovery of the golden disc in Spain and the unearthing of the Cretan palace and remains of Princess Hemite. These were finds that a professional archaeologist would be proud of, let alone a mere amateur, a linguistics professor. But somehow, with everything else that had gone on, they had hardly registered, and when Dan did think about them it hurt because they reminded him of Korina.

He couldn't help but smile at some of the memories of her though: her cheeky grin as she had served him a large helping of Antonio's disgusting eels in Mallorca; the days and evenings spent together on the boat, including the rather enjoyable Pankration lesson; her staged look of bewilderment as she chastised him in Crete for forcing her to make off with the disc and smug look of victory when she hooked him with the prospect of finding the palace; and of course last but not least, her brilliant performance as Priestess Ariadne, sentencing him to the labyrinth and then discreetly slipping the phone with the app into his pocket.

Dan had tried to contact Korina but in vain. She was not answering her mobile. He had rung the villa and left a message on the voicemail. He had inquired at the university in Naples but she had not returned. He had also rung the university in Chania but they said she had taken indefinite leave of absence; they either didn't know or wouldn't tell him her whereabouts. He had finally tracked her down, after watching her interview with Alexia on CNN, to the head office of her father's business in Heraklion, but she had refused to take his calls. Her secretary had been very open and had not sought to make excuses. She had told him honestly that Korina didn't want to speak to him.

Dan missed her. He was also worried about her. She was strong but to lose both parents in such tragic circumstances would be hard for anyone to bear. She must feel very alone. But why would she want to talk to him? He had used her. She must by now have worked out that Dan had arranged with the Rector for her to chair his lecture. She probably felt their entire time together had just been a lie.

Dan was in the lecture hall in central Naples at the university's Department of Humanities. He had just sat down after giving his final public lecture before his planned sailing trip round the Mediterranean. He had been looking forward to it for so long. He had mapped out an itinerary which would take him to many of the places mentioned in the ancient texts: Syracuse in Sicily, the ancient cities of mainland Greece including Corinth, Epidaurus and Athens, and then onward to the islands of the Aegean and the ancient cities on the coast of Turkey, such as Troy and Ephesus. He had arranged to hand back the yacht in Alexandria in Egypt, from where he would fly home to Boston. This could be his last chance for a while to go off on such a long trip. But he was no longer sure he wanted to do it. He didn't have the same enthusiasm for it any more. He thought he might just head back to Boston and skip the trip. He hadn't felt so depressed since he lost Aliah in the MSF tragedy in Afghanistan nearly three years ago.

Dan had been passed a note just before his lecture asking him to include the story of Theseus and the Minotaur in his presentation. He had told many other tales from the ancient texts during his stays in Naples. Such stories were a great way of livening up the audience and grabbing their attention right at the beginning of his lectures. He would often return to them at the end to round things off and finish his lectures powerfully and with humour. Of all the tales he had told, his rendering of the Minotaur story had proved to be one of his audiences' favourites.

But today it hadn't worked. He hadn't been on form. The tale had just left him feeling empty. He could feel the disappointment among the audience, many of whom had been to his lectures in the past. Gone was his customary lively and entertaining delivery. Gone was his natural ability to connect with his audience. This was supposed to be the grand finale to his summer lecture series but it had surely been his worst performance yet. On this form he probably wouldn't be invited back. But he really didn't care. He just wanted to get it over with, get out of the lecture hall and catch a plane back to Boston.

The chairman, plainly disappointed, thanked him rather perfunctorily. He opened the floor for questions. There were fewer questions than normal and Dan could barely concentrate on them. Then the audience fell silent. The chairman looked at the clock and, in the hope of prompting the audience, said there was time for one more question.

"I have a question," said a large Carabinieri officer sitting near, but not at, the front. He wasn't fat. He was just massive in a way that even his well-cut uniform couldn't disguise. "Tell me, Professor Baker, are we sure Theseus left Ariadne rather than the other way round?"

Dan smiled at the Brigadier General's question. "A very perceptive question, Brigadier General, and if I may say so an appropriate one for a senior Carabinieri officer. It has been suggested that the whole thing was actually a cover story invented by Theseus to save face. Perhaps by the time they got to Naxos Ariadne had had enough of him. Perhaps it was she who dumped him!"

For the first time today there was laughter from the audience.

The chairman, encouraged that things were finally livening up, said,

"Any further questions?"

"Yes. I have a question for the Professor. It's related to the Brigadier General's question," said an American-sounding voice coming from directly behind the Brigadier.

The Brigadier was so tall and broad that the person asking the question was completely obscured from the chairman's and Dan's view. Not that Dan was really looking at the audience anyway. He was mainly just staring down at the speakers' table.

"Please stand and state your name," said the chairman.

Ignoring the instruction the person asked, "Professor Baker, let's suppose your version of the story is right and it was Theseus who betrayed Ariadne and abandoned her on Naxos. If Theseus were given a chance to re-consider, do you think he would take Ariadne with him on his Mediterranean voyage?"

Dan looked up to see an attractive dark-haired woman standing behind the Brigadier General. From her neck hung a golden pendant depicting two bees with their wings outstretched, clasping a honeycomb into which they were placing a small drop of honey. She was dressed in a white T-shirt and jeans. Printed in large black letters on the T-shirt were the words:

Good girls go to heaven.
Bad girls go to Benidorm.

THE END

Acknowledgements

The Cretan Prophecy combines my love for adventure thrillers with a life-long passion for ancient history. Of all the ancient Mediterranean civilisations, the Minoans hold a particular fascination for me. Here was an ancient people whose influence spread throughout the eastern Mediterranean and who, while Britons were still living in thatched huts, were building vast palaces and dwellings decorated with stunning artwork and equipped with elaborate plumbing, sewage and heating systems. Yet we still know comparatively little about them. Like the Mycenaean Greeks under whose influence the Cretan palaces later came, the mighty Minoans were already a distant memory for the classical Greeks, the stuff of myths and legends.

The historical characters, places and events in the novel are largely fictional, although the Pharaoh Userkaf, founder of the Fifth Dynasty, the Great Library of Alexandria, the Villa dei Papiri, Roman Allon and the *Bou Ferrer* shipwreck are all real enough, as are the fabulous ruins at Knossos and Phaistos and the temple of Anemospilia, where evidence has been found of a darker side to Minoan Crete. I hope I haven't offended too many archaeologists and historians by fictionally extending the palace period back to the middle of the third millennium BC. Current evidence suggests that Minoan Crete did not become a centralised society until four to five hundred years later.

Stelios' villa with its underground labyrinth is of course fictional, although the idea for the novel was inspired by Labyrinth Cave, a huge artificial cave south of Heraklion quarried for stone by the Minoans and later by the Romans. For readers who have not yet visited the beautiful island of Crete with its amazing sights, welcoming people and terrific food, I would recommend that you try to do so before long. Let me assure you that the dark activities of the Minoan Cultural Society, its sinister Inner Sanctum and the corrupt policemen and officials described in the novel are purely fictional. I have invariably found the Cretan people to be, like Stelios, friendly and only too willing to help.

Many of the locations in Italy and Spain also exist, although again the characters are fictional. In particular the fabulous Naples Archaeological Museum, the spectacular La Seu Cathedral in Palma, the lovely little town of Altea, the Alfaz tram stop (with its Sunday afternoon jamming session) and of course Benidorm are all real. The Albir lighthouse walk is one I have done many times when visiting the beautiful Northern Costa Blanca, although happily I haven't yet bumped into Antje!

I should express my thanks to family members, friends and colleagues who have helped me with the novel, including my wife Susan and daughter Isabel (for helping me shun the uncool - well some of the time!); Dianne for her comments on multiple drafts, cover and blurb; Vanessa for generously sharing her thoughts on the plot and her distilled wisdom on the art of fiction-writing as a debut author herself; and, last but not least, Sarah Luddington, best-selling author of the Knights of Camelot series, and her team at Mirador Publishing, for helping me turn my manuscript into a publishable novel and their honesty in telling me when something was not up to scratch. I cannot recommend the Mirador team highly enough to any aspiring author.

Finally, I would like to say that I would love to hear from you. Please email me at the address on my author's page. I would love to know what (and whom) you liked in the story and also what you didn't.

Printed in Great Britain
by Amazon